Praise for *Between Shadow's Eyes*

Jill Hedgecock knows first-hand that every rescue animal possesses their own "magic." Her gifted storytelling, which has helped countless animals find their own forever families, now creates a fun, clever adventure for all to enjoy!

—Elena Bicker, Executive Director, Tony La Russa's Animal Rescue Foundation

What I loved about *Between Shadow's Eyes* was the mystery of it all, the not knowing. Ms. Hedgecock has a keen descriptive style that keeps a reader in suspense, always wondering whether a character is good or bad, lost or found, heading toward shadow or heading toward light. She creates a compelling protagonist in the woman Sarah, a person both terribly young and terribly old, caring for a rescue dog named Shadow. Ms. Hedgecock triumphs over other dog stories by making the dog a dog, with a pre-science different from our own, with a different sense of mystery and a different sense of loss. **Read this book.** I guarantee you will keep turning pages, learning the answers with Sarah and Shadow, and likely you will find yourself wondering what your life would be like if there were a zip-per-nosed Doberman who needed a home …

—Kevin Fisher Paulson, *San Francisco Chronicle* columnist

Sarah Whitman should be in high school, getting dressed for her prom. Instead she is prematurely forced into the role of a grown-up, isolated by grief and a secret. Shadow, her adopted Doberman, who sees things that may or may not be there, is Sarah's lifeline and, perhaps, her undoing. But for better or worse, the pair's destiny is intertwined and their devotion to each other, unwavering. *Between Shadow's Eyes* will reel you in close from the first few lines, then quickly shove you to the end of your seat, where you will remain through twists and turns, intrigued, until the surprising ending.

—Deborah Stevenson, author, *Soaring Soren: When French Bulldogs Fly*

Solid characters abound in Jill Hedgecock's latest novel, *Between Shadow's Eyes*, taking the reader on an unexpected journey. Focused around a pet zipper-nosed Doberman, young Sarah must face dangers that push her to her limits as she struggles to remain undiscovered as a minor living alone after the death of her father.

—William Gensburger, *Spotlight on Writing, Books N' Pieces Magazine*

Jill is a master of detail that leaves the reader with vivid imagery of each setting. She doles out just enough new information in each chapter to stoke the suspense while gradually unfolding a mystery. If you like tales of dogs or paranormal activity, this will be an enjoyable read.

—*The Diablo Gazette*

A stirring tale of love, loss, and the paranormal. Prescient Shadow and his teen owner are characters you will remember long after you close the book.

—B. Lynn Goodwin, author of *Never Too Late: From Wannabe to Wife at 62* and *Managing Editor of Writer Advice*

Between Shadow's Eyes beautifully captures an amazing bond between a girl and her Doberman. This compelling story will transport you to a place where everything isn't always as it seems. Jill Hedgecock crafts a world that leaves the reader begging for more. This wonderful journey explores the depths of a young girl's strength, thanks to the undying loyalty of her beloved dog. Suspense and excitement grip the reader in a way that makes it all too easy to become engrossed in this exciting story of danger, suspicion, love, and hope. You won't soon forget this amazing journey.

—John Walter, DobermanPlanet.com

Hedgecock beautifully captures the essence of the Doberman breed's intelligence, loyalty and devotion to their human in this fast-paced novel about a teenage girl facing great loss. Struggling with the pain of isolation and the secrets she needs to keep, she is drawn into a tenuous relationship with a veterinarian who promises to help her with her dog's barking problem. Between Shadow's Eyes will keep you riveted from the very first paragraph to the highly-charged finish.

—Diane Walsh former board member of the Illinois Doberman Rescue and Owner of East SF Bay's Endless Pawsibilities Pet Services

For all the dog rescuers that steel themselves to enter shelters on a regular basis knowing that they can't save them all. For the fosters that take in the tired, the sick, and untrained canines and who do the hard work to transform these neglected animals into adoptable pets only to make the heart-wrenching sacrifice and give them up. You are admirable. You are brave. You are heroes.

CHAPTER ONE

O n my sixteenth birthday, I wished for an ordinary life. All I wanted on that special day six months ago was to be a teen girl who got good grades in high school, a girl whose mother hadn't died in childbirth, and whose father didn't have cancer. If only I could turn back the clock and stand in front of that pink cake with its flickering candles knowing then that my father would not survive no matter how much I wanted a different outcome. I would ask instead for a life without secrets and a dog that didn't bark all day while I was away at work.

As I steered my car onto Cherryglen Lane and maneuvered it into my driveway, I knew my post-birthday requests would never come true. Especially the one about my dog. The presence of a white envelope wedged into the screen door confirmed Shadow's barking was still causing problems. Because animal control had already contacted me by phone, the letter was not a surprise. This was the third citation triggered by my dog's behavior.

I pressed my forehead against the steering wheel letting

the vibrations of the idling engine travel through my tired body. I really had no idea what to do. Since Dad died, decisions overwhelmed me. The Game Plan Rules he left behind for me to follow didn't address barking dogs. His guidelines were designed for me to keep a low profile and out of the foster care system. Dad would have found the solution in his rules anyway. He stormed through life armed with a spreadsheet of all the possible alternatives. I tended to try the quickest and easiest fix. My approach seldom worked, and then I let things slide until the problem reached a tipping point. We had always been very different people.

Sometimes I wondered if we were even related. Dad and I hadn't even looked alike. He was tall—about six feet to my five foot four. His graying hair had once been a mousy brown, while my dark chestnut locks bordered on black. Dad said that my eyes looked just like my mother's— an opaque hazel with a hint of yellow. I had never seen her eyes. As I slipped into this world, she slipped out.

I switched off the engine and listened for my dog's distinctive bark. All I could hear was the whistle of the wind. I slowly raised my head to stare at the dreaded envelope that flapped in the breeze like a loose sail.

Dad would say find Shadow a new home. He would warn me that the more the authorities poked around the recently purchased house that I inherited from him, the more likely a representative from the social services agency would discover that I was underage and living alone. But even though Dad had told me enough stories about his childhood experiences with his foster parents for me to agree that living on my own was my best option, I would never give up Shadow. My one-year-old Doberman, my affectionate, sweet, goofball of a dog had an uncanny ability to sense when a meltdown was imminent. She would crawl onto my lap, lick my face, and bring me back from the brink. She was the glue holding me together. Shadow helped me cope with my impossible new life.

I threaded an arm through the strap of my purse, tucked it against my body then braced myself as I opened the car door. The blast of unseasonably crisp April air bit through my thin cotton blouse. Strands of hair whipped my face as I stepped outside.

I hip-checked the door shut then leaned into the wind to walk the short distance to the porch of the one-story rancher I now called home. "SARAH WHITMAN" was written in large, bold letters on the notice. Fear fingered its way down my spine. I didn't need to open the envelope to know what it said: Violation of Ordinance No. 630, Section 12(b)/Title 6.27.140, disruptive animal. This third warning meant an investigation by an animal control officer, which meant a possible court date pending the investigator's findings. I snatched up the wretched thing.

My attempts to quiet Shadow weren't working. The tipping point had been reached. Before Dad died, I swore to him that I would follow his Game Plan Rules. I hadn't realized this also meant that I would not be able to ask anyone for help. Like so many other challenges I faced in the wake of my father's death, I must figure this out on my own.

I unlocked the front door and stepped inside to where my sweet pooch awaited. Her shortened tail wagged a mile a minute. Shadow's brown eyes stared up at me as if she had been the perfect pet in my absence. The notice in my hand suggested otherwise.

The skinny dog I had taken home had put on weight and shed her dull coat. She was now a shining example of her heritage with a sleek, reddish-copper body and pops of golden color in all the right spots. I suspected her parents had been show dogs, champions even.

"Shaa-dow," I sighed.

I reached down and scratched behind my dog's pointy ears. Her long snout sported a distinctive ridge—a recessive characteristic of the Doberman breed called a zipper nose. Her muscular body made her look formidable, yet she had a gentle temperament.

Her behavior suggested prior obedience training. A quick hand signal, a vertical slash through the air, sent my loyal dog scurrying into heel position so that I could close the door. She leaned her sixty-five pounds against my leg. She was petite, even for a female Doberman, probably the runt of the litter. Maybe that's why she barked so much— her only means to show she was a big girl in a small body.

"What am I going to do with you?" I said.

Her tail drummed the floor. I couldn't help but smile. It was hard to stay annoyed with her when she was so happy to see me.

I moved through the entry and dropped the citation and my bag onto the dining room table. A stupid act of rebellion led me to buy that piece of furniture, and every time I looked at it, I remembered that I betrayed one of my father's dying wishes: to be financially responsible. Now my remaining meager funds put everything in jeopardy. What had the banker guy called it?—a glitch in probate? The bank had frozen the account, and I couldn't withdraw any of the money my father left me. Dad had been so sure that I could handle things without him. These last few weeks have shown me just how unprepared I was to face the adult world on my own.

The clack, clack of toenails alerted me that Shadow had followed me. It hadn't taken me long to name her. From the moment I brought her home, Shadow accompanied me everywhere. This was pretty typical of the breed. They were loyal, intelligent, and bonded deeply with their owners.

One of her feet impatiently pawed at the ground then she took my fingers gently in her mouth and guided me to a corner of the dining room. She released my hand then made her strange muttering noise. I swear she was trying to talk to me and explain the problem. I had already tried everything I could think of to keep her from barking. A variety of new toys, chew bones, and leaving the television on had not kept her from disturbing grumpy old Mrs. Cromwell next door.

A visit to a veterinarian last week reassured me that Shadow's behavior was not the result of a medical problem. Dr. Fullerton referred me to an animal behaviorist. Following Dad's Game Plan Rule #6: Don't spend money you don't have, I was waiting to make an appointment until after my financial issues were resolved.

"I don't understand," I told Shadow.

She barked, reared up and jumped against the blank, green wall. Her nails created divots in the paint.

"Hey," I said. "Stop that."

Shadow hung her head.

When I went to smooth out the damage, the wall felt ice cold to my fingers. Unease wiggled a path under my skin. What the heck?

I sank into a dining room chair and reached into my purse to pull out the envelope that I turned to whenever I felt at a loss or overcome with despair. The frayed edge of the flap revealed how many times I had handled it. I extracted the letter, smoothed the creased folds, and read: *My Dearest Sarah.* A familiar ache settled in, so I pushed the paper across the table. I shouldn't indulge in pity when what I really needed was guidance. I extracted the laminated card with Dad's Game Plan Rules that he had included with his last letter to me. I closed my eyes to center myself then studied each rule:

Game Plan Rules

#1. *Don't make rash decisions.*

#2. *Never ignore Serious Business.*

#3. *Always prepare for the worst.*

#4. *If you have a chance to fix a wrong, do it.*

#5. *Keep a low profile.*

#6. *Don't spend money you don't have.*

#7. *Stay away from Odd Ducks and Nosy Neighbors.*

#8. *Always demonstrate good manners and use proper English.*

#9. *Take one step at a time.*

#10. *Listen to the voice within.*

As I read them, a knot formed in my throat. If Dad were here, I would be such a disappointment to him. It wasn't only Rule #6 that I violated. Keeping Shadow had been a rash decision, so I had broken Rule #1 too. I re-read the rules, looking for one that applied to my current problem and paused on the ninth rule that said I should take one step at a time.

Okay. Read the citation. I started at the top, determined to read the full document for any information that might help me find a solution. My eyes traveled across the words next to "Complaint Source" then backtracked to re-read them. The name of my neighbor to the east, Mrs. Cromwell, who initiated the other two citations, wasn't there. Instead, M. O'Shawnessy filled that space in bold font.

Mr. O'Shawnessy? After the second complaint, when

I asked my nearest neighbor if he heard Shadow's barking, the elderly man assured me that my dog didn't disturb him. This sweet old man was supposed to be my friend. His fondness for Shadow had visibly grown with each encounter. He had started calling her "Shaddie"—a pet name I sometime used too. He even carried dog biscuits in his pocket in case we happened to walk by. The sting of betrayal and dull ache of disappointment filled my chest.

My dog sidled up beside me. A low rumble erupted from her throat. I cringed. Not again. This was how it always started.

"Shadow," I groaned.

As usual, her growl rolled over into the second phase: a ruff, a hesitation, then her staccato, high-pitched bark. Sometimes she would spin in a circle a few times, whimper, and erupt in a frenzy of growls that seemed to come from deep in her chest—a noise that sometimes made me a little frightened of her. Shadow's full-blown barking would then continue until she ended her routine with the crescendo, a plaintive howl.

As if the audience yelled "encore," Shadow would repeat this routine, over and over until I managed to calm her into silence. According to this citation, her barking had occurred nonstop throughout the day this entire week. I really couldn't blame Mr. O'Shawnessy. The racket had only been going on less than a minute, and I was ready to jump in the car and escape.

"Shadow," I yelled over the din. "Shadow, chill."

I pulled her tense body close to me. She continued to direct her displeasure at the barren space in the far corner of the room.

"Enough," I yelled.

Shadow's barking only became more frenzied. I stood and rummaged through my purse as she tipped her nose to the ceiling, imitating the profile of a coyote baying at the moon.

"Arrruuuu, arruuuuu."

My fingers located the business card the vet had given me: *Dr. C. Griffin, D.V.M, Certified Animal Behaviorist.* Calling for help felt like my only option.

"Quiet," I screamed and stamped my foot.

Shadow stopped and gave me a sheepish look.

I hurried to make the call while the silence lasted. As I dialed, I ticked off the two Game Plan Rules I was ignoring. Rule #1: Don't make rash decisions. Rule #5: Keep a low profile. Above all, Dad had cautioned, keep your interactions with others to a minimum. Yet, I was following Rule #10 to listen to the voice within and Dad said this was the most important rule of all.

While I waited for someone to answer the phone, my dog cycled back into her early growling phase. Once again, her gaze fixed on that same empty corner. There wasn't anything there. Not even windows where she might see a bird or a cat. What could possibly be upsetting her?

I took a deep breath. I had read that dogs are sensitive to their owner's emotions. If I calmed myself, maybe

I could quiet her. I focused on the air moving in and out of my lungs until my anger slipped away. This seemed to disrupt Shadow's typical behavior pattern long enough to book an appointment with Dr. Griffin that very afternoon without having to shout over Shadow's barking. Yet, when I hung up, Shadow's growl resumed. Poor dog. She must feel miserable.

"What is it, girl?" I whispered.

I rubbed the ridge between Shadow's eyes, her favorite place to be stroked. Normally, this relaxed her, but her body remained stiff and unyielding. I tilted my head, listening. No scurrying sounds suggested squirrels on the roof or rats in the walls. Then for a moment, a diamond pattern flickered against the solid green wall where Shadow nicked the paint. The same place where the surface had been cold to the touch. I turned my head looking for a reflective light source, but when my gaze returned to the wall, for a split second, I could have sworn an unusual pattern of light formed a pair of eyes above the diamond shapes.

My hand froze on my dog's head. The image had been a momentary flash as if I was fast-forwarding through a television commercial on a recorded show. Had exhaustion taken over? Had I momentarily dozed off? I blinked hard. The original geometric shapes returned. There had to be a rational explanation. Leafy branches blowing in the wind might cause something like this if there were any trees near the window—but there weren't. Car headlights? Yeah. That would explain it—if it weren't a sunny afternoon.

CHAPTER TWO

I entered Dr. Griffin's clinic with skepticism at my side and Shadow at my heel. Dad always said that it was hard to get last minute appointments with people who were skilled at their jobs. How good could this animal behaviorist be if she fit me in within an hour of my phone call? She had also answered the phone. Apparently, she didn't even have a receptionist.

Several forms lay on the unmanned front desk of Dr. Griffin's office. On a yellow sticky on the top sheet was Shadow's name. A placard in red type announced that all fees must be paid in full at the beginning of the session. Great, just great. My account balance flashed through my mind. I was hoping to set up a payment schedule.

I picked up the paperwork then made my way to a yellow-ochre chair so small that the plastic seat must have been part of a student's desk at some point. Shadow lay at my feet while my pen scratched out the requested information. The last question asked about the dog's early life. I wrote in "unknown."

I always knew if I ever adopted a dog, it would be a rescue. I hadn't gone to the shelter three weeks ago with the idea of bringing a dog home though. I went to inquire about volunteering, but after I arrived, when the volunteer coordinator told me I would need my parent's signature on the forms, I left the office with no intention of returning. When I stepped outside and headed to my car, a harried woman with a screaming baby on her hip intercepted me.

Before I had a chance to protest, she thrust a dog leash in my hand. At the end of the lead was a painfully thin red Doberman with eyes that glowed with intelligence. With her arm freed, the mother patted the baby's back and bounced the infant until it quieted.

"Please," she said, "she's a stray and I really don't want to take her in there, but I can't take her home and we don't have a local Doberman rescue. I already have three dogs. Could you take her?"

"I really can't," I said, trying to hand the lead back.

"Look," she said, "this stray has been living in a drain-pipe near my house for weeks. I've put up flyers and posted on my neighborhood NextDoor and across social media. No one has come forward to claim the dog. It seemed to magically disappear whenever animal control showed up. She has been uncatchable until today. This morning, she slunk into my front yard. I gave her water and some food and she didn't protest when I put the collar on. She's very sweet, rides well in the car, knows sit and down."

I had wanted a dog ever since I was three years old and

fell in love with Clifford, the Big Red Dog. But this wasn't part of the Game Plan.

"I wish I could, but—"

"She's a really good dog. My veterinarian is really reasonable and first visits are free. I'll even give you the extra bag of dog food I just bought at the grocery store. Please take her. She likes you. Look at her."

The Doberman leaned her body against my leg and stared up at me. When I put my hand down so she could sniff it before I tried to pet her, she pressed her nose against it and inhaled so deeply that she snorted, I laughed, something I hadn't done in the months before Dad died. That moment changed everything. I gripped the lead and asked for the veterinarian's address.

The door to Dr. Griffin's inner office swung partway open interrupting my thoughts. A faint scent of urine infiltrated the lobby where I sat. I leaned forward trying to see who might be on the other side.

"Dr. Griffin," a woman's voice said, "at your service."

She still hadn't poked her head into the room or even called Shadow's name. How did she know who she was inviting in? I stood and walked around the door.

A blonde-haired woman wearing thick glasses and a black T-shirt that proclaimed Save the Living Unicorns! smiled at me. She was way younger than I expected— probably in her late-twenties, though I couldn't be sure. A turquoise flower was tucked into her hair. The color matched her blue tortoiseshell glasses. The thick-rimmed style was popular now, but somehow they looked odd on Dr. Griffin. Her spectacles reminded me of the grouchy librarian at my high school. That old biddy surrounded herself with giant dictionaries, yet her vocabulary consisted of one word: shush.

"Hello," Dr. Griffin said in a deep voice that didn't match her frail frame. She stepped to the side. "Please come in, you must be Sarah."

I nodded then followed her with Shadow at my side. The large, oak desk positioned against the far wall looked empty and exposed. No papers, no pens, no computer covered the surface. Rather than being centered, the furnishings had been shoved to the right-hand corner of the room.

A colorfully framed document hung on the wall above the brown, leather office chair behind the desk. Several photographs covered the lemon-yellow walls, each depicting different dog breeds engaged in various activities. I was impressed by those examples of canines showing good behavior—fitting decor for an animal behaviorist. One framed photo showed a red Doberman that resembled Shadow sitting at attention next to a police officer. Was this a sign that maybe I had made a good decision?

As I made my way toward the empty seat in front of the desk, Dr. Griffin followed closely at my heels as though the vet feared that I would change my mind about the appointment and might bolt for the exit.

From behind me, the vet squealed. I dodged to the side as she darted around me and pitched forward to the far corner by the desk. Her displeasure seemed to be aimed at a plain section of wall. Shadow stiffened and did that weird vocalization of intermittent guttural moans she sometimes made that sounded like Chewbacca from *Star Wars*.

"Shoo, shoo," Dr. Griffin said, flicking her wrists.

The short fur on Shadow's back bristled. My dog repeated her low growl-bark.

Dr. Griffin straightened up at the very same moment that Shadow quieted. Then the veterinarian who wanted to Save the Living Unicorns! turned to face me. Below the words on her shirt was the profile image of a pink rhino. Maybe animal behaviorists didn't need to wear green scrubs, but I had expected her to at least be wearing a white lab coat.

"Sorry about that," she said. Her gaze darted to the corner. "Uh ... spiders."

Really? Shadow barked at many things, but bugs didn't interest her. And shouldn't I have seen brown dots skittering across the wall? But what if those eight-legged creatures were heading my way? Why hadn't she squashed them or captured the vile insects and removed them from the building? Dad taught me how to cover them with a cup, slide a sheet of paper under the opening, then release the creepy crawlies outside. I had never heard of anyone who tried to frighten them out of a room.

"You try to scare spiders out of your office?" I blurted.

Her smile revealed picture-perfect teeth that were white enough for a toothpaste commercial. My nose caught a whiff of peppermint.

"Of course." Dr. Griffin cocked her head to one side. "These little creatures see some big animal coming near them, they're bound to run away. If you were a spider, wouldn't you hightail it in the other direction?"

"Err ... I guess." In truth, I'd never contemplated the spider's perspective."

"Sit," she said, waving in the general direction of the chair. A command, not an invitation. Shadow's bum hit the ground, but I remained standing.

The doctor glanced down as if noticing Shadow for the first time, as if my dog were an afterthought and not the reason for my visit. "And this must be Shadow."

Well, duh. I stifled the urge to say something sarcastic because Game Plan Rule #8 indicated I must always display good manners. So, I pasted on a smile.

"Yes," I said. "This is Shadow."

Dr. Griffin got down on all fours and rubbed noses with my dog. I couldn't believe it. What was she, an Eskimo?

Shadow didn't seem to mind this woman's eccentricities. My dog's hind end shimmied as though Dr. Griffin was her long-lost master. The doctor rose to her feet and extended her hand, waving her fingers with impatience at my dog's leather lead until I surrendered the leash.

The vet squatted down and then hefted all sixty-five pounds of my dog onto her desk. Shadow was unusually small for a female Dobie, but it still took quite a bit of strength to lift her. Dr. Griffin walked around behind the massive oak furnishing and sat in the leather chair, as though placing dogs on wooden work surfaces was an everyday occurrence.

I took the seat on the opposite side, sitting on the edge. Nothing she had done so far had put me at ease.

On the wall, her college diploma announced she had earned her Doctor of Veterinary Medicine from the University of California at Davis. This prestigious university degree might have given me some comfort if not for the fact that her certificate was matted with a fluorescent orange border, and the ensemble displayed with a green border with daisies at each of the four corners. This crazy frame coupled with the slump of her shoulders and her wispy unkempt hair made me feel she was not going to be able to help me.

Dr. Griffin followed my gaze, turning her shoulder to examine the framed document.

"Oh. The city makes me display that, but it's so stuffy. I livened it up."

Stuffy? That stupid floral frame diminished the significance of her hard work. Her statement further served to confirm that coming here had been a mistake. Yet, I was at a loss as to what else to do.

Shadow didn't seem the least bit upset about standing atop a desk, even though she knew furniture was off limits. My dog lifted her head in the regal manner of a Westminster show dog. Her red coat shone copper under the fluorescent lights. Dr. Griffin's chair creaked as she leaned forward. I couldn't see the veterinarian's face, but a pale hand reached out to stroke my dog's belly.

"Shadow, sit," Dr. Griffin commanded.

Shadow's rump settled onto the desk surface and Dr. Griffin dropped the looped end of her lead. My dog's lower jaw dropped open into a lazy pant, exposing her pink tongue. Behind my dog's seated form, I could now see Dr. Griffin's face. She craned her neck around Shadow's back and cupped her hands around her mouth like she was about to call a child in from outside.

"You have some things for me?" she said, her voice muffled by her strange behavior.

I felt like I had fallen down a rabbit hole into the world of *Alice in Wonderland.* I was too stunned to speak. My hands seemed to act on their own without the permission of my brain. They handed her the form I had filled out in the waiting area and my check for seventy-five dollars. She stood and took the items with her dainty fingers. She thrust my paperwork with the information about Shadow unread into a desk drawer. The signed rectangular paper that relinquished almost all of my meager savings to her was folded and slipped into her pocket before she sat down.

Why had I handed over her fee? Now it was too late to take Shadow and leave. Stupid, stupid, stupid. Well, at least I could get proof to show the Animal Control officer that I was trying to solve Shadow's problem.

"Uh, I'll need a receipt," I stammered.

Dr. Griffin raised an eyebrow that had been plucked

good manners. "I'll be sure to schedule an exorcism."

"Please," she said, coming out from behind her desk. "Don't go. You've booked a full half hour."

Yeah. A half hour too much. I considered asking for a refund, but I needed the receipt for the Animal Control officer. I strode to the door without responding, well aware that she followed us. The Doberman in the photo seemed to smirk at me as I passed by. Dr. Griffin's office was nothing but smoke and mirrors.

"Wait. You obviously love your dog."

She ran and intercepted us at the door that led into the waiting area. Concern shone from those startling blue eyes of hers. "Your dog needs help." She pressed a business card in my hand. "In case you change your mind."

She sprinted through the reception area then darted toward the exit. I thought Dr. Griffin might block my escape route. Instead, she opened the barrier as though she were a door attendant at an expensive hotel. I felt her watch me stride to my white Honda Civic.

Dr. Griffin remained fixed in the doorway as I loaded Shadow into the back seat. I drove out of the lot under her unsettling gaze. With a depleted bank account and no clue how to keep Shadow from disturbing the neighbors, I was worse off than when I arrived.

CHAPTER THREE

I shut my front door a little harder than necessary, tossed my keys and cell phone on a shelf in the entry, then hung Shadow's leash on a peg next to the doorframe. My pup panted and wagged her tail at the speed of a hummingbird's wings, as if to say, "Don't be upset, this will all work out." I was in no mood for her charm. I felt like an idiot the whole drive home. I couldn't believe I wasted seventy-five dollars on that wacko vet.

Ghosts? Give me a break. My flip-flops slapped across the hardwood flooring in the entryway and into the dining area, making an empty, hollow sound.

Afternoon light fell on my new oval, oak table. The polished surface sparkled, and the familiar wave of shame passed through me. Twice in less than a month, I managed to violate Game Plan Rule #6: Don't spend money you don't have.

It had been stupid to buy this table during my fit of rage. I had been sitting at our old, rectangular, cherry table envisioning Dad engrossed in the morning newspaper. It was a memory of the way Dad peered over the headlines when I joined him at breakfast that sent me over the edge. All of a sudden, one question consumed me: How could he have left me? That's the thing about grief, it could descend at any time. It wasn't rational. Once it grasped my heart-strings and cinched them tight, it wouldn't let go. It twisted, contorted, and delivered blows of unbearable pain. That's what happened every time I had looked at that table. Some-how that four-legged, wooden piece of furniture came to represent the whole of my misery.

I became convinced that as long as our old table re-mained I couldn't shake the image of Dad's broad grin spreading across his face before delivering his standard line, "Morning, Pumpkin. How'd you sleep?" This had been his daily morning routine until he was hospitalized. Even when I rolled my eyes and told him for the millionth time that I'd grown too old to be his pumpkin, he just laughed and shook his head.

I fought hard against the pain the memory brought, slamming my fists on the table. Poor Shadow scrambled into the back bedroom as I screamed up at the ceiling, "Come back and call me Pumpkin. Right now. Do this RIGHT THIS SECOND or I'm gonna hate you forever." Breathing hard, blood singing in my ears, I tipped over the wooden symbol of my former life, stormed to my computer, and ordered the first oak table that popped up on my Google search. I broke Rule #6, Rule #1: Don't make rash decisions, and Rule #3: Always prepare for the worst. I failed to keep the promise I had made to my father while he lay dying: Follow the Game Plan. I had demonstrated that I was a poor excuse for a daughter.

Now Dad's letter lay face up on the polished tabletop. Even though I knew I shouldn't, even though I knew that once I started, I wouldn't stop reading, even though that familiar stab of loss would reopen the wound, my eyes sought the words anyway.

My Dearest Sarah,

First and foremost, I want you to know that you are the best thing that ever happened to me. I just wish I could start over. I have so many regrets, and I have made many mistakes. I wish I had been a better father.

I'm sorry, Sarah. I'm sorry I did not give you the fairy tale childhood. It's not fair that you never had a mother to tuck you in at night. I'm sorry you never had the white picket fence. I moved you around so much. I wish now that I had given you that puppy you always wanted.

I'm sorry you won't see me glow with pride at your high school graduation. I wish I could be there to settle you into a dorm room and to walk you down the aisle on your wedding day. I would have enjoyed being a grandfather to your children.

But KNOW this. Know this without doubt, without reservation. You were loved. And so I offer you one final gift.

The enclosed laminated card holds all you need to face the challenges that lay ahead. As I write this, we have already talked through the Game Plan Rules. I hope that when you read them now you will not see tips or guidelines, but the love and heartfelt wishes behind each and every one.

Use them, be safe, be happy.

All my love, Dad

The words "*You were loved*" scrawled in my father's familiar, loopy handwriting caused my chest to seize up. I caressed the signature with the tip of my thumb, wishing I could tell him not to be sorry, that I couldn't have asked for a better father. He had been brave. Right up until the end. In his strength, I found courage too.

Death is an intimate affair. Those last few days we held hands constantly—something we hadn't done regularly since I was in fourth grade. Surrounded by all those beeping machines, he brought up past grievances, apologized for leaving me, and professed profound love. In turn I laid myself bare. Right before he died, Dad called me in closer and closer until our foreheads touched and we breathed in each other's air. There wasn't anything left to say at that point. His train was barreling toward a destination where I couldn't follow. We both knew it, and we were both powerless to change its course.

Dad used to tell me I was like the Brazil nut. Of all the fruits, this one has the toughest outer shell. He told me I was so strong that I could handle anything. Whenever he gave that speech, I knew what was coming. Another work transfer for him. New school for me, new city for us. After a while, I started to believe my heart had changed into one giant seed from that South American tree, and I could handle anything. Anything … except losing my dad.

The hurt slammed into my chest. I staggered backward distancing myself from the table that represented betrayal. It was so strange, but its newness somehow represented the knowledge that my father wasn't coming home. In some part of my brain, the memories of sitting around my old table had been transferred to the new shiny surface of this tabletop. It became a physical reminder that there was no escaping the tangled knot of sorrow that my father's passing left behind. I learned the sad fact that the anguish I felt couldn't be thrown out with the furniture.

My knees slumped together, and I sagged against the wall for support. Shadow whined and leaned against my legs. Even my dog couldn't lessen the searing pain that washed over me like a rogue ocean wave.

I wouldn't let the tears out. Just like at the hospital, just like at the funeral, just like at the gravesite where I had tossed dirt and tulips onto the coffin lid, I would not give in to the sadness. To cry would be to start to let him go. As long as I held strong, he would remain close. He would stay a part of me. Each passing day it seemed harder and harder to hold on, and I was so tired. So very, very tired.

My legs gave out, and I slid down the wall. I gathered Shadow in my arms. I had to pull myself together. Breathe. Just breathe I told myself. I closed my eyes pressing my forehead against my dog's muscular chest. She leaned into me, licked my hand once then opened her mouth so that her teeth clutched my thumb in a gentle bite, so tender it was as though she lifted a newborn pup. She did this sometimes in bed at night. Her way of just holding on and making sure I didn't go anywhere after she fell asleep. That small, loving gesture was enough to center me. Shadow always seemed to sense exactly what I needed.

"Good dog," I said.

I took a few deep breaths, squared my shoulders, and straightened my spine. Shadow once again brought me back.

Okay. Now what? My brain rifled through the Game Plan rules until I found one that applied. Game Plan Rule #9: Take one step at a time. I released my dog, stood and, once again, shoved my feelings into my deep, dark place.

Only then did I notice the captain's chair. I could have sworn the green-and-pink-floral, upholstered cushion had been tucked under the table before we left for the vet appointment. Dad was a fanatic about having me align the seats in their proper positions—a habit that I still maintained. Perhaps I had been too distracted to notice because of Shadow's barking and the shock that Mr. O'Shawnessy turned in a complaint to Animal Control without talking to me first.

I glanced at the official form on the table. Dad had said to stay away from the authorities. I promised him that I would do whatever it took to keep my age a secret. Could

I? Could I give up Shadow? But if I didn't find her a new home and her barking resulted in me going into foster care, I wouldn't be able to keep my dog anyway. She would probably be sent to the animal shelter. I shook off the image of her locked up in a cage.

I assumed that if I flashed my receipt from Dr. Griffin to show that I had taken steps to address Shadow's barking, Animal Control would give me a break. Was I kidding myself? Even if my good faith effort kept me out of trouble for a while, sooner or later another grievance would be filed. Sooner or later, a court appearance would be required if I couldn't find a way to keep Shadow quiet. If I could only figure out what triggered her barking. It wasn't being left alone. She barked even with me here. Maybe I overlooked the obvious. Maybe she was only hungry. I hadn't tried feeding her more. It was worth a try.

"Hey, pup," I said, reaching down and patting her head. "Let's get you some food."

Shadow didn't charge into the kitchen at the word "food." Instead her attention remained riveted on the captain's chair. With her feet planted and her docked tail standing erect, the short, spiky fur along her spine rose to attention.

"Shadow." I placed my hand on her back. "Oh, sweetie. It's only a piece of wood."

Dr. Griffin's diagnosis was that Shadow saw ghosts. I remembered that strange diamond pattern and what I thought were eyes. I recalled the coldness to the wall. Could a spirit have moved into my dining room? Perhaps Dad had come back from the grave to show his displeasure at my foolish purchase. I shook my head. Yeah, right.

"Rururururururu." Shadow sounded like an obstinate car engine that refused to turn over.

"Shadow," I said. "You have to stop doing this."

I grasped the back of the chair to shove it into place so my dog would see there was nothing to fear. When my fingers curled around the smooth, wooden back, cold encapsulated my hand as though I had plunged it into a bucket of ice water. Alarm ricocheted through my brain and spiraled down to my toes. My heart reverberated like a jackhammer as I jerked my arm back.

That stupid vet. She planted the idea that a ghost lived here. Now I overreacted to a cool draft of air. No way did I believe that animal behaviorist's bogus claims.

When I lifted my arm to push the chair into place once more, Shadow launched into full-out barking. I gripped the top of the chair. No ice, no wind chill factor this time. The wood remained at room temperature. Shadow had no reason to be unhappy with an inanimate piece of furniture. I would show her that the chair posed no threat.

I reached down to smooth the cushioned seat. My fingers tingled as though a jolt of electricity passed through my hand. The fabric was warm. Someone *had* been sitting there recently.

Fear pierced me. Shadow had probably picked up the scent of an intruder. Probably the creep invaded my home whenever I left the house. This jerk must have a key, entering at will. Shadow had been barking at the intruder. This time I nearly caught the person red-handed.

A shiver originated at my neck and traversed the length of my body. Was the prowler still inside my house? Maybe lurking in my closet? I should call the police. No. They would ask where my parents were, and my secret would be revealed. We had no choice but to leave.

I backed away then turned and dove for the door. From where I stood, I still had a clear view of the crooked chair. I shoved my cell phone and keys into my pocket and pulled Shadow's leash from the peg.

"Shadow. Come on, Shadow." I kept my voice light in case the prowler was within earshot. "Let's go for a walk."

Shadow trotted to my side, but her eyes remained fixed on the chair as though the intruder still sat there. My hand fumbled around Shadow's neck for the ring on her collar. She quivered with tension, becoming more and more anxious until her whole body shook. She skittered out of reach every time I tried to attach the lead. I squatted next to her and rested my hand on her head. Rather than calming her, she issued a volley of growls at the chair. Her body stiffened. The air grew still. The seat hadn't moved, yet something had shifted.

As I tried to figure out what was wrong, a hazy image materialized behind the vacant chair. A boy about my age appeared before me like a photograph developing in a dark room. The teen wore a collared shirt covered with diamond-shaped designs. Diamonds. The same pattern I glimpsed in that exact spot earlier.

The youth's bell-bottom pants flared at the ankle—an outfit befitting John Travolta from that classic movie, *Saturday Night Fever*. I blinked hard. This couldn't be real. Shadow lunged toward the translucent form, but now I had a firm grasp on her collar. The young man tipped his head back and laughed as his see-through body faded.

And then poof. Just like that, the image was gone. What the hell just happened? When I was a little girl, Dad assured me that Casper, the Friendly Ghost, lived only in books, that there was no such thing as spirits. I had believed him. I still believed him.

There must be another explanation. I hadn't slept well for weeks. Last night I tossed and turned until four in the morning. We learned in science class that extreme sleep deprivation causes hallucinations. That must be the cause.

"There's no such thing as ghosts," I said to the empty chair.

I straightened my spine in righteous indignation. The seat I tried to push into position scooted completely out from under the table all on its own. I clutched Shadow to my chest from my crouched position. The chair tipped backward and clunked to the floor with a decisive thud.

Still, my mind rejected the idea of a ghost. There must have been an earthquake. Except why hadn't I felt it? Maybe one of the chair legs had loosened. Things fall over. Gravity has its own set of rules.

"I don't believe in ghosts," I said to convince myself.

The tipped chair lifted off the ground discrediting the idea that the Earth's pull had something to do with this insanity. I took a deep breath. The intruder went to great lengths to scare me. The chair must be rigged with fishing line. Probably the creep wanted me to flee so he could rob me. Yes, leaving would be a good idea right about now. I stood and stepped backward toward the front door.

My new wooden chair descended to the floor. Rather than tipping over, the four legs landed rooted to the ground as though nothing had happened. Shadow's growl grew into a frenzied bark. She pulled forward, and I lost my grip on her collar. Her bared teeth snapped at the empty seat.

Shadow's bravado buoyed my courage. I stormed over and swiped my arm between chair and ceiling expecting to find the invisible lines. My arm met empty air. I stumbled backward as though this inanimate object might decide to attack me.

I couldn't swallow, I couldn't breathe as the realization hit me. There was no intruder. My house really was haunted by a kid in disco clothing. And no ordinary ghost. My new home came with a poltergeist that could move objects. I had to get out of here, but my feet would not move.

The captain's chair rose into the air once more. Shadow's barking grew louder. Her bravery spurred me into action. My trembling fingers grabbed her collar. I fled to the entryway, dragging my dog with me. At the door, I was finally able to attach the leash.

"Heel," I commanded as I opened the front door.

Shadow gave a final bark and scurried out onto the porch. I slammed the door behind me and bolted down the driveway. My faithful companion fell in stride beside me as I raced along the deserted street. It wasn't until we reached the intersection that I realized we had no one to turn to and nowhere to run.

CHAPTER FOUR

The green rolling hills of Stone Ridge Open Space, just a few blocks from my house, was the only place I could think of to go. Adrenaline coursed through my veins as I sprinted up a brush-covered hill near the entrance. I couldn't seem to stop running. Could Dr. Griffin have been right? Even if I could convince myself that I imagined that spectral boy, chairs didn't levitate by themselves. If it were true and my house is haunted, I sure as hell didn't want to go back there. These preserved, hilly grasslands strewn with boulders and shrubs felt like a haven in comparison.

The path was so steep I could extend my hand straight out and touch the hillside. The jingle of dog tags informed me that Shadow trailed right behind me. I had huffed and puffed my way up this precipitous grade the last time I came here, carefully choosing my footing. Today, I scrambled, grasping at shrubs to keep my balance. The pungent scent of sage filled the air as branches snapped.

I crested the ridge, my heart thundering in my chest. My hands clutched my knees as I gasped for air. When I caught my breath, I continued at a walk. This section of trail was an easy hike but offered little protection from the wind. Ahead, a large boulder would provide shelter from the incessant wind and be a great place to regroup. Moments later, I collapsed and leaned into the giant rock.

Shadow nudged her cold nose between my arm and ribcage, poking her zipper-nose snout through to sneak a kiss. I remember reading somewhere that a person could see their soul in the eyes of a dog. What I saw in her brown eyes was unconditional love. My own heart did seem to stretch whenever she was nearby.

I reclined against the coarse stone. Shadow panted in my face but I didn't mind. It was so nice to sit without my hair whipping my eyes. I felt safe for now. The receding light of the afternoon sun reminded me that I couldn't stay here all night though. I needed a plan. Okay, if I accepted that there really was a ghost, who was he, and what did he want? Dad said the prior owners had moved away to retire in Florida. Was that disco kid their deceased son? If so, what happened to him?

Ghosts. I hadn't believed Dr. Griffin. Yet look at me trying to sort out the spirit's identity. I gave Shadow an affectionate squeeze. I had been thinking of her as psycho dog. I should have thought of her as psychic dog. Except what should I do now?

"Who ya gonna call?" The theme from that old movie, *Ghostbusters,* spilled into my consciousness. Who could I reach out to when cops weren't an option?

If only I could contact my Aunt Sally in Nevada. I had never met her. She and Dad had lived in different foster homes. Dad said she wasn't well in the head and I should pretend she didn't exist. Anyway, he once told me she collected newspaper clippings on the paranormal the way most homemakers collected recipes. I imagined she would probably hop on a plane, don an aluminum foil hat, and call the local news media. A group of reporters swarming my house would violate Game Plan Rule #5: Keep a low profile.

"Hey," a male voice startled me so badly that I jumped to my feet. "Look. There's the new girl."

Two teen boys jogging side by side along the relatively flat portion of the ridge slowed to study me. They appeared about my age and both wore friendly smiles. I wasn't afraid, especially with Shadow at my side.

One was tall, muscular, and blond, the other one skinny with windblown red hair—his curly locks shifting across his brow. Both boys stopped dead as my dog barked and pulled back her lips to reveal her sharp, white teeth. This was actually Shadow's version of a smile. The bark held no malice, but I didn't mind that the boys were afraid. The guy with the bulging pecs had treated his hair with enough gel to prevent the wind from ruffling it. There was an awkwardness to the skinny one that I found attractive and an arrogance to the tall one that annoyed me.

"What a beautiful dog," the redhead said. "What's its name?" he added at exactly the same time the blond boy asked me what mine was.

I debated not answering either of their questions, but Dad wouldn't want me to be rude—that would make me memorable. Still, I could deflect the question.

"This is Shadow," I said, pretending I hadn't heard the blond boy's request for my name.

"I'm Paul," the blond announced. "This here is Kyle. You live over on Cherryglen, right?"

How the hell did he know that? I bit my lip to hide my shock. I had been so careful to follow Rule #5 and keep a low profile. Where had I slipped up?

Kyle offered a goofy half smile, and I liked him immediately. A single red curl covered one eye in a sexy kinda way. He tilted his head as if in expectation then raised his eyebrows. I realized I hadn't responded to Paul's question.

Keep it together Whitman, I chastised myself. Remember what Dad said about keeping your distance. Don't you dare answer the question, Dad's voice agreed in my head. Trust the Game Plan. We rehearsed these situations.

"Nice to meet you," I gushed with a little too much enthusiasm. "But I gotta get going. My dad will kill me if I'm late for dinner."

"Yeah," Paul said. "I know how that is. Well, see ya."

"Be careful going down that hill," Kyle said. "There's a gravelly patch, and it's easy to lose your balance."

"Thanks," I said.

I smiled, and he grinned showing adorable dimples. My cheeks flushed with warmth. I turned my head away before Kyle could see me blush.

"Let's do another sprint along the ridge before we go," Paul said, elbowing Kyle and setting off in the direction they had come.

I knew I shouldn't, but this was the first time I interacted with anyone my age since moving here. It was the first time I hadn't felt alone in this town.

"Sarah," I called out after them. "My name is Sarah."

Kyle stopped, grinned, and waved. I lifted my hand and headed in the opposite direction, as Dad would have advised. He had told me not to befriend anyone my age.

It was a steep descent. I skirted the rocky section as Kyle suggested. My heart filled with gratitude that he cared enough to warn me. When I reached the park gate, I pulled out my cell phone. I was dying to call my best friend, Tess, from my old school and tell her about Kyle. I keyed the number then immediately hit cancel before the first ring. Dad had insisted that any correspondence with my friends be through texting. I opened the messaging program and punched a few buttons.

Hi How are you? I typed.

OMG. Cant talk. Getting hair done for prom.

Prom. I had forgotten. I pictured Tess and Derrik posing for pictures later tonight, dancing to hip hop, eating prime rib. What a different world she lived in. I couldn't even imagine describing the events of my day. Would she be worried about me? Would it ruin her evening? Or would she even believe me? If she did, what could she do anyway? I couldn't tell her where I was. She thought I now lived in Nevada, not here in California, a mere two-hour drive from her.

Kay. My fingers typed. I added. *TTYL.* I hoped that Talk To You Later would happen after I resolved my problems, and I could enjoy her detailed account of dress colors and juicy gossip. It might even feel as if I had been there and not missed the fun.

The temporary lapse into my old life helped me forget my predicament, but now I was at a loss as to what to do next. I couldn't go to my neighbor's house. Mr. O'Shawnessy had complained about Shadow. Jeez, this whole thing, the Game Plan, moving to a house in a new city where no one would know my age was such a …" I rifled through a list of my former English teacher, Mrs. Lutz', vocab words to describe the situation and settled on "calamity." It was clear I wasn't coping well with the transition.

The week before my father died, the school counselor had called me into the office. I never liked Miss Tuppenheimer. Her pinched face always seemed unhappy.

"Sarah," she had said, "Ms. Lutz and Mr. Mulkin have brought it to my attention that your grades have been slipping. I've heard your father has been hospitalized."

She thrust a paper across her desk. I picked up the sheet. Across the top was the Hospice logo of a white dove. The heading said, "Helping Teenagers Cope with Grief and Illness."

"As you can see," she continued, "falling grades are a

sign that you might be having trouble dealing with your father's health issues. I know this is a difficult situation. I'm sure never having experienced a mother's love makes it all the harder."

The brochure listed warning signs of teenagers' possible behavior when they were under a great deal of stress such as alcohol or drug abuse, sexual experimentation, and sleeping difficulties. It was true that my grades had dropped, but I managed to maintain at least a B in most of my classes and my lowest mark was a C. I hadn't taken drugs, but exhaustion ruled my world. Then the last bullet on the list of warning signs caught my attention: denial and acting overly mature. That was me.

I folded the sheet in half and thanked Miss Tuppenheimer without admitting that I might need help. I promised to work harder on my studies and told her not to worry, that I had survived sixteen years, five months and three days without a mother. And then I lied and said that my dad was doing much better. As soon as he was released from the hospital, we would be moving, so I probably wouldn't be completing the school year here. As I left the office, I wondered why acting mature was a bad thing when it was what my father expected of me from as far back as I could remember.

Paul and Kyle might be coming down the hill soon, so I knew I had to leave because I told them I needed to get home for dinner. I guided Shadow out the gate and up the block then sat on the curb to think.

The day Dad announced the tenth and final Game Plan Rule he prefaced it by saying that there was a solution to every problem. He went on to declare that there were seven directions—north, south, east, west, above, below and within. Traveling north, south, east or west would get your body wherever it needed to go. Looking above to the sun and stars would orient you in time and space. The ground below would show you where your feet were planted. "But," he said, "the most important direction in life comes from your voice within."

I closed my eyes and focused on my inner thoughts. Nothing. No blast of inspiration. I squeezed my eyes tighter. Still nothing. Maybe I was trying too hard. I softened my muscles trying to relax. I became aware of the edge of my phone digging into my skin. I shifted my weight, and as I pulled my cell from my pocket, Dr. Griffin's business card tumbled to the ground. Shadow sniffed at it then licked my cheek as if endorsing the idea of calling her. She encouraged me to reach out, even after I scoffed at her advice. I fingered the card.

"Okay, girl," I said at last. "We'll give it a try."

"Yes?" Dr. Griffin's low voice answered after two rings.

"Dr. Griffin," I said. "It's Sarah. I—"

"Is Shadow okay?" she interrupted.

Jeez. Was my dog the only thing she cared about? What about me? Then again, I stormed out of her office, claiming I was going to see my priest. I judged her as incompetent because she looked and acted different. I hadn't taken her seriously because of her strange behavior. Why should she be concerned about a rude teen girl?

"She's fine," I replied. "It's just … well, there was an … incident."

I relayed the paranormal events that occurred. The phone remained silent after I finished. Considering that she was paid to give advice, Dr. Griffin sure didn't have much to say.

"What should I do? I mean, should I buy some garlic or something?"

Silence. I couldn't even hear her breathing. Was she wondering if I was a danger to myself or others?

"Please say something," I said. "Recommend a crucifix or at least tell me you don't think I need a straitjacket."

"Uh-huh, uh-huh," Dr. Griffin said. "Yep, yep, yep."

Was that a yep to the loony bin or to the cross? I shouldn't have bothered to call. My finger sought the off button.

"Wait," she said as though she sensed my intention. "Give me a minute. This is a lot to take in."

"Ya think?" I said.

We both laughed. The next thing I knew she reeled off her home address, directions, and an invitation to dinner. I could even spend the night if I wanted. A home-cooked meal sounded like heaven.

"Thank you, thank you. I'll see you soon." I punched the off button.

At least Dr. Griffin believed my crazy story. How many

other people in this town would accept the idea that my house was haunted? I gave my dog a pat. Shadow liked her from the start.

I stood and headed for home. Shadow took the lead. When she turned and looked over her shoulder, sunlight glinted in her eyes. I caught my breath.

When I had called for the appointment, Dr. Griffin asked me if I had ever noticed anything unusual about Shadow, other than her constant barking. I said, "No," without thinking. I now realized there was something very odd indeed about my dog. Something that hadn't registered as significant until now. Hadn't Dr. Griffin wanted to take a picture of Shadow before we left her office? Could she have known?

Is this quirk about my dog connected to her ghost-viewing ability? I needed to show my printed photos of Shadow to Dr. Griffin. To get them, though, I had to go back inside my house.

* * *

I hesitated on the threshold of my front porch. The setting sun reminded me it would be dark soon, the witching hour. Was there such a thing as a ghosting hour? I only needed to grab a few overnight things, dog kibble, and the glossy pictures of Shadow then get out fast. Problem was I didn't want to go in there at all.

"Let's get this over with Shadow," I said as I unlocked

the door.

My dog whined, sat down, and braced her feet. I couldn't blame her. What if I had come to the wrong conclusion, and there was no ghost? What if a real-life intruder lurked inside? What if this guy watched a slasher film last night and decided to embark on a new level of crime? I shuddered. Suddenly, facing a poltergeist didn't seem half bad.

I shoved the door open before I lost my nerve then poked my head inside. I could peer to the right, through the entryway and into the dining room without setting foot in the house.

Fading light illuminated the dining room chairs. All stood upright. The one that had been askew and tossed around was now in its proper place. Its four legs cast eerie, dark shadows across the glossy shine of the hardwood floor.

Was it possible that I had imagined the levitated chair —a combination of lack of sleep and the power of suggestion? My purse still sat on the table, as did Dad's letter. A burglar would have taken my bag, wouldn't he? But would a ghost have righted the chair it had pushed over? Perhaps the poltergeist anticipated that I would call the police. If I had, the cops would have thought I was crazy. Sure, kid, the chair fell on its side then righted itself. Oh, sorry, you're right, it fell over *twice*, floated in the air, and picked itself up. Then I would find myself subjected to drug testing or a breathalyzer analysis. And by the way, they'd ask, where are your parents?

Well, too bad for you, Disco Boy or Creeper or whoever the hell you are. I ruled out going to the authorities. You tidied up your mess for no reason.

"Come on, Shadow," I said, stepping inside. "This is our house."

Shadow's rear stayed on the porch. I tugged on the leash. She rooted her feet and made that odd moaning sound when she didn't want to do something. Her eyes were so wide I could see the white edges. Poor girl. She was terrified.

"Okay, okay," I said, patting her head before tying the leash to the rain downspout. "You can stay outside. I'll go in alone."

I strode through the entry and turned left toward the back of the house, steering clear of the dining room for now. The bed covers were crumpled, just the way I left them this morning before I departed for my dreadful vacuum cleaner sales job. The room seemed undisturbed.

I tossed my gym bag on the bed and stuffed in a change of clothes, a few toiletries, sweat pants, and one of Dad's T-shirts that I used as pajamas. The photos of Shadow that I wanted were on top of my dresser. I packed those too. My heart rate steadied as I worked. As far as I knew, the ghost hadn't ever come into this room. Shadow's barking fits almost always occurred in the dining room. I remember it happening once in the kitchen. Now that I thought about it, she never barked after sunset either, which seemed strange.

Weren't ghosts supposed to be active at night?

The mirror above my chest of drawers reflected my image. The tan blouse Dad had bought me blanched my skin a murky brown. I preferred to wear vibrant colors like peach that made my skin glow, and teals and jades that accentuated the green in my hazel eyes. My nose looked less freckled than normal, but that would change with the summer sun. I fingered the tips of my ears, wishing I had ignored Dad's insistence that I let my triple piercings close up. Did Kyle like girls with ... Stop it, Sarah. Part of the Game Plan was to stay away from other teens. I pursed my lips remembering how Kyle had grinned at me. I tipped my head to the side. The lame silver balls in my lobes lacked the sparkle and style I wanted to express. I tucked a few loose strands of my hair behind my ears then froze.

Had I heard a noise? I held my breath.

Nothing. Not a sound. Even Shadow was silent on the porch.

I shouldered the gym bag. Best to get the kibble from the kitchen and get the hell out of here. For that, I had to pass through the dining room. I swung by the entryway first where I had left the front door open. Shadow hadn't budged. She whimpered at the sight of me.

"Stay," I said, even though I knew she had no intention of coming inside.

Steeling myself, I tucked my chin against my chest and plowed into the dining room, like a bull charging a matador's cape. I snagged my purse then swooped up Dad's letter and the laminated Game Plan card and shoved them into the bag before heading into the kitchen. I snatched the five-pound kibble bag from under the sink. Now to cross the dining area again.

I took a deep breath and stepped through the doorway. The musky scent of cologne accosted my nose. The smell was strong, right next to my shoulder. I raised my hand. Cold air encased my wrist like a metal bracelet as though a hand grasped my arm.

Dead air filled my lungs. I couldn't breathe. This was no hallucination.

Outside, Shadow burst into a fit of barking. Not her normal routine but a strange, primal sound. Anger replaced my fear. How dare this ghost terrify my dog. How dare this phantom boy try to scare me.

"Let. Me. Go," I said and jerked my arm.

The icy grip tightened then released. I rubbed my cool skin and clutched the dog food. A dining room chair slid across the floor and blocked my escape route. I had to get out of here.

Leaping over the obstacle, I slung both duffel and my purse over my shoulder. Behind me, the other three dining room chairs snapped to the ground in quick succession, making loud smacks like enemy gunfire. Shadow's barking reached a new crescendo. Why didn't my neighbors come to see what happened? Were they too accustomed to her yapping?

Still hugging the dog food, I slammed the front door

behind me. My knees buckled and I collapsed on the front porch. I dropped everything and gathered Shadow into my arms, rocking her back and forth, as though she were the one in need of comfort.

CHAPTER FIVE

The whole chair-tipping incident seemed surreal the closer my car got to Dr. Griffin's house. My foot eased up on the gas as I turned onto her street. One-story single-family homes bordered the straight road on both sides. Dad and I had lived in many places just like this one. Small, semi-upscale houses designed for people who were only passing through town until their next job assignment took them elsewhere. Dad would have called it a cut above economy seating, suitable for the business crowd, definitely not first class.

Only one beater car interrupted the middle-class feel to the street. The rust-covered hood of the Toyota Corolla and scratched bumper were unmistakable. I had seen it before parked in front of Mr. O'Shawnessy's house though I had never seen the owner, who I assumed was either the gardener or maybe a housekeeper.

The numbers 242 on the mailbox at the end of the cul-de-sac confirmed I was headed in the right direction. No cars were parked curbside. Was street parking forbidden or were people not home? My Civic slid into the empty slot next to a yellow VW Bug in front of Dr. Griffin's garage.

I sat for a moment, the car engine ticking in protest as if it wished I would restart it. The street was silent. No kids in the yards, no sign of people, no dogs, not even a cat. The neighborhood felt deserted and eerie, as though people were hiding in their houses.

What was I thinking coming here? I didn't know anything about this woman. I had violated Game Plan Rule #1: Don't make rash decisions. This whole excursion suddenly seemed like a bad idea.

Shadow squeezed into the front passenger seat as Dr. Griffin emerged from her house. The vet was all smiles. A flowing black-and-tan sari replaced her "Save the Living Unicorns!" rhino T-shirt and khaki pants. She, well, she floated toward the car. That was the best description I could come up with for her smooth gait. Her chin swept side to side as if her head was loose on her neck. Something about the combination of her mannerisms and her physical appearance set my nerves on edge. With that pale skin and wispy blonde hair, she could have been a ghost herself.

I sighed. It would be rude to leave now. I would stay for dinner then decide whether or not to spend the night. I gave Shadow a command to stay and stepped from the car.

"Sarah," Dr. Griffin said. Her blue eyes shone with eagerness behind horn-rimmed glasses. "You made it."

My dog wagged her tail at the sight of her, let out an excited yip, jumped up, and pawed at the window. Shadow's fondness for the doctor should have comforted me, but I was too annoyed. I didn't get this kind of response from her when I returned from work.

"I so miss having a dog around," she said. "I just lost my sweet girl a few months ago and haven't found the right match yet."

No dog. This was welcome news because Shadow typically growled at her fellow canines.

"That's good," I blurted. Color rose to my cheeks as I realized what I just said. "I mean, I'm sorry for your loss. It's just that Shadow doesn't get along with other dogs."

"I expected as much," she said. "Other dogs probably sense she's different."

Different? How could other canines know Shadow was a ghost-seeing dog? Maybe Dr. Griffin was thinking of herself. She was most definitely "different."

A yellow haze settled on the street. It would be dark soon. My empty stomach ached for food. Shadow was probably ready for dinner, too.

When I opened my trunk to get Shadow's kibble, Dr. Griffin followed and snatched up my overnight bag. It took all my will power to squash my instinct to grab the duffel out of her hand and tell her I changed my mind. How could I, though, when even I didn't have a plan yet? So I did nothing.

A breeze kicked up, pushing spiky bangs into my eyes. The air was brisk. I pulled my arms against my side and suppressed a shiver.

"Brrr." Dr. Griffin shook her whole body like a dog emerging from a bath. "Let's get inside where it's warm."

Shadow clawed vigorously at the car door as if she intended to dig through the steel to escape to the outside. I told her to sit and waited until she listened before opening the door and attaching her leash. She lunged, vying to get closer to Dr. Griffin.

"Good dog," Dr. Griffin said. She leaned down to pat her head, while hugging my bag to her chest like I was a purse-snatcher. "Follow me."

She pushed open the front door, revealing a living room comprised of one tan leather couch, a floor lamp, one college-style bookshelf made of cement blocks and a single wooden plank, and a coffee table. The wooden surface held an assortment of rhino figurines placed in a circle with a silver-winged object at its center. Next to this strange arrangement, a picture frame that lay face down so I couldn't see the enclosed image. Where was her television? Didn't everyone have a TV in their front room?

"Come in, come in. Make yourself at home. Shadow can roam free."

I stepped inside. Shadow followed on my heels. A framed poster of Seurat's *A Sunday Afternoon on the Island of La Grande Jatte* hung above the couch. My art teacher had obsessed over this painting. He spent an entire class describing the way the use of color and millions of dots created this serene, carefree setting. My hands itched to pick up my own paintbrush as I marveled at how all those tiny spots of paint transformed into women with bouffant butts posing under umbrellas and men in suits lounging on the grass.

Seeing this print on Dr. Griffin's wall surprised me. It didn't fit her personality or the rest of her furnishings. I was trying hard to keep an open mind, but something didn't feel right about this place.

Shadow danced around my legs, tangling the leash around my ankles as she did her characteristic prance of excitement. Her red fur shimmered in the fading dusk light that filtered through the front window. I unclipped her lead.

My dog made a beeline for the coffee table. I squinted at the silver object in the center of the ring of rhino figurines that captured her interest: a molded, chrome eagle with outstretched wings. Had this once been the hood ornament of a car? What an odd thing to display. And what was the deal with the rhinos?

As if reading my mind, Dr. Griffin spoke: "The rhino is my spirit animal. It represents an ancient warrior clad in armor and serves as the ultimate protector because it will charge when challenged."

I wanted to ask about the central silver eagle that Shadow now sniffed, but my dog's reaction distracted me. Her stubby tail quivered then shook like a rattlesnake. I knew from reading up on dog behavior that a wagging tail could be a greeting or a warning, and that I needed to read Shadow's body language when we approached other dogs.

This wag, a rattler imitation, was the bad kind—the kind where I better steer Shadow in the opposite direction.

"Hmm." Dr. Griffin looked smug as though she just earned the highest test score in the class. Then she leaned forward and whisked the chrome trinket away, causing the folds of her sari to billow. "I'll just put this out of sight."

She disappeared down the hall to the right, still clutching my bag. My insides clenched with unease. What the heck was going on here? Shadow gazed up at me then wandered off to smell the couch. Her agitation vanished as she explored.

My own curiosity to take a peek at the hidden photo on the coffee table threatened to overwhelm my better judgement. It was odd. If she didn't want me to see the photo inside, why hadn't she moved it to another room? My fingers itched to flip over the frame to see what picture it held. The hair on the back of my neck prickled to attention at the idea. My voice within screamed *Don't you dare. Don't even think about spending the night here either. Okay, okay,* I told my inner voice.

I scanned the room for other photos. Maybe there was one of Dr. Griffin's recently departed pet. The vet would be the small breed type. A Lhasa apso or a dachshund. Dr. Griffin seemed too frail for a big dog. Not a single snapshot—canine or human—personalized the walls or the bookshelf. Maybe the tipped frame held her dog's image, and she missed her beloved pet too much to keep the image in view. But that wouldn't explain why there weren't any photos of loved ones on display. I wasn't surprised at the absence of a spouse's image since she wasn't wearing a ring, but the woman must have parents.

Dr. Griffin emerged from the hallway still holding my duffel. Her finger pushed her glasses up toward her eyebrows, while she cleared her throat four times in quick succession.

What a nut job. Instinct told me that I should absolutely follow Game Plan Rule #10 and listen to my inner voice.

"Whoops, I meant to put your belongings in the spare room," Dr. Griffin said.

"Wait," I said, intending to tell her I wasn't staying. The woman clutched my duffel to her chest. The gesture held desperation and something else that made grasshoppers dance inside my stomach. I hesitated but decided now was not the time. "I . . . uh . . . I want to show you something I brought."

"Let's wait till after dinner," she said clinging to my overnight bag as though she expected me to rip it from her hands. "Everything's ready."

Again, something in her tone, in the inflection in her voice at the word "everything," set me on edge.

Dr. Griffin disappeared into the hallway again then re-appeared moments later empty-handed. I followed her through the arched doorway that led from the living room to the north end of the house. A waist-high counter separated her kitchen and dining room giving the two rooms an open feel. A chandelier cast a soft light over her dining room table. The aroma of cooked pasta and butter renewed my stomach rumbling. Was Dr. Griffin like the witch in Hansel and Gretel, fattening me up before she stuffed me into the oven?

"Shall I feed Shadow?" she asked.

"No, I'll do it," I said.

She handed me a metal dog bowl. I measured out Shadow's kibble and placed her food next to a water bowl that Dr. Griffin had set on the tiled kitchen floor.

As my dog gobbled her dinner, I surveyed my surroundings. In the dining room with its rectangular oak table and four straight-backed chairs, a formal setting for two had been arranged with dinner and salad forks, and both wine and water glasses. No plates though, as if food was not the main purpose of the meal.

"Please, sit," Dr. Griffin said.

I did as I was told, taking in the smaller, fluted glassware. She was serving wine. With Dad's make-over, I knew I could pass for eighteen but twenty-one? Perhaps this was part of her plan to keep me here—provide enough alcohol so I couldn't drive home and take "her" precious Shadow away.

During Tess' sweet sixteen party, I had tried zinfandel. She had snuck a bottle from her parent's wine cellar. I was one of three friends invited to sleep over that night and the four of us drank the whole thing. Of course Tess' parents noticed the missing wine. They blamed me, the new girl in town, for corrupting their daughter. Since Dad and

I moved so often, this was a common occurrence. Parents always wanted to blame me for their kid's behavior. They wouldn't have believed it was Tess' idea, not mine, even if I had ratted on her, which I hadn't.

I had enjoyed the fuzzy feeling from the wine and the way everything seemed so funny. As tempting as it might be to take a sip or two tonight, I knew I needed to keep a clear head. So even if Dr. Griffin offered me wine, I wouldn't accept her offer.

The vet migrated to the refrigerator and extracted one clear and one dark-colored wine bottle. She filled her wine glass with a chardonnay then filled my stemmed glass from the dark green bottle. I recognized the bubbling, light amber fluid as sparkling cider and felt foolish for thinking she had planned to get me drunk. Obviously my "new look" hadn't fooled her into thinking I had reached drinking age.

In moments, a green salad and a plate of steaming pasta, smothered in a rich cream sauce nestled against a mound of broccoli, appeared in front of me. A basket of sliced bread completed the meal. Everything looked delicious.

"Eat up," Dr. Griffin said as she took her seat.

I cheated and took a mouthful of fettuccini before tackling the salad. Mmmm. I savored the hint of basil and sautéed mushrooms in the sauce. Dr. Griffin could add a diploma in gourmet meal preparation to her office walls—preferably without flowered borders. Even the silly plaid dinner plates rimmed with Scotty dogs didn't diminish my enjoyment of the food. "Delectable," Mrs. Lutz whispered in my head. I silently shot back, "Shush."

Whenever I had complained about Mrs. Lutz's vocabulary tests, my father said my teacher explained on Back-to-School Night that these weekly quizzes had a proven track record of improving SAT test scores. Not that it mattered now. I had missed my SATs because Dad had been hospitalized the night before my scheduled test.

"So," Dr. Griffin said, "you work for Cyber Vacuum Service."

She paid closer attention to my forms than I expected. Dad had told me that if there wasn't a question, I didn't have to respond. And never, ever offer information. I also wasn't supposed to be rude, so I nodded.

I maneuvered a bite of pasta onto my fork and took another mouthful. Shadow finished her own dinner and now her head warmed my thigh under the table. I reached down and patted her.

"I think I've heard of the company," Dr. Griffin added, with a hint of disapproval in her voice. "Don't they mostly hire college students?"

Again, I nodded. Dad had insisted I apply for that very reason and because they were lax on background checks. Many people didn't agree with Cyber Vacuum's practices. They offered a free carpet cleaning to get their young employees into people's homes. We were trained to convince reluctant customers to let us in by telling them that the business earmarked fifty dollars for our college expenses for every room we cleaned. This was true. It often worked because helping out kids that were trying to better themselves tugged on people's heart strings. I asked the company to set aside my extra earnings for U.C. Davis for next year, explaining I decided to work for a year before starting college.

Some thought Cyber Vacuum exploited young people. I didn't think it was a bad deal. We got a cash bonus if we sold a vacuum in addition to the minimum hourly wage and the fifty bucks in school money if we scored a carpet cleaning.

I stuffed another huge forkful of food in my mouth to discourage further questioning. Dad would be proud of me. I was following Game Plan Rule #5: Keep a low profile.

Dr. Griffin took a swig of wine. She nibbled a few bites of her dinner. No wonder she was so skinny. Aquamarine eyes peered at me through those awful tortoiseshell glasses.

"So, what are you studying in college?" she persisted.

Dad and I had practiced my responses to this line of questioning. I set down my fork, chewed, then swallowed hard. I had prepared for this scenario.

"I missed the application deadlines because I was caring for my father. I'm saving money and working right now."

"Yes, I saw on your form that your father had passed away," she said. "I'm sorry. I'm sure he was proud that you plan to attend college. Do you know what you're going to major in next year?"

That was a harmless enough question.

"I haven't decided," I said, "probably art history or maybe architectural design."

"Were either of your parents architects?"

"Nope," I said. "My mother was a housewife before she died giving birth to me. My dad opened up new restaurants."

An image of my father in his business suit formed, causing that familiar tightening of my chest. He had been so pleased when his boss began calling him "The Starter"—a twist on "The Closer."

I hadn't been happy though. It meant we never settled in one place. Though now I wouldn't care if we moved every month if I could have Dad back in my life. I pushed my plate away. I wasn't hungry anymore.

"Sorry. I shouldn't have mentioned your father," she whispered. With the palm of her hand she hit her forehead a few times. "Dumb, dumb, dumb."

Dr. Griffin stabbed a large piece of broccoli and stuffed it in her mouth. Dad always said I should get people talking about themselves if things became too personal. I waited for my host to swallow, before asking my question.

"What made you specialize in animal behavior?" I said.

The woman cocked her head, as though listening for an answer. She picked up her fork. The silverware slipped from her grasp and bounced off the edge of her ceramic plate before clattering to the floor. Shadow startled from her position under the table, scrambled away, and planted her rear in the far corner of the dining room, still facing us. Her ears pricked forward as though curious about what would happen next. Dr. Griffin got down on the floor.

"It's oo-okay," Dr. Griffin crooned to Shadow. "Did I scare woo?"

I wasn't an animal behaviorist, but even I could tell my dog wasn't that frightened. The woman crawled over to her. She stroked the top of Shadow's head and whispered something. I strained to hear, but I only caught a word here and there.

"My fault," she said. "Long ... not used to being around people ... couldn't ..."

What the hell was she mumbling about? I leaned across the table under the guise that I wanted a piece of French bread. Shadow's nose tracked the food in my hand. She wiggled away from Dr. Griffin to establish herself next to the table in case I dropped a few crumbs. Dr. Griffin nodded at me as if to say I think she's going to be fine then returned to the table bearing a lopsided grin.

I remembered Shadow's photos. After mentioning that I had something to show her, I navigated back through the dark living room and down a narrow hall. My bag was on a bed in a room across from the bathroom. I retrieved the envelope with the pictures and didn't linger. I didn't like leaving my dog alone with this woman.

"You had asked me if there was anything unusual about Shadow," I said as I reentered the dining area. I handed the packet to Dr. Griffin. "Take a look at these."

"OOOhhh," Dr. Griffin removed the dozen or so carefully arranged headshots from the envelope. "My favorite poochy-pooch."

Jeez. What a freak.

Dr. Griffin breezed through the next five photos. Nothing remarkable about those, other than the fact that Shadow either had her head turned away from the camera or her eyelids were always squinted closed. The last few were the ones that held the surprising images.

The woman squinted as she reached the bottom of the stack. She sat up straight in her chair as she studied the indoor shots where I had used a flash. Her lips tightened, and she kept her eyes downcast. Really? She didn't have anything to say about Shadow's strange eye color? Dr. Griffin's fingers dropped the last photo ceremoniously onto the top of the pile.

"Our Shadow isn't ... what's the word? Ah, yes. Photogenic. But we wuv her, don't we?"

Our Shadow? She was my dog, not hers. Shadow's tail went thump, thump under the table. She always wagged her rear end at the sound of her name. Why hadn't Dr. Griffin commented on Shadow's eye color?

The odd woman propped her elbows on the table, fingertips together. Her upper teeth bit her lower lip. My face must have given away my uneasiness.

"I'm sorry," she said. "I shouldn't have had any wine. Yep, yep, yep. Bad idea. I'm feeling all woozy-snoozy. But if you give me a moment, I think I can explain."

Dr. Griffin went through the doorway toward the living room without another word. What a whack-a-doodle! How did this strange woman ever graduate with a veterinary medicine degree? I considered following, but in the end, I settled back into my chair.

Dad used to say you could tell a lot about people by how they decorated their home. Clearly, Dr. Griffin loved animals, especially canines. Rhino salt-and-pepper shakers seemed to be the only objects not dog-related. Cloth placemats even held the word WOOF in the center.

A small wall-mounted television faced the kitchen table but could be swiveled toward the granite island so she could watch shows while she prepped her meals. Apparently, she didn't see the need to have a TV here and in the living room.

I drummed my fingers on the table. What was taking her so long? Various species of dogs adorned the face of her wall clock. A dachshund image represented the six and a black lab at the top instead of a twelve. It was 8:30 (poodle-dachshund), then 8:35 (poodle-boxer). A black Doberman took the 11 spot, which made me smile. Finally, she breezed in with a stack of photos in one hand and the picture frame that had been face-down in the other.

"My dog died," she said.

She had already told me. Maybe her dog's death was the reason she was acting so weird. My grief counselor had said everyone reacts differently to loss.

"Wasn't Celeste the cutest puppy?" Dr. Griffin gushed

as she sat down across from me and presented a stack of glossy pictures that showed a puppy with bandaged ears.

Celeste. That would be a name she would choose.

Then as if presenting a diploma, Dr. Griffin presented the framed photo of Celeste as an adult.

I almost gasped. The outer gold frame surrounded a close-up view of a sleeping Doberman. The front paws extended out toward the photographer. The head, resting on the extended leg, sported the distinctive copper eyebrows and muzzle. What struck me the most was the characteristic ridge of the recessive zipper-nose trait. While Shadow had prominent orange coloration from her paw to just above the joint on her left leg, the copper highlights on Celeste's visible leg in the photo were more yellowish and extended almost up to her chest. The dog in this picture could easily be from the same lineage as Shadow, especially given the shared zipper nose. Is that why Dr. Griffin had hidden the photo?

I returned my attention to the pup with bandaged ears. A pink collar studded with metal stars encircled her neck.

"Aw," I said wishing photos carried the scent of puppy breath.

In the next picture Celeste was older. This, too, was a shot of the dog's head, angled to get a profile view.

I rifled through a half dozen similar photos. Each time, Celeste had managed to avoid looking at the camera. Dr. Griffin reached across the table and snatched up one of Celeste's photos from the bottom of the stack. She pressed the picture against her heart. Her breath came in short intervals like she was trying not to cry.

Guilt swept over me. Maybe Shadow, a Doberman just like her former pet, reminded her of her loss. Perhaps having a four-legged pooch in her home caused her pain. The dog clock ticked as I struggled to find something to say.

"She must have been very special," I whispered at last.

"She was," Dr. Griffin took a deep breath, "in so many ways." She pulled the photo from her breast and placed the picture of her dog before me. "This afternoon in my office, well, now you see why I knew right away that Shadow could see ghosts. Because Celeste used to bark at them, too."

My hands trembled, and my abdominal muscles clenched as I stared at the image. This photo was snapped at night. The typical "red-eye" effect was absent. Just as in Shadow's portraits, Celeste's eyes glowed fluorescent purple.

CHAPTER SIX

The screech of Dr. Griffin's chair against the hardwood floor jarred me back to reality. How long had I stared at Celeste's photos? Shadow emerged from beneath the table. I massaged her neck. Ghosts, huh? Those purple-eyed photos offered compelling evidence. My poor dog was cursed.

"Do you think it's a Doberman trait?" I asked.

Dr. Griffin shrugged. Other questions fill my head. Where had Celeste come from? Could she be related to Shadow? How could she be so sure there was a ghost?

"How did you figure it out? That she saw ghosts, I mean."

Dr. Griffin's whole body stiffened. She stood and went into the kitchen without responding. She turned her back to me and wiped at her eyes. Shadow's ears pricked forward. She rose and trotted in the opposite direction toward the dark living room. I followed my dog to give Dr. Griffin a moment to compose herself.

Shadow crossed the living room then disappeared into

the corridor that led to the bedroom where my bag was. I followed the sound of her clicking nails that sounded like one-fingered typing.

A hall light illuminated a hardwood floor. This was a bit odd since the living room and bedrooms were all carpeted in the same drab tan color. To my right, an open door offered a glimpse of the master bedroom. A black comforter dotted with white stars and yellow moons covered a queen-sized bed. A print of Van Gogh's *Starry Night* hung above the headboard. All that swirling air with the cobalt blue sky and scattered stars left me feeling unsettled.

Unsettled. That was a good word to describe Dr. Griffin. It wasn't that she fidgeted or even acted nervous. She just seemed uncomfortable in her own skin.

The bathroom door was open. My overnight duffel lay on the double bed in the bedroom across the way. Straight ahead, my dog stood silhouetted against a closed white door at the end of the hall. The short fur on Shadow's back had straightened up like fresh-mowed grass.

When Dr. Griffin had whisked away the hood ornament, she turned left in this passageway. Had she put the object in that closed room? Is that what was upsetting Shadow? She growled then lifted her forepaw and scratched at the door.

Whatever lay beyond that barrier, Shadow wanted in. Perhaps Dr. Griffin used the room as a home office and had files that smelled of dogs and cats. That would explain my pet's reaction.

A gurgle of running water emanated from the kitchen. I imagined Dr. Griffin splashing water on her face to compose herself. I still had time. It felt wrong, but I snuck down the hall to peek at what lay behind the white door. I grasped Shadow's collar so she wouldn't bolt inside the room, and ever so quietly twisted the doorknob. Locked. A chill spread from the base of my spine and traveled down to my toes.

"Sha-dow? Sar-ah?" Dr. Griffin called.

Her voice came from the living room just around the corner. I jerked my hand off the doorknob as though I had been burned and let go of Shadow at the same time. She darted toward the living room, her tail wagging a greeting. I stole into the bathroom.

"Just using the restroom," I called out.

I closed the bathroom door and leaned against it. Who locks rooms in their own house? What didn't she want me to see? And what did I really know about her? Suddenly, spending the night at home with a ghost seemed preferable to sleeping in this odd woman's house.

I turned on the faucet and stuck my hands under the cold water. The green eyes staring at me in the mirror were too wide. I removed the rubber band and released my dark brown hair then tucked an errant strand behind my ear. Dad had insisted that I keep my locks contained in a ponytail, but I preferred my hair loose like this. He had blown a gasket when I dyed a bright red stripe down the center of my part line like a colored Mohawk. That was my response to the news that his cancer was terminal. The disappointment and sadness in his eyes, and his soft protest about how pretty my natural hair color was, not the angry rant that followed, convinced me to dye the stripe back to its original brown.

Dr. Griffin's soft voice wafted from the living room when I emerged from the bathroom. I paused in the hallway, listening. I deciphered words like "good dog" and "there, there." I peeked around the corner. Dr. Griffin and Shadow snuggled together on the couch. My dog rested her pointy, reddish-brown muzzle on the woman's thigh and gazed up at her with a soulful expression. I couldn't understand. Why wasn't Shadow leery of this woman?

The vet fused her index and middle finger and placed them in the space between Shadow's eyes. One of Shadow's quirks was that she LOVED being stroked along her zipper nose. But Dr. Griffin wasn't really petting her. Her fingers stayed motionless while she scanned the room. This was too weird. No question about it now. No way was I spending the night here either.

I tiptoed back down the hall and closed the bathroom door with a thud as though I had just emerged. Then I walked into the living room. Dr. Griffin dropped her hand as if she were a kid caught raiding the cookie jar. Shadow nuzzled closer to her.

"That was a lovely dinner," I said. "But I always sleep better in my own bed and Shadow's never barked in the evening so the ghost must stay away at night. I'm thinking I'll go home after all."

"Oh, but you can't." Dr. Griffin clutched Shadow to her. "We haven't even had dessert. There's a slice of key lime cheesecake with your name on it. I'll make us both a cup of coffee, too. And tomorrow's Saturday. There's no need to go to bed early."

Shadow slurped a kiss. A tingle of jealousy in me spilled over into irritation. She was my dog, not hers.

"No, thanks," I said and took a step toward the hall to collect my things.

"Perhaps you would consider leaving Shadow then?" she said.

What? I paused and turned to face her. No way. She was so enamored with my dog it wouldn't surprise me if she fled the state so she could keep Shadow. She must have read my expression.

"Surely you want to do right by your dog. Taking her back to your house where she feels threatened is, well, it's just plain cruel."

Cruel? How dare she accuse me of animal abuse.

"In that case," I said, "I'll drive to Sacramento. We can stay at my sister's."

"That's a long drive," Dr. Griffin's right hand clutched Shadow's collar.

The vet's expression was one that you would expect from a wounded animal trapped in a cage. Maybe unsettled hadn't been the right word to describe her after all. Perhaps tragic would be a better term.

Tragic. What a loaded word. Warning bells jangled.

I should never have gotten involved with this woman. I had enough of my own problems. I walked through the hall and into the spare bedroom to retrieve my things. She didn't follow, but I could feel her presence thick and heavy in the next room.

"Trust me." Her unsteady voice called out. "It would be better if you stayed."

How dare she presume to decide what was in my best interest? I wanted to yell back that I was an adult, capable of making my own decisions. Then realizing where my choices had led me, the lie stuck in the back of my throat, and I said nothing.

What did she mean by "it would be better," anyway? Was that a threat? I grew cold inside. Would she barricade the door? My trembling hand searched my purse contents. Nervous fingers located the soft leather of my tan wallet, passed over the crinkly plastic of a Kleenex packet, until they encased the smooth hard case protecting my cell phone. This link to the outside world calmed the thundering rhythm of my heart. I could threaten to call the police if she tried to stop me from leaving. I shook my handbag listening for the clink of metal against metal to find my keys then exited the room armed with car keys in my right hand, an iPhone in my left.

Dr. Griffin stood by the front entrance. Her expression held only resignation. She had leashed up Shadow, and her outstretched arm offered me the end loop of the leather lead.

"I'm sorry," she said. "I only wanted to help. For Shadow's sake, please call me tomorrow."

She seemed so vulnerable standing there with the leash extended like a peace offering.

Thank you for dinner," I said.

I snaked my hand through the looped end. Dr. Griffin opened the front door. Shadow sat on her haunches and whined.

"Come on, Shadow."

I tugged at her leash. She planted her feet. I squatted to brace myself for handling the weight of lifting her, but she lunged from my grasp.

I felt uncertain. Shadow didn't want to go home. She would probably balk about going inside our own house. Wouldn't it be better for her to spend the night here? Now that I knew Dr. Griffin wouldn't stop me, I felt silly. I really had nowhere else to go. Splurging on a hotel room that I couldn't afford violated Dad's Game Plan #6 about money. She was odd, but harmless enough. And while something felt wrong, returning to a house where chairs floated in the air and skittered across the room to block my exit seemed stupid. True, I had stumbled across a locked room, but what did that really mean?

I glanced toward the hallway. Maybe Dr. Griffin had a wad of cash stashed inside. After all, she didn't know me any better than I knew her.

"Well," I said. "Shadow sure doesn't want to leave." I set my bag on the floor. "Maybe . . ."

"Great," Dr. Griffin said as she shut her front door with a decisive thud. "Now how 'bout some pie and coffee?"

Shadow barked and jumped up against my thigh. Dr. Griffin grinned. Two of us were pleased. My voice within, however, rattled with indignation.

CHAPTER SEVEN

Shadow lay on the plain, tan comforter at the foot of Dr. Griffin's guest bed. I still wasn't sure if I had made the right choice, but it was too late to change my mind about spending the night. The bedroom door locked from the inside. Yet, my nerves remained on edge.

My eyes closed and I focused on my breath. Exhaustion should have hijacked me into a coma by now. When was the last time I slept through the night? A week ago? Two? How was I even functioning? I worried that my tired body and mind clouded my perceptions. How was I supposed to make good decisions if I couldn't think straight?

For the hundredth time today, I wished my father were still here. I sniffed Dad's T-shirt, but his scent had faded. I was losing more of my connection to him every day. I still had his letter. I folded up the precious sheet of paper and tucked the frayed envelope beneath my pillow as I had done every night since the funeral. My bedtime ritual complete, I reached up and switched off the light.

"Good night, Dad," I whispered.

Blackout drapes must have covered the windows because the moment the lamp went out, I couldn't see a thing. Shadow whimpered. I called her up to the head of the bed and lifted the sheets. She dove beneath the covers then circled around so that she could poke her nose out to breathe. I stroked her sleek fur until I relaxed.

I was on the verge of dozing off when Shadow jumped to her feet, lifting the sheet off me so that a waft of cool air startled me awake. If Dr. Griffin had tried to come in without knocking, I would have heard a key inserted in the locked door. Shadow must have heard an outside noise.

"Down, Shadow," I said then pulled the covers around me.

It was so dark in this pitch-black room that a murderer could be standing over me with a knife poised to stab me, and I wouldn't even know it. My hand patted around until I found my dog. Her whole body was taut. I listened to hear if anyone was in here. Nothing.

A low growl came from Shadow's throat. Unease overloaded my senses. I fumbled for the switch on the bedside lamp. The light snapped on. I squinted though I could still make out shapes. No hulking form stood near the bed. I blinked a few times until my vision cleared. The closet door stood open just as before. I could see that the scattered shoeboxes and random clothes on hangers had not been disturbed. Nothing seemed out of place.

"Go to sleep, Shadow," I said, reaching for the light.

My dog stared at the empty wooden chair in the corner

and curled her lip. Holy crap. I didn't want to believe it, but if a ghost sat there, her behavior would make perfect sense. If Dr. Griffin's dog Celeste had seen spirits, wasn't it possible that I had traded staying in one haunted house for another?

The old-fashioned chair cushion did not match the décor of the rest of the room. Even the color scheme was off. The avocado green embellished with yellow ochre diamonds clashed with the tan comforter and patterned blue-and-beige curtains. Shadow inched forward like a lion stalking its prey. The diamond pattern reminded me of the ghost's clothing I had seen in my own house.

I pulled Shadow into my arms. I kissed my poor dog's zipper nose then stroked her head. A flicker of movement at the edge of my vision drew my attention, but when I turned, nothing was there. Was it fatigue? Power of suggestion? Could there really be a ghost? If the seat wasn't cold, that would be proof that there was no spirit in this room. There would be no sleep if I didn't check. I flung off the covers and swung my legs over the side of the bed. The fur between Shadow's shoulders rose to pointy spikes.

"Stay," I said.

I tiptoed forward. Shadow's growl turned into full-out barking. Crap. She was going to wake up Dr. Griffin.

"Quiet," I snapped.

She whimpered then grew silent. I braced myself and approached the chair to touch the outdated fabric just as Dr. Griffin pounded on the locked door.

"Sarah," she screeched. "Sarah, are you and Shadow all right?"

Her extreme reaction only frightened me more. I clutched my arms to my chest, suppressing a shiver. Still, I had to know if I was alone in this room or if a ghost sat in the chair.

"Yes, yes" I called. "Just a minute."

I gathered my courage. My hand snaked out. Just as I had experienced in my own house, I felt a wall of icy air enclose my hand all the way to my elbow. I backed away.

"Get out," I shouted. "Go away."

Oh crap. Dr. Griffin probably thought I had spoken to her. I regretted my outburst because suddenly I wanted another human nearby, even if it was a potentially crazy woman. A few short steps and I opened the door.

Dr. Griffin's expression sent icicles spiraling down my spine. Her eyes had a glazed look. Instead of looking distressed, her face twitched as if she could barely contain a smile. I remembered how she had pretended there was a spider in her office earlier today. Had a ghost been there too? Well, two could play at this lying game.

"A spider," I said. "There was a spider. But it's gone."

"It's okay," she said in a flat monotone. "I'll talk to him."

She stared at me without recognition. I passed wiggling fingers in front of her face. She didn't blink. Was she sleep-walking?

Shadow hadn't moved off the bed. Her tail moved in a

lazy, uncertain way as she looked toward us. My dog cocked her head to the side as if awaiting an answer to a question.

Dr. Griffin didn't seem to notice Shadow at all. She was either in a very deep trance or a very good actor. How could she have been calling my name and banging on the door one moment then lapse into this catatonic state the next? And what did she mean by she would talk to him?

"Who?" I said.

A coy smile passed her lips. Dr. Griffin wore a slinky, blue teddy that matched her eye color. Her sexy nighty seemed completely out of character.

"Oh, where are my manners?" She grinned. "Allow me to introduce you to David."

She wrapped her arms about her torso as if giving herself a hug and swiveled side to side. Pale blonde hair swayed across bare shoulders. Years of aging melted off her face. The woman before me transformed into a smitten schoolgirl.

Holy crap. This was way, way, way too weird. I tried to control my breathing. Was this really happening? Could my extreme tiredness be causing hallucinations? I blinked and shook my head. Nothing changed. The frozen expression remained on Dr. Griffin's face.

I should grab Shadow and get the hell out of here. No. Game Plan Rule #1: Don't make rash decisions. Right.

I would wait till she left and fell back asleep to make my escape. I managed to shake my head up and down.

"Hello, David," I said imitating her calm, flat voice and

nodding at the chair before turning to address Dr. Griffin. "Maybe you should take David to your room."

She extended her hand out like a child wanting to hold her mother's hand as she crossed a busy street. Shadow let out a single, sharp bark. Dr. Griffin's fingers curled into a loose fist then she turned toward the direction of her room.

"Good night then," she said. "Don't worry. I'll make sure he understands."

I shut the door and pushed the button on the lock. I turned around so that my back braced the door then my knees gave out, and I slid to the floor. Holy crap. I was stuck in a house with a woman who had a ghost for a boyfriend. I had stepped into a situation worse than the chair-tipping ghost at my own house. The sooner I got out of here, the better.

Shadow jumped off the bed and came to my side. She leaned into me and gazed up with somber, brown eyes. My dog seemed more confused than frightened.

"So," I whispered, "I suppose you know what this David looks like."

Shadow licked my cheek then wiggled her hind end as if to say he's okay—as long as he stays away. I heard the click of Dr. Griffin's bedroom door closing then nothing. I contemplated getting up to turn off the lamp but decided against it. Maybe the light would keep David away.

I stroked Shadow's head until she laid her head over my heart and closed her eyes. She may be fond of Dr. Griffin, but she was still mine. We sat like that together until my dog dozed off. I waited a while longer until I managed to convince myself that Dr. Griffin was asleep too.

Shadow stiffened as I inched her sleeping form off my lap and to the side to prepare to open the door. She had balked at leaving earlier this evening. Maybe she would be more cooperative without Dr. Griffin standing nearby. I put my ear to the door and listened. Nothing. I had left Shadow's leash on the coffee table. I would retrieve her lead, and we would make our escape. I had worn my old gray sweat pants and a T-shirt to bed, so I only needed to fetch my belongings, locate the flashlight that I had brought, and sneak out before Psycho Woman woke up again.

I stood and slowly turned the doorknob, holding the button so it didn't pop out with a click. Shadow stood, stretched, then hovered by my heels. Not good. I patted the bed, and she jumped onto it.

"Stay," I said in a hushed voice in the meanest voice I could manage.

I waited until she lay down and dropped her head between her paws then I edged the door open. A waft of cold, icy air crept into the room and encapsulated my hand. It took all my will power not to scream. I shut the door fast. The cold receded even before I engaged the lock.

David stood watch outside the door. Even if Dr. Griffin slumbered on, we were still stuck. Imprisoned by a ghost.

CHAPTER EIGHT

I frowned at my watch and set it back onto the night stand. It was only 3:04 a.m. I flipped over onto my belly. My mind kept trying to convince itself that the cold air outside my door could have been nothing more than a draft. Except if it had only been a breeze, why did my voice within, the one that had wanted me to leave earlier this evening, now demand that I stay put?

Hours of sleeplessness stretched before me like a vast desert plain. I stuck my hand under my pillow and clutched the envelope that held Dad's letter. Holding it never failed to comfort me. If he were still alive, I wouldn't be in this mess. I wondered if he had ever considered that his Game Plan could put me in danger. No one knew where I was. Tess thought I was in Nevada. Mr. O'Shawnessy had never been inclined to stop by to visit. Our encounters were outside when I walked Shadow. It could be days before he realized I had gone missing. Even my company probably was used to no-shows since they employed college kids. I had remained aloof with my fellow sales representatives, another precaution to keep my secret safe. Aloof. Another of Mrs. Lutz's vocab words had slithered into my brain. "Aloof," she had announced in her scratchy smoker's voice that day, "when used as an adjective, it means to be distant, either emotionally or physically."

I sighed. Did Dad realize that secrets devour you from the inside out? I felt like I would forever travel on a path of eggshells in a world where not only did I have to be quiet, I had to keep my dog silent too.

Maybe there wasn't even a ghost. If only I could see what my dog saw. I remembered the flash of movement I had seen when petting Shadow tonight, and hadn't my hand been on her head when the ghost-like teen had materialized in my dining room? I saw Dr. Griffin search the living room tonight while her fingers lay between Shadow's eyes. Perhaps if I touched my dog's zipper nose in that spot, I could see this David that Dr. Griffin talked about. I would know whether a ghost stood outside my room. The trick would be to keep Shadow quiet.

Shadow stirred as I sat up then stood to retrieve my purple headband from my overnight bag.

"Good dog," I whispered as I wrapped the soft material around her muzzle to keep her from barking.

She leaned against me as if to let me know she didn't mind.

"Stay," I said as I moved to the bedroom door and opened it.

A cool breeze swirling around the doorframe entered

the room and hovered just inside. Shadow jumped to her feet but remained on the bed. She growled, though as I had hoped, she didn't bark. I went to her, turned to face the doorway, pulled in a deep breath, and placed two fingers between her eyes.

At the threshold of the bedroom, an image started as a flicker, like a light bulb dimming, then resuming full illumination. I sucked in my breath as the black-and-white silhouette of a male materialized. His head formed a billowy shape that faded in and out. I snapped off the bedside light. The solid outline of a body glowed. Other features soon emerged like a developing photograph.

David was young, maybe eighteen or nineteen, clean cut with a military buzz, and decked out in a tuxedo. His eyes were darkish, as was his hair. He probably would have appeared brown-haired and brown-eyed if he had appeared in Technicolor. Maybe it was his youth, or maybe I was shell-shocked by everything else that had happened, but I found myself unafraid of him.

David's glowing, transparent form loitered in the doorway as though mistletoe hung above him, and he waited for a kiss. He twisted his head to the left, looking in the direction of Dr. Griffin's bedroom door. He didn't seem threatening. He just stood there, like a wallflower waiting for someone to ask him to dance.

"Hi," I said.

The spectral being lifted a semi-transparent hand and waved. A friendly gesture. A smile crossed his dark gray lips. I wanted to ask him all kinds of questions. Who was he? Why was he here? But how could he answer?

The worried frown that appeared whenever his attention shifted back to Dr. Griffin's bedroom disturbed me. Had Dr. Griffin warned him to stay away from this room? Except what could she possibly do to him? He was already dead.

"She scares me too," I said.

Shadow moved her head, shifting my hand, so I didn't see the ghost's reaction. David's features blurred like a camera out of focus. I repositioned my fingers, and he came back into a recognizable view. This time a hint of blue coloring tinted his eyes, and his skin held a slight peach hue. The ghost looked toward Dr. Griffin's door again.

"Is it safe to leave?" I whispered.

David's head swiveled in my direction. His eyebrows lifted, and he shook his head no.

Shadow growled and flattened her ears. My free hand grasped her collar. David lifted both palms as if telling my dog he meant no harm. Shadow whimpered. Her whole body remained stiff.

The ghost brought his hands to the ten-and-two position as if holding on to a steering wheel. He moved his curled fists as though driving. Then he lifted one hand and swiped it across his throat a few times.

"My car is dead?" I guessed aloud.

David nodded and pointed at Dr. Griffin's bedroom door. Had she disabled my car so I couldn't leave? A doorknob rattled in the hallway. Crap.

I jumped off the bed and closed the door as quietly as I could. I heard shuffling footsteps. Thank goodness, I had turned out the light earlier, and my sweet pup had stayed quiet on the bed.

The soft whisper of careful footfalls suggested Dr. Griffin stood outside my door. I held my breath. Time stretched. At last, I heard slippered feet retreat down the hallway. Perhaps, David had somehow told her all was fine. I paused a moment then pushed the lock. I couldn't risk another "conversation" with David with Dr. Griffin roaming the house.

I went to Shadow and removed the headband, massaging her muscular neck while she licked my cheek. There was nothing more to do but try to get some sleep. David had said it wasn't safe to leave, and I believed him.

CHAPTER NINE

The smell of bacon and eggs roused me. I sat up, feeling groggy and disoriented. When my gaze fell on the chair with the yellow and green cushion, the strange encounter with David the Ghost flooded back.

My dog stirred, then stood, arching her back in the manner of a cat engaged in a luxurious full-body stretch. Her pinkish brown nose sniffed the air, and her docked tail wiggled back and forth.

Had it only been a few hours ago that I had seen Dr. Griffin in a zombie-like state? That David the Ghost barricaded the hallway and told me that Dr. Griffin had tampered with my car so I couldn't leave this house. Would I be allowed to step out the front door this morning? A gentle knock interrupted my thoughts.

"Sarah? Are you awake?" Dr. Griffin said through the door.

Shadow rushed to the door full of exuberant energy. My dog's opinion about Dr. Griffin hadn't changed, but I had come up with my escape plan. When Griffin was within earshot, I would make a fake call to "my friend Charlene" to confirm our lunch date. I would even add that there was outdoor seating, and I planned to bring Shadow. Above all, I would act as if everything was normal, which meant I would have to make nice with Psycho Woman.

"Yeah," I said.

"Breakfast is ready." Dr. Griffin's muffled words filtered through the door.

"Okay," I said. "I'll be out in a moment."

I whipped back the covers and changed into a pair of jeans and a cobalt blue top. Easing the door open a crack, I reminded myself to appear calm and relaxed. The empty hall suggested Dr. Griffin had returned to the kitchen. Shadow headed in her direction.

"I'm just going to throw on some makeup, and I'll be right there," I called. "Can you let Shadow outside?"

"Sure," she called back.

So ordinary, this exchange of words. I rummaged through my handbag as I carried it into the hall bath. My car keys lay at the bottom. I would know soon enough whether my car would start. My cell phone charge indicator showed only one bar. Well, no matter. Even if it died, I only needed to make a pretend call anyway.

I washed my face, applied eye shadow, blush, and lip gloss then ran a brush through my dark hair. I patted tan cover up over the dark, saggy flesh under my eyes. My body desperately needed sleep, and it showed. With a straightened spine, I made my way to the kitchen. Eating a quick breakfast would keep up the appearance that nothing unusual had happened last night. Things were under control.

"What can I do to help?" I asked. The food smelled so good I didn't even need to force a smile.

"Nothing," Dr. Griffin said, flitting around the counter with a pitcher of orange juice in one hand and a plate of sizzling bacon in the other. She had donned a pair of blue jeans and a white, frilly blouse as if she too wanted everything to appear normal this morning. The only thing odd about her was those hideous eyeglasses.

"Here," I said. "I'll put those on the table."

She relinquished the items. Her expression held only warmth and gratitude. She went to the stove to scoop a giant mound of scrambled eggs onto a platter. The sunshine flooding through the windows, the scent of bacon and the genuine kindness in Dr. Griffin's demeanor jarred me. In all the scenarios I had conjured last night about how this morning would play out, having a pleasant breakfast with Dr. Griffin had not been one of them.

"Sit, sit," she said. "How did you sleep? I was a rock."

It was all I could do not to let my jaw drop.

"Great," I managed to strangle out.

She didn't remember getting up and wandering the halls? Could sleep deprivation have caused me to confuse reality with a nightmare last night? Or maybe I had a weird reaction to her coffee? Perhaps she bought her beans from some organic store and natural herbs had caused me to hallucinate. Was it possible nothing extraordinary had happened, and I imagined all those weird events of last night?

No, my voice within said. *You are tired but you are NOT CRAZY. She's messing with you.*

That would explain why she was pretending not to remember knocking on my door in the middle of the night after Shadow's barking episode.

Shadow. Alarm bells went off. My head swiveled left to right as my panic grew.

"Where's Shadow?" I said, forcing my voice to remain steady.

"Oops," Dr. Griffin said. "She's still in the backyard. Celeste used to scratch when she wanted inside."

I went to the back door and opened it. My regal red dog stood right at the threshold awaiting reentry. Relief flooded through me.

"Sorry, girl," I said peeking out into the backyard. "Didn't mean to strand you outside."

The fenced yard was small like most newer homes, but well-groomed. Flowerbeds bursting with yellow daffodils bordered the fence. A single walnut tree offered the only shade, reminding me of the sugared walnuts my dad used to bake as an afterschool snack. My breath hitched at the memory. I gripped the doorframe until my knuckles paled. I hated the way the most obscure things caught me off guard and threatened to pull down the barricade I had constructed around my grief.

"Are you okay, Sarah?"

The last thing I needed to do was fall apart in front of Psycho Woman and give her an excuse to keep me from driving away from this Haunted Mansion. I swallowed hard. I put on my best Brazil-nut face and turned to Dr. Griffin.

"Uh … yeah. I was just wondering … do you ever get walnuts off your tree?"

"Walnuts? Never," she said. "This whole development used to be an orchard before …"

A strange expression crossed her face, as if she had said too much. How odd. Shadow bounded to her. Dr. Griffin patted my dog's head, and the moment passed.

Shadow wandered over to investigate the kibble and water in matching silver-colored dog bowls. She had never been much of a chowhound. Never chewed on furniture, never soiled the carpet, never been anything but sweet and loving. Her only fault was her loud, menacing bark that annoyed my neighbors.

"Coffee?" Dr. Griffin asked.

I sniffed the pungent aroma. She had the pot poised over an I-Love-My-Doberman mug with a red heart next to the word "love." I had gotten hooked on coffee during the long hours at the hospital. I could have used the caffeine, but what if her coffee really had caused my hallucinations?

"Uh, no thanks," I said sinking into the chair. "I'll just have orange juice."

The clear pitcher held a pulpy fluid. Fresh-squeezed.

This woman had gone all out. She poured a generous amount of juice into a clear glass and set a plate full of steaming scrambled eggs in front of me along with a napkin that pictured yet another Doberman. A black version of the breed decorated her coffee mug. If anyone ever needed a new canine companion, it was this woman.

"Maybe it's time you started looking for a new dog," I said.

I knew instantly that I had said the wrong thing. Dr. Griffin's piercing, aquamarine eyes filled with pain. How could I be such an idiot? She was still grieving.

"No dog could ever replace Celeste," she said. "I even saw her birth. She came from the third litter of my clinical trial."

Clinical trial? As in research? I shoveled in a mouthful of steaming food to hide my frown of disapproval. I had never liked the idea of dogs being used for science. Dad, however, said that animal studies were necessary for the good of humanity. Medical research hadn't saved him though. Maybe something good, like a better cancer drug, came out of her investigations.

"What kind of studies?" I said somehow managing to keep my voice light.

Dr. Griffin sat in the chair across from me with only two pieces of dry toast and a small serving of salad on her own plate. No wonder she was so thin.

"Dr. Humphrey used beagles." Dr. Griffin picked up a napkin and placed it on her lap. "I suggested Dobermans would be a better breed for our purposes."

Better for what? She hadn't answered my question. Dr. Griffin sipped her coffee then puckered her lips. She picked up her spoon then set it down. Just when I had decided she wasn't going to answer my question, those blue eyes peered straight at me through the thick lenses.

"A smart, working dog and the breed's emotional sensitivity would be so much more likely to detect movement," she said. "And with their repertoire of vocalizations, they might make a unique sound to alert us to the presence of ghosts. I was right, at least in part. Unusual barking, erratic bristling of fur. I was convinced the dogs were seeing ghosts. But Dr. Humphrey was too arrogant to see that our selective breeding program was making progress."

Ghosts again. She had studied the paranormal in college. That she had tried to breed dogs that could see spirits somehow didn't surprise me.

"My professor's colleagues considered our studies unscientific," Dr. Griffin continued in a chatty tone. "The funding for our studies was depleted by the time I graduated vet school."

I chomped on a piece of crisp bacon, while imagining a bunch of old codgers laughing behind their hands at their colleague who studied a dog's reaction to ghosts. This wasn't the kind of research a prestigious university would want to advertise.

"In appreciation for my work," Dr. Griffin nibbled the crust of her toast, "Dr. Humphrey let me adopt one puppy.

The remaining dogs were slated for a psychology study on communication through body language."

I suppressed a yawn. My tired brain tried to keep up, but jumbled thoughts made it hard to focus. My eyes latched on the stack of pictures of Celeste that still lay at the end of the table. The head shot of her pet did depict the same odd, purple eye color that I had seen in Shadow's photos. A ridge on Celeste's head sat in the same spot where I had touched Shadow and discovered that I could see David. Perhaps that was how Dr. Griffin knew to touch Shadow there. Taken together it seemed plausible that she could be telling the truth.

"Celeste's ability to see ghosts didn't develop until she was eleven months old," Dr. Griffin continued. "I was interning at a vet clinic here in Walnut Acres by then. I tried to locate the other dogs from her litter, but the lab informed me they had contracted the Parvo virus and had either died or been euthanized."

"How awful," I said.

"Even then I thought they were lying." She frowned.

Wait. What? A conspiracy? It was all I could do not to roll my eyes.

"And I think Shadow is proof." Dr. Griffin continued. "She has to be related to Celeste."

Could one of Shadow's parents be the equivalent of an escaped lab rat? This would explain her ghost-seeing ability. Shadow wandered to my side and leaned into my leg. I massaged the prickly fur under her jaw.

"So, you see," Dr. Griffin leaned forward. "I don't want just any other dog, I want Shadow."

I sucked in my breath. She had been going gaga over my dog, but I never expected her to admit she wanted to take her from me. The nerve of this woman.

"Are you out of your mind?" I picked up my empty plate, stomped into the kitchen, and dumped the dish in the sink. "She's my dog. She's not for sale, and you can't have her."

"Heyyyy." Dr. Griffin stood; hands raised as if surrendering at gunpoint. "Take it easy. I know she's your dog. I was hoping we could come up with some arrangement that would benefit us both. Maybe you could bring her by my clinic while you're working. That way Shadow would have company during the day. She wouldn't be barking and annoying your neighbors. I swear that's all I'm suggesting."

She would probably skip town and take my dog. I didn't even know if she would try to stop us from leaving today. I needed to get out of this house.

"I hate to eat and run," I said. "But I have a full day today."

"I'm sorry." Her gaze seemed filled with regret as she looked at Shadow. "I overstepped. You don't have to run off."

Now seemed like a good time to implement my escape excuse. I whipped out my cell phone and punched the asterisk and pound keys. While a woman's voice announced the number that I had dialed was not in service at this time,

I uttered a sugary hello and "confirmed my lunch arrangements with Charlene," just as planned. I hit the off button on my phone.

"I'm glad you were able to stay for breakfast," she said.

Her words seemed sincere enough. Shadow's tail thumped the ground. She adored her. Would my dog react this way if she were a psychopath? I would know soon enough if my suspicions had merit if my car started.

"Breakfast was delicious," I said. "Thanks again. I'll just get my things."

To my relief, she didn't follow me into the guestroom. I tossed my sweats in my gym bag and surveyed the room for anything I had missed. The crumpled sheets lay bunched at the foot of the bed. I felt a pang of guilt. I probably should strip them or at least straighten the sheets and comforter, but I did not want to linger here any longer than necessary, so I turned with my duffel on my shoulder and walked out.

Dr. Griffin had already leashed up Shadow. She smiled and opened the front door, handing me the bag of dog food and my dog's lead as I crossed the threshold. Shadow followed me outside without any of her former theatrics. She pranced toward the car while Dr. Griffin stood on the porch, watching.

I looked up and down the empty street. No witnesses, no one to turn to for help. Even the familiar dilapidated car was gone. This was not good.

With my gym bag and Shadow's food secured in the trunk, I loaded my dog into the back seat. I slid in behind the wheel, inserted the key, and twisted. The car started, and the engine settled into its familiar purr.

Dr. Griffin waved from the front stoop. I had no plans of ever seeing her again. I shifted the car into reverse and backed out of the driveway. My car seemed to be operating just fine. Had my Civic been functional last night, or had Dr. Griffin only temporarily disabled the car then fixed the problem this morning? Or had David lied? Was there even a David? What proof did I have that he existed? I was too tired to puzzle it out or try to make sense of anything.

CHAPTER TEN

My little white Civic turned onto Cherryglen Lane without incident. I planned to grab my phone charger at home then figure out where to go next. So much had happened that I expected my street to look different. Yet, as I drove along the asphalt stretch to my new home, the same trees yawned their shade, the same pansies bloomed pink along grassy borders. This quiet neighborhood shouldn't include a haunted house.

I pulled into my driveway. The Toyota Corolla that had been on Dr. Griffin's street last night was once again parked next door. In the morning light it was even more obvious that the front bumper had suffered many a scrape. The patches of rust dotting the hood also seemed more pronounced. The little red car had seen better days.

A black-haired girl about my age positioned a walker on the passenger side where Mr. O'Shawnessy struggled to get out of the car. This hunched old man in no way resembled my spry, elderly friend. Had he fallen ill enough to need a nurse's aide in these last few days?

I still couldn't believe my sweet neighbor had complained to the authorities about my dog. He was the only resident on this quiet lane who had come by to welcome us when Shadow and I first moved in. The sight of Shadow never failed to bring on his grin.

I enjoyed our conversations, though it was sometimes a challenge trying to decipher his mix of Irish brogue intermingled with a Scottish accent. I waved. An infectious smile spread across the round face of the short, bald man. Mr. O'Shawnessy lifted his hand in greeting. The young girl with him looked up but didn't smile. Shadow yipped in excitement. Her wiggling hind end whacked the seatback again and again with an enthusiastic thump, thump, thump.

Leaving Shadow in the car, I walked down the driveway to the street. I would retrieve the mail and morning paper for the sweet old man and ask why he had filed a complaint.

"Top o' the morning to ya, bonnie lass," my neighbor said.

Mr. O'Shawnessy's words were not spoken with his usual ... effervescence. Mrs. Lutz' nasal voice rang in my ear. Effervescence. This woman's vocabulary words seemed to follow me everywhere. The definitions would come unbidden: Excited. To behave in a lively way.

The old man's crisp, white shirt and lime green slacks might have been stylish in the 1970s. If he added a green top hat, a passerby might mistake him for a leprechaun. A lot of girls at my previous high school would have made fun of the old man's outfit, but I found his quirky clothes endearing.

"Mr. O'Shawnessy," I said, nodding at his helper, "are you two-timing me?"

His escort shot me a wary glance, like I was some kind of freak. What was her problem?

"Nay, nay." Wrinkles formed as he chuckled. "'Tis always a sight to behold, your pretty face. You remind me of me eldest child. This here be me granddaughter. She's come to live with me for the next year. She's moving in next week while her parents travel the world, aren't ye? Maggie, meet Sarah."

His granddaughter, of course. The one he said had a 4.0 GPA. Smart and gorgeous, blessed with arresting, green eyes and the blackest hair I had ever seen. No wonder he felt proud.

"Oh, Grandpa," she said with a self-indulgent whine. "How many times do I have to remind you? It's Margaret."

Margaret turned her back on me and guided her grandfather toward his porch. I had been dismissed. She hadn't inherited her grandpa's charm.

I jogged to Mr. O'Shawnessy's mailbox at the curb, retrieved his mail, then stooped over to fetch the newspaper. By the time I had caught back up to them, they had only progressed halfway up the walk. The short distance to the front door had winded him. He stopped to catch his breath.

I handed over a few pieces of junk mail and the folded

Centennial newspaper to Maggie who accepted them without saying thanks. My neighbor's face appeared sunken. His pale skin had shriveled to sharkskin gray. Each breath was a raspy wheeze. I had wanted to ask him about Shadow's barking, but now was not the time.

"Hey, where's Shaddie?" Mr. O'Shawnessy said, glancing around, as though he had read my mind.

He let go of the walker. When his hand reached into his pocket, he wobbled a bit. Maggie moved in to support his elbow and glared at me. Her upper lip lifted into a scowl.

"No treats for Shadow today," I said quickly. "Do you need a hand, Maggie? I could unlock the front door."

"It's Mar-gar-et," she corrected, drawing out her name as though I were mentally challenged.

Silky black waves shimmered as she whipped her head back and forth in an emphatic "no."

"Okay, then," I said, turning my back on Mar-gar-et.

"Mr. O'Shawnessy," I said, "you take good care of your granddaughter."

His chuckle followed me to my own mailbox. I removed the contents and headed toward my front porch. As I passed my car, Shadow pressed her nose against the opening in the window and moaned. She had balked at entering the house yesterday. Hadn't Dr. Griffin emphasized that forcing her to go inside would be cruel? I would leave her in the car for now.

I wasn't keen on the idea of going indoors either. When I opened the door, the first thing I noticed was that the dining room table and chairs were all in order. The "ghost" chair was aligned perfectly under the table. I strode straight to it and clenched the wooden back. No blast of cold air coated my skin. The cushion felt the same as the air temperature. Still, I did not want to remain here any longer than necessary. I made my way to the kitchen.

The doorbell rang. That was odd. I peered through the peephole. A grim-faced Mar-ga-ret stood on my porch. Had something happened to Mr. O'Shawnessy? I jerked open the door.

"Look," she said, "I've been staying with my grandpa off and on the last few days because he hasn't been feeling well. I may even be moving in permanently sooner than expected. Your dog's barking is intolerable. All that noise keeps Grandpa awake when he's trying to nap."

She thrust a handful of colorful pamphlets in my hands.

"My grandfather doesn't need you to get his mail for him. He needs you to get rid of that obnoxious creature."

"I'm sorry," I said. "I—"

"Because of your stupid dog," she spat, "I'll have to miss my prom. That beast has made Grandpa so sick he can't be left alone."

Prom? She looked too old to be a junior in high school.

"Wait," I said. "You can still go to the dance. I'll stay with him."

"It's too late."

Margaret turned on her heel. She breezed by my car. Shadow yipped a greeting.

"Shut up," she screeched in Shadow's direction.

How dare she yell at my dog. Shadow woofed then excitedly shifted from one paw to the other as she watched Margaret's retreating form. My dog seemed capable of finding the good in everyone. Maybe that explained her reaction to Dr. Griffin.

Margaret stormed across Mr. O'Shawnessy's lawn. At the front door to her grandfather's house, she turned and glared at me. It dawned on me then. M. O'Shawnessy. The M. stood for Margaret. She was the one who had filed the complaint against Shadow, not my elderly neighbor. Thank goodness I hadn't said anything. Mr. O'Shawnessy might have gotten mad at Margaret, which would have increased her hatred toward me and possibly put my secret more at risk. For Shadow's sake, I would have to find a way to win over Margaret.

I glanced down at the leaflets she had handed me. The same ones that had been included with the first Animal Control warning notice:

Why Debarking Your Dog Isn't Always Cruel
The "NO-BARK" Collar
Ten Tips to Keep Your Dog Quiet

I had already read all these pamphlets. I crumpled up the one about debarking. Mutilating my dog wasn't an option. The NO-BARK collar was too expensive. An Internet search revealed it was not always effective, besides the idea of shocking my dog into a quiet state seemed wrong. None of the ten techniques I tried had worked, probably because none of them addressed "What to do when your dog sees ghosts."

I dropped the useless brochures onto my dining room table then leafed through my stack of mail. I inserted my finger under the seal of my VISA bill and removed the folded statement. I held my breath as if the paper announced an Academy Award winner. I scanned the new charges: $50.00 for Mount Vista Veterinary Clinic. $150 total from the Chevron gas station because my job required a lot of driving.

Next, I opened my bank statement and stared at the balance in my personal account: $63.04. My finances were in worse shape than I thought. This was my allowance for the next week. I tossed the papers onto the table that I had impulsively purchased, a move that led me down this path of ruin. What was I going to do now? I didn't have enough funds to stay anywhere else.

Outside, Shadow let out a howl. I could practically feel Margaret's wrath descending on me. I grabbed my keys, a banana, and Shadow's dog bowl, filled a sports bottle with tap water, then launched myself out the door.

CHAPTER ELEVEN

Shadow was content to share my blanket and bask in the spring sunshine while I sat cross-legged next to her. Across the park, an Australian shepherd mix caught a Frisbee in mid-air. A yellow lab and a golden retriever played tug-of-war with a rope looped into a figure eight. Dozens of other dogs played with happy owners within the fenced, off-leash area. What would it be like to own an ordinary pet?

I couldn't let Shadow frolic with these dogs. Unfortunately, she dealt with her insecurities using a tough-gal routine, posturing and growling at other members of her own species. Her breed's unfortunate reputation as an attack dog made other pet owners leery. Thus, the off-lead area was off-limits to Shadow.

Ironically, the dog park was the reason I brought Shadow here. The leash-required section of park was almost guaranteed to be dog-free. The south end of the park didn't have picnic benches to entice park users, so it tended to be vacant.

My lids grew heavy as the sun warmed my face. Perfect napping weather. I eased onto my back. If only I could relax enough to sleep. But worrying about where we were going to stay tonight kept me from nodding off. It would be a disaster if Tess responded to my text, and I slept through it. I didn't have a Plan B if she didn't come through with an invitation for Shadow and me to visit for the rest of the weekend.

I still didn't know what to do with my dog on Monday morning. Muzzling Shadow for a full day to stifle her barks wasn't an option. The only way to guarantee the contraption would stay on while I was at work would be to cinch it tight, but she wouldn't even be able to drink water. What if she vomited? She could die. My only other idea was to take Dr. Griffin up on her offer, but relinquishing her to Psycho Woman, even for a short time, was also unacceptable.

Shadow's tail thumped the blanket. She yawned and turned her head in my direction. I leaned against her and Shadow rewarded me with a flick of her tongue across my cheek.

Disturbia lyrics originated from my purse. At last, Tess was getting back to me. Even if a sleepover wouldn't work, I was dying to know all the details from her prom night. As I fished through my bag, it dawned on me *Disturbia* wasn't my text ringtone. Someone was calling.

I examined the gray screen, just like Dad had always insisted. I could still hear his unrelenting reminder. Don't answer if you don't know who's on the other end.

Caller ID announced C. Griffin. I put the phone away without answering. I had seen enough of this strange woman who was smitten with a teenage ghost named David.

After a few minutes, the phone strummed, announcing a new text message had arrived. Tess. Finally. I extracted my cell once more.

"OMG. Missed curfew last night. No sleepovers, no cell for 2 weeks. For being 5 minutes late. Can you believe it? Crap. Mom's coming to confiscate my phone. gtg."

Two weeks. Poor Tess. Her parents were so extreme. I pushed the off button. Tess had a Facebook page, but Dad had forbidden me to start one. I noticed I still only had one bar on the charge indicator. Crap. I had forgotten to pick up my battery charger.

A message flashed indicating I had a new voicemail. I wasn't interested in what Dr. Griffin had to say. When I opened my purse to replace the phone, I glimpsed the laminated Game Plan rules nestled in the bottom.

Oh, crap. My stomach knotted. Dad's letter. I left it under the pillow in Dr. Griffin's guest bedroom. That paper held the last message from my dad. I had to get it back.

Another realization hit. How could I have been so stupid? With the information in that letter, all she would need to do was an Internet search and find the story about a rise in cancer in younger men. My father would never have agreed to his boss talking to a reporter about his condition if he had known the article would mention me. The piece not only included my name but also my age. One look at the story and Dr. Griffin would know I was underage.

Dad would have said it served me right. If I had done the right thing and made the bed before I left, I would have found the letter. Maybe that's why she called. Maybe she had discovered the envelope when she went to strip the sheets. When I left this morning, I had been sure I would never step foot in Dr. Griffin's house again. Now I had no choice. I had to get Dad's letter back. My fingers typed in my password then hit the number one to listen to the message.

"Hi, Sarah," Dr. Griffin said, her voice flush with excitement. "It's about 4:00 p.m. Hey, I came across this journal article."

Journal article? What was she talking about?

Dr. Griffin gushed on. "I have great news. There might be a biochemical reason for Shadow's ability to see ghosts. And there's medicine she can take to fix it. Call me. 555-0105."

A beep sounded. Was it possible she had found a solution? What were the odds that she had come across that study in the few hours since I had left her house? None. This must be a trick so she could see Shadow again.

A stilted electronic voice asked me to push the number 2 to save or 7 to delete this message. My finger hovered over the 7 then shifted. I found myself hitting 2.

I had to get Dad's letter anyway. Besides, what if she really had an answer to Shadow's problem? This could mean no more citations, no more neighbors annoyed at my barking dog. I would be able to spend the night at my house again with Shadow. Better yet, after today, no more Dr. Griffin. My dog and I could go about our lives blissfully unaware of ghosts.

My fingers dialed her phone number. Once again, I had violated Game Plan Rule #1: Don't make rash decisions.

"Hello," Dr. Griffin answered on the first ring

"It's—"

"Oh, Sarah," she gushed. "It's amazing. Truly amazing. I was reading *Veterinary Medicine Today* where a veterinarian in Oregon published the results of his clinical trials on a new medication for Dalmatians."

I wished she would slow down but Dr. Griffin was on fire. She spewed words like an erupting volcano. I envisioned her flinging her hands in the air as she spoke.

"…because their liver fails to detoxify uric acid, this particular breed is subject to bladder stones. The experimental medicine is supposed to allow Dalmatian liver cells to absorb uric acid."

"What does this have to do with Shadow?" I said when she paused to take a breath.

"Oh, sorry," Dr. Griffin said. "It's just so exciting. During my dissertation, one of the things I noticed in the blood work of our dogs during the paranormal studies was a high percentage of a derivative of an amino acid called taurine. This doctor in Oregon, Dr. Baum, noticed that a side effect of this medication was that taurine appeared in the dog's tissues. This organic acid is normally found in ox bile, not dogs. Dr. Baum indicated all of the Dalmatians had excessively high concentrations."

"O-kay," I said.

Make your point, I wanted to add, but didn't. Shadow nudged my hand with her cold nose. I had stopped petting her after I placed the call. She pawed my hand. Neither one of us would get an "A" for patience.

"The eyes of the dogs in the clinic trial, in every single documented photo, glowed purple two weeks after they'd taken this experimental drug."

So? That would mean the drug induced a ghost-seeing ability. How would that help my dog?

"And?" I said.

"It was in a footnote," Dr. Griffin replied. "He put this huge, enormous finding in fine print. Dog Number DM775-2X, this dog, and only this dog, had been treated with a medicine for diarrhea, and his eyes didn't glow. This antidiarrheal drug could be a way to remove Shadow's paranormal ability."

I let hope seep through for a moment, then skepticism descended. She had probably made this up. My inner voice was telling me not to believe her.

"I called a colleague and ordered a metronidazole prescription for Shadow," Dr. Griffin continued. "The clinic is only a few blocks from your neighborhood. It'll be ready about 4:30 or so. I can pick up the drug and drop the medicine off at your house."

Crap. I hadn't anticipated she would want to come to me. I had to get back into her house. I had to retrieve that envelope with Dad's letter before she found it.

"That's okay," I stammered. "I'm not home. Let's meet at your place."

"That'd be even better," she said. "Shadow will need to be observed after she gets the first dose. You never know. She might have a bad reaction."

I hadn't planned on sticking around. Grab the medicine, grab Dad's letter, and make a quick escape.

"You can stay for dinner," she added. "I'm making pork chops."

Maybe sharing a meal while I was there wasn't such a bad idea. I could slip away from the table and retrieve the envelope while she was in the kitchen, rather than storming into her house and heading straight for the guest bedroom.

"Sounds nice," I said.

"I'll see you around 5:30. Okay?"

"Okay," I said. But before I said I couldn't stay long, my phone died.

Shadow pawed my leg again. I rubbed behind her ear. Even if the medicine didn't work, at least I would get Dad's letter back.

CHAPTER TWELVE

I turned my car onto Cherryglen Lane. Shadow lay on the backseat sound asleep. The prospect of returning to my house yet again left my stomach flopping about like a beheaded chicken. I didn't have much choice. I needed my phone charger.

An unfamiliar Lexus stood in front of Mr. O'Shawnessy's house. Two figures hovered next to the classy, silver car. The dark-haired person had to be Margaret. The guy standing next to her with his back to me must be her boyfriend. There was something familiar about his broad shoulders. The boy stiffened then folded his arms across his chest.

The blond-haired young man speaking to Margaret was dressed in a formal black tux. Black shoes shone in the late afternoon sun. Bedecked in skinny blue jeans with holes in the knees and a white tee, Margaret looked like a drab female bird next to a colorful male in resplendent plumage. The boy was dressed for prom, the dance Margaret was missing because of me.

When she told me earlier that she would skip her prom, I hadn't realized she meant tonight. This was so stupid. I could stay with Mr. O'Shawnessy. I would even have an excuse not to linger at Dr. Griffin's house. It could work out for both of us.

I pulled up alongside the couple. As I rolled down my window, I remembered Father's words: "Your biggest flaw is your impulsiveness." That's why Game Plan Rule #1 had been "Don't make rash decisions." But what could go wrong with this plan? Everyone benefited.

"Margaret," I said, "go get ready for the dance. I already told you that I can stay with your grandfather."

Prom Boy turned to look at me. OMG. It was Paul. One of the boys I had met in the open space.

"Sarah," he said. "That would be awesome." He scowled, and his head jerked back in Margaret's direction.

I had a sinking feeling that I had just made a huge error.

"What the hell?" he said, squinting at Margaret. "You said you couldn't find anyone to help out."

Going to prom was obviously very important to him. I had to fix this.

"Margaret," I said. "Really. You can go. I'll take good care of your grandfather."

"No," Margaret shot back.

"Margaret, what's your problem?" Paul said, kicking his car tire. "It's prom. Our prom."

"You can't be serious. I'm not leaving him with *her*.

How the hell do you know her name anyway?"

"What? I can't talk to other girls now? Kyle and I ran into her and Shadow while we were jogging."

"Shadow?" Margaret screeched. "I suppose you like that stupid dog too."

Paul stumbled backwards. He shook his head from side to side.

"What is wrong with you? As a matter of fact, I think Shadow is a pretty cool dog."

When I met Paul I thought he was arrogant, but perhaps I misjudged him. And he liked Shadow. For the first time, I noticed that the clear plastic package in his right hand held a wrist corsage of white carnations.

"I don't believe you." Paul clenched his right hand tighter and tighter until the outer plastic cracked, crushing the flowers inside. He dropped the mangled corsage and jerked open his car door. "We're done."

"Paul. Don't." Margaret's hand covered her mouth.

It was too late. Paul got into his vehicle and slammed the car door. The Lexus roared away, flattening the corsage into a nice, thin pancake.

What had I done? I had only been trying to help. How could things have gone so horribly wrong?

"Oh," I stammered. "Oh, Margaret, I'm so sorry."

"You," Margaret shrieked. Her cheeks puffed in and out. Green eyes as cold as lime popsicles bore into me. "You and that ugly dog of yours. Thanks. Thanks a million."

Margaret's ponytail swung like a pendulum as she

turned and ran. I drove to the end of the street and completed a U-turn. My car crawled by Mr. O'Shawnessy's house. Margaret still stood on the front porch. Her murderous gaze followed me as my Civic pulled into my driveway.

Oh, how I wished I could fix the mess I caused. Even if Paul decided to go to the dance, he probably wouldn't be able to enjoy it. Shadow's barking and my impulsiveness had ruined a special night for two people. And what about their friends? Where did the ripple effect end?

I took a deep breath then hunched my shoulders and ran for the front door like an old woman caught in a rainstorm. The inside of my house wasn't as intimidating as facing Margaret right now.

The dining room remained unchanged. My poltergeist had behaved during my absence. An empty grocery bag lay crumpled on the kitchen counter. On impulse, I snatched it up before heading for the fridge. A plan had formed. I had some nectarines and a couple of Fuji apples. I would suggest we have fruit salad for dessert. When Dr. Griffin went to put the produce away, I would retrieve Dad's letter then I wouldn't have to stay for dinner.

After the fruit was packed, and I retrieved an open can of dog food from the refrigerator for Shadow's dinner and added it to the bag, I spotted the last bottle of wine from my father's stash. A pinot noir from Napa Valley.

This time I would follow Game Plan Rule #3: Prepare for the worst. Even if my speedy escape plan failed, having

Dr. Griffin enjoy a glass of wine or two during the meal might allow me to leave after dinner without her making a fuss. I snatched the bottle off the counter. At the same moment, a cold icy grip encircled my wrist. Two things registered at the same time. The ghost was here, and it was touching me.

I screamed. The neck of the bottle slipped through my fingers. Liquid and glass shards splattered in all directions as it hit the floor. I shook my arm until the cold grip released.

As wine puddled across the floor, I backed out of my kitchen, turned, and fled.

* * *

My hands still shook as my car traveled along the main drag through town. With Dr. Griffin's house only a few streets over, I really needed to compose myself and act like nothing had happened. If I revealed how the ghost at my house grew bolder with every encounter, it would give Dr. Griffin a reason to insist that I spend the night again.

I flipped on the radio to find music to calm my rattled nerves. "She held me spellbound..." Lyrics from The Eagle's "Witchy Woman" triggered another bout of unease. Witchy Woman. Now, that was a fitting description of Dr. Griffin. I changed the station and an instrumental version of one of Dad's all-time favorite songs, "How Do I Live?" filled my ears. Tears pricked my eyes. I punched the sound off and rubbed the moisture away. The weight of my sadness sent a tremor of exhaustion through me. I shook my head to clear it.

A flash of light caught my attention. It must have been caused by the sun glinting off the hood ornament of an oncoming vehicle. It took a moment longer for the obvious to register. A tan sedan had swerved onto my side of the road heading straight for my Civic. I clenched the steering wheel, waiting for the driver to veer the car back into its lane.

The car accelerated but remained on course for a head-on collision. I straightened my spine, pounding my hand on the front of the steering wheel. Where was the horn? My foot depressed the brake pedal to give the driver more time to recognize their mistake and return to their lane. The distance narrowed. Five car lengths, four, three. Oh, holy mother. Can't they see me? Panic seized my muscles, and I froze. The encircled upside-down "Y" on the hood of the Mercedes bore down on me. Move back, move back, MOVE BACK.

At the last second, at the moment of certain impact, I jerked the wheel to the right, popping up onto the sidewalk. The other car barreled by, less than a foot from my car door. I glimpsed a flash of the gray-haired driver. The elderly woman hadn't even seen me. She peered straight out through the front windshield, without even glancing my way.

Somehow my car stopped. A loud noise blared in my

ear. I looked down and discovered my body had slumped against the horn on the steering wheel. I leaned back, and the racket stopped.

The quiet was even more unsettling, just the tick, tick of the engine. I couldn't remember turning off the car. Shadow nudged my arm then finagled her way into the front seat. She seemed unhurt and didn't appear freaked out by the accident. Behind me, the old woman had pulled over. Her car faced the direction of oncoming traffic, but she had guided her vehicle up onto the curb so that traffic could still pass.

My father's words played like a repeating tape recorder: "A car is like a loaded gun, you can kill yourself, and you can kill other people." This was the closest I had ever come to a collision. My father was right. We could all be dead if I hadn't steered the car out of the way. My hands shook, and a wave of nausea coursed through me.

I clutched my head between my hands and concentrated on breathing. Moments later, red lights flickered in my rearview mirror. I turned around and through the rectangular glass of my rear window, noticed that a cop now stood next to the elderly driver. Traffic slowed in both directions as rubber-neckers coasted by. My stomach hitched. There were no Game Plan Rules to handle this situation. How was I going to keep my secret now?

A knock on the car window startled me. Shadow barked, but she sat and quieted as soon as I commanded. A uniformed police officer motioned for me to roll down the window. He was blond and barrel-chested, a formidable presence, but his expression was kind. I turned the ignition key one click, hit a button, and the glass barrier disappeared downward.

"You all right?" he asked.

I nodded.

"I need your license, proof of insurance and registration," he said.

Why? I hadn't done anything wrong. My expression must have revealed my fear.

"Is there a problem?" he asked.

"Uh, no," I said, hating the quake in my voice.

I pulled paperwork from the glove compartment then fumbled in my purse for my wallet. My hand trembled as I passed the items to him.

"I'll be right back," he said.

He sauntered toward his black and white cruiser. A red-haired pedestrian rushed over and intercepted the cop. They chatted then she followed him to his car. He nodded, jotted down a few things, then spoke into a radio receiver.

Shadow crawled into my lap. She placed her head on my chest as though checking my heart rate. I pressed my face into her sturdy body.

"I'm okay," I whispered. "But you need to get in the back seat."

I gave her a light shove, and my dutiful dog hopped into the rear passenger side. I turned to give Shadow a pat and saw the officer was once again heading my way.

When I shifted my legs, a whiff of wine drifted up from my damp jeans. I had been in too much of a hurry to get out of my house to change my clothes. Would the officer smell alcohol and assume I had been drinking? I knew I would pass a Breathalyzer test, but he would probably want to call my parents. Crap.

The cop had a stiff-legged gait. Not quite a swagger, but he moved with a briskness that left no doubt he was in charge. For some reason, I found this comforting rather than intimidating.

"You won't need to come to the station," he said, passing my documents back through the window.

That was a relief. If I stayed in the car, maybe he wouldn't smell the wine. All I needed to do was stay calm.

"I observed the near miss myself. And there's a second witness, as well." He nodded toward the red-haired woman standing nearby. He handed me a form and a blue pen. "But I'll need a statement. It'll only take a few minutes."

I nodded and forced a smile. Sweat trickled down my temples, and my heart beat so fast I felt like I might pass out. I took the clipboard from the cop somehow managing to keep my fingers from trembling. A business card clipped to the upper left-hand corner indicated his name was Officer Donald Stone.

"How long you been drivin'?" he asked.

"A few months," I said.

He nodded. "You did the right thing, pulling to the side

of the road like that. I don't think your car was damaged, but I'll check it over while you fill this out."

Dad had advised that I was always to put the welfare of others above keeping to the Game Plan. I peered through the rearview window. The old woman had not stepped out of the car.

"Is she okay?" I jerked my head in the direction of the lady sitting in the vintage Mercedes.

"She's a bit rattled. She's ninety-two. Can't imagine how she passed the eye exam for her renewal. I doubt that woman can see five feet in front of her. Then again, she is a Canton. There seem to be different rules for that lot."

Canton. The name sounded familiar. Then I remembered why. The Cantons had been the former owners of my current house. Were they related to this old woman?

Officer Stone continued, "The Canton dynasty won't buy her out of this one though. Her license will be revoked. The accident could have been deadly if you hadn't pulled out of her way."

I glanced at the form. Officer Stone bent over to examine the left tire then moved to the front of my car. The paper had an assigned case number. Blank lines indicated where to add my name, date of birth, and address. A full paragraph described my rights. The remainder consisted of empty lines like a piece of binder paper. While the officer circled the car, Shadow yipped and scratched at the window—her enthusiastic reaction reassured me.

"Good news. Not even a scratch," Officer Stone said.

"And your dog. Is it okay?"

"She's fine," I said.

"I love the Doberman breed," he said. "I used to be in a K-9 unit car. My partner had a Dobie. Stanley was such an amazing animal. He could bring down a fleeing suspect that we never would have caught in a foot race."

It occurred to me that my dog might help deflect further questioning.

"Shadow sure likes you," I said.

I pushed the button to roll Shadow's window halfway down. She stuck her head out, lapping her tongue as if to lick the officer. He laughed and scratched behind my dog's ears while my shaking hand filled in the necessary facts.

"Do you want me to call your parents?" he asked. "You look a little shaken up."

I bit my upper lip, remembering how Dad and I had practiced for this question over and over again. Dad said it was acceptable to mislead the authorities. The answer I was supposed to give wasn't really a lie.

"It's only me and my dad," I said. "He's away for the weekend."

I saw a way to embellish my answer that might appease the cop, though it meant going through with dinner at Dr. Griffin's house.

"I'm staying with a ... family friend," I added. "She just lives around the next block. A short drive. I'll be all right."

I refocused my attention on the paperwork. My pen hesitated over the blank lines where I was supposed to describe the incident. It had happened so fast. Yet, details were now returning. "Witchy Woman" had been blaring on the radio. The circular hood ornament on the Mercedes had glinted in the sun. It had been that flash of light that had first alerted me to the car's presence on the wrong side of the road. Those few added seconds may very well have given me the extra time I needed to get out of the way.

The elements important for this report made their way onto the page. I summarized the events in four concise sentences then signed and dated the bottom and returned the pen and paperwork. He signed and dated the form then passed me a pink copy.

"Where are you headed again?" he asked.

"Witchy woman's house," I blurted. Heat rose and colored my cheeks. Dang. What a moron. "I mean ... uh ... next block over."

Officer Stone looked at me askance. Would he ask me to step out of the car? Would he demand that I give him my parents' phone number? But he only laughed.

"Welllll," he drawled, "not too fond of her, huh? Sorry about that. Anyway, I wouldn't want you going any further than that. Take your time before you drive off. A close call can shake you up more than you realize." He hit the side of the car door twice, like a cowboy patting the rump of a horse to get it moving. "Be safe."

I pulled in a few deep breaths. That was too close. I couldn't believe he hadn't grilled me about my parents. The officer headed toward the tan Mercedes. He helped the ancient-looking woman out of her car and escorted her into his cruiser. I twisted the key, turned on my blinker, and merged my "loaded gun" onto the road.

Officer Stone turned to watch me leave. With no choice but to continue to Dr. Griffin's, I accelerated into the turn onto Walnut Grove Court a little too fast. A nectarine tumbled from the grocery bag. The policeman had been right. I was shaken up.

Something niggled at me about the near miss with the Mercedes. The image of light glinting on the hood ornament reminded me of the way Shadow had reacted to the silver eagle that had been on display on Dr. Griffin's coffee table. She had hidden the strange object in that back bedroom. I had forgotten about the locked room. What else lay behind that closed door?

A breeze whipped through the open car window. I gazed at the bank of clouds rolling in from the coast. The charged air held the threat of an imminent storm.

Straight ahead, Dr. Griffin stepped onto her front porch. She folded her arms across her chest like a mom annoyed with a teenager coming home late from a date. I remembered then. In my rush to get away from the ghost at my house, I had forgotten my phone charger yet again. If things went wrong at Witchy Woman's house, I didn't have a way to call for help.

CHAPTER THIRTEEN

Like a train fixed on rails, onward my car rolled toward the blonde woman standing on her porch. Dr. Griffin's home lay dead center at the end of the cul-de-sac. Walnut trees, no doubt remnants of a former orchard for which Walnut Grove Court was named, lined each side of the two-lane road. As before, not a single soul worked outside, no children rode bicycles. Warning bells jangled in my brain loud enough to rival a five-alarm fire. Coming back here felt like a mistake.

As I pulled into the driveway next to Dr. Griffin's yellow VW bug, I felt a twinge of déjà vu, except I really had just done this yesterday. It was a little after 6:00 p.m. Because of my close call with the Mercedes and the aftermath of the incident, I was a half hour late though I wasn't about to explain what happened.

Shadow yipped and danced in the back seat. At least she didn't have any qualms about returning. Dr. Griffin rushed to open my car door. She wore the same jeans and white top from this morning. I steeled myself, hoping I didn't look flustered after my ordeal. Must Act Natural.

It wasn't until I stepped from the car that I noticed how crookedly I had parked. My left bumper would prevent Dr. Griffin from backing out of her own driveway, but I would be leaving soon anyway.

"Sorry I'm late," I said as I offered her the grocery bag. "I brought some fruit for a salad."

Dr. Griffin frowned at my parking, but her look of annoyance faded as my dog caught her attention. Shadow wiggled and scratched at the window in the back seat. I opened the car door. A red bundle of enthusiasm leapt out of the car and did what I called a zoomie lap around the front yard. She returned to circle Dr. Griffin while lifting her nose in the air and sniffing in the direction of the food.

"Shadow's calling dibs on the whole bag," I said, hoping to keep things light.

Dr. Griffin laughed, but she paused and wrinkled her nose. "Sarah, have you been drinking?"

"No, of course not," I said, pointing at the legs of my wine-splattered jeans. "I was going to bring you a bottle of wine as a thank you gift, but I ended up dropping it on the kitchen floor."

"Oh, well, don't worry about it. What's important is Shadow," she said. "Let's get her inside and started on the medicine."

I retrieved my sweat pants from my car trunk to change into then caught up to Dr. Griffin who already stood in the entryway to the house. The living room carpet held the pattern of fresh vacuuming. The scent of lemon cleaner drifted from the coffee table. Shadow went straight to it and sniffed at the circle of rhinos. The silver eagle wasn't in the center. Instead, the framed purple-eyed photo of Celeste now lay surrounded by the rhino figurines.

Was the hood ornament still locked away in the back bedroom? What had I been thinking returning here?

Dr. Griffin ushered me into the dining area. A Polaroid camera and an open laptop computer were on the wooden table. So that's how she planned to test whether the medicine worked. Dr. Griffin had thought it through. The pictures would capture the absence of purple eyes, but why not use her iPhone camera? The answer dawned on me a moment later. Unlike a digital photo, the images from a Polaroid couldn't be altered.

"Is Shadow's medicine in pill form?" I asked.

"Yes," she said. "But let's take a picture before we treat her," she said. "I want a baseline photo."

"Come, Shadow," Dr. Griffin called.

My dog trotted over, sat at her feet, and stared up at her. Dr. Griffin hit the button on the camera and a shiny, white paper square whirred out. She tugged on a tab and enunciated the word "Polaroid" aloud. Dad had used this trick on his old camera. Reciting the word allowed the proper amount of time to steadily remove the cover sheet off the photo for proper development. Dr. Griffin showed me the picture. As always, her purple eye color appeared. The color was accurate so at least we knew the camera would provide a good measure of the effectiveness of her treatment. The next step was to give her the first pill.

"I see you brought some canned dog food. We can hide the pill in a chunk of it," Dr. Griffin said. "I don't like shoving things down a dog's throat."

"Sounds good," I said.

"I don't think there will be an immediate change in Shadow," Dr. Griffin said. "Still, I'd like to keep watch over her. You wouldn't mind chopping up the fruit, would you?"

So much for my plan to grab Dad's letter and run. It didn't matter though. I couldn't go yet. I needed time for Officer Stone to deal with the Mercedes and leave for the station with that old woman. Anyway, the task would give me time to settle my nerves. I still felt pretty shook up. The red wine splatters on my dark blue jeans weren't noticeable and had already dried, so I abandoned my plan to change clothes.

"Not at all," I said glancing around for a knife.

Dr. Griffin settled into a chair at the dining table in front of a laptop. Because the dining room and kitchen were one large room with only a granite counter and a sink separating them, I could keep an eye on Shadow and Dr. Griffin while I worked. A wood block with two knives, a cutting board, pans and the various utensils were out on the counter. Two plastic-wrapped pork chops rested on a ceramic plate ready to be tossed into a frying pan.

An amber pill bottle with a child-proof cap sat on the counter. I picked up the container. It held twenty 250 mg capsules of metronidazole. Shadow's name was on the label with instructions to give her one pill twice a day until the diarrhea cleared up. Had Dr. Griffin broken an ethics rule when she lied about Shadow's affliction?

A few scuff marks marred the cap, which seemed odd. Had Dr. Griffin taken a used pill bottle with her when she filled the prescription? It appeared as if a new sticker had been plastered over an old one. D. Valley Veterinary Hospital had been typed in bold letters at the top, with a business address and phone underneath.

"Will this cause her to become constipated?" I asked.

"Add a little fruit to her diet, and it should all even out. Just not grapes. They can be toxic to dogs."

"Really?" I said. I didn't give people-food to Shadow, so she had never had any kind of fruit.

"No grapes," Dr. Griffin repeated. "And most dogs don't like citrus. Pears are great. Chop up a small slice and mix it in with a little food. She probably won't even notice."

After inserting a round, white capsule from the container into a teaspoon of wet dog food from the can, she called Shadow over. My dog swallowed the offered morsel without pausing to chew.

"I'll take another picture thirty minutes after this first pill, at about 6:45 p.m.," Dr. Griffin announced. "Then one about 7:45 p.m. and again on the hour for the next three or four hours, assuming we don't see her eye color change in the photos at any previous stage."

A mental calculation suggested the last picture would

be taken at about 10:45 p.m. or more. I planned to be long
gone before then, but I didn't say a word. Maybe the first
picture would show that the medicine had worked. Or
maybe her eyes would glow periwinkle in the next picture,
preliminary evidence that the drug had kicked in.

Shadow tilted her head as though waiting for a command. Dr. Griffin stroked her head. My dog soaked it up,
nudging her for more when her hand stilled.

The apples were chopped, and I had started with the
nectarines when Dr. Griffin asked me to switch gears and
tenderize the meat. Pork chops sizzled in the frying pan
when Dr. Griffin's watch alarm beeped. It was time for the
thirty-minute photo. She picked up the old-fashioned camera and moved to where Shadow dozed under the dinner
table. I set down the knife and came around the counter.

Shadow completed a couple of spins then sat next to
my feet. I reached down to scratch behind my pup's ears.
Her paw came up to shake hands. Her favorite trick.

"Don't be disappointed if there's no change," Dr. Griffin said. "Metronidazole doesn't absorb very quickly."

I nodded. She raised the camera and pressed the button. When the time came to pull the protective sheet, I
moved closer to watch the picture materialize. The outline of Shadow's dark head was clearly visible against the
contrast of the tan hardwood floor. Slowly, dark grays appeared along the outline of her head and highlighted the
fur around her muzzle. The eyes lightened to a dark gray
then the purple hue appeared. My ghost-seeing dog was

not cured. The objective scientist nodded her acceptance of the result. I tried not to be disappointed, but I was.

"Yep, yep, yep," Dr. Griffin said. My face must have revealed my frustration, because she patted my arm. "Better prepare yourself. It could take days for the medicine to work."

Days? I had expected a quick fix. I returned to the counter, felt around the grocery bag and removed the last two nectarines. The sooner we ate, the sooner Shadow and I could leave. I extracted the pit from one while Dr. Griffin labeled the first picture. She pulled a thermometer—the kind that measured temperature in the ear—from a backpack next to her chair that I hadn't noticed before.

"Do you mind?" she asked, pointing at the instrument.

I nodded my assent. Dr. Griffin called Shadow to her. But my pooch must have sensed something was up. She bolted for a corner of the room. Dr. Griffin whispered and cajoled until she trapped her at the far side of the dining room table. From my vantage point at the counter, I could see my dog's back and tail with Dr. Griffin kneeling next to her. Minutes ticked by. The scent of cooking meat filled the air. The temperature reading was taking a long time.

When I reached for the knife, a nectarine rolled to the other side of the counter and fell to the floor. I circled the island, and when I bent down to retrieve the fruit, I noticed the thermometer on the floor. If she wasn't taking her temperature, what the hell was she doing?

I shifted my position, peering through the chair legs.

Dr. Griffin had an arm hooked around Shadow's neck and two fingers of her free hand placed between Shadow's eyes. Well, well. Was this another way of testing the medicine's effectiveness or was she checking the room for David?

She hadn't noticed my gawking, so I retrieved the wayward nectarine. Why hadn't Dr. Griffin informed me that I could see the ghosts that Shadow could see if I put my fingers in the right place? Did she think only she could do that?

I returned to the counter where I could see the outline of her rounded back. What else hadn't she told me? How deep did her deception go?

"How's her temperature?" I asked.

Dr. Griffin startled and released my dog. Shadow trotted over. I patted her head.

"Normal," Dr. Griffin said. "Can you flip the chops?"

While I turned the meat, she returned to her seat in front of the computer. Her pale fingers flew across the keyboard, tapping away. What was she writing? Was David standing nearby? No. If a ghost were around, Shadow would bark.

The scuffed-up pill bottle caught my attention. What if the container held a placebo? Maybe she had lured me here under false pretenses. Perhaps this treatment was all a ruse to get Shadow back so that Dr. Griffin could visit with David.

"The fruit salad is ready," I said. "I'd like to see that journal article now."

Dr. Griffin stiffened. Her hands froze over the keys. She

turned in my direction. A fake smile formed.

"Oh," she said, "there was only a short footnote reference."

"Even so," I said, "I'd like to read about the study. It sounds interesting."

Dr. Griffin shrugged.

"All right." She pointed to a stack of journals in the living room. "It's the one on top. I'll show you after dinner. The test drug is patented so it's only distinguished by a series of random letters—XVZ-6 something, something. I already sent an email message out to Dr. Smith with a dozen questions. So, I would prefer to be the point of contact." She tossed her head like an uppity racehorse. "A lot of veterinarians are hard-core scientists that don't believe in the paranormal."

Dr. Griffin's precautions did make sense. The researcher could have critical information, and if a dog owner contacted her instead of a fellow veterinarian, he or she could withhold clues that might help Shadow.

"Don't worry," I said. "I don't want to interfere. I'm just curious."

Dr. Griffin nodded. She tapped a few more letters. Her blonde hair fell across her face, masking her expression. What kind of notes could she possibly be taking? Shadow lay curled under the table like a roly-poly. I imagined the entry.

Time: 1838

Minutes since initial dose: 38

Behavior: dog resting.

I removed the chops from the pan and turned off the gas. Dr. Griffin stretched her arms over her head and yawned. She closed the lid to her laptop then glanced at her watch.

"We've got another twenty minutes or so before the next picture. I'll be back in a few."

I don't know what got into me, but when I heard the bathroom door click shut, my legs guided me to the computer. I lifted the top. The screen had gone dark.

My hand snaked out and jiggled the mouse. Instead of a Word file, the screen showed the home page of Google. Maybe she had been emailing her observations to the vet in Oregon in real time. Except something didn't feel quite right. I knew I shouldn't, but I hit the down arrow in the address tool bar to see her search history.

Six website queries were listed, including several medical journals and the website for D. Veterinary. The one at the bottom struck me as odd. It was www.diablocentenniel. com. The newspaper? The string of characters that followed was 875cherryglenlane. Why would she query my home address on the local paper's website?

I clicked down. An article from June 6, 1985 appeared. The headline read: Teen Boys Killed Playing Chicken. What did this have to do with my house? I scanned the text. Two boys, apparently in a snit over a girl, had decided to duel it out in their cars. The teens, David Westley and Gregory Canton, had ... Wait. David. As in David, the ghost in this house? It wasn't possible.

The street name in the piece caught my eye. When I had Googled for directions to Dr. Griffin's, I had put in Walnut Grove Drive. There wasn't a Walnut Grove Drive, just Walnut Grove Court. The street that I was on now. Had they changed the street name when they added the housing development? If so, this house could be dead center over the scene of the accident where they had smashed their cars and died. Why in the world would Dr. Griffin have decided to live here? How did my home address fit into the picture? I browsed down the page. At the very bottom of the article, I found a reference to Cherryglen Lane. Alice and Fred, parents of deceased teen Gregory Canton, held a viewing of the body in their home at Cherryglen Lane—at my house.

Dad had purchased a haunted house for me to live in. The teen ghost at my residence had to be Greg, and the girl they had been fighting over had to be Dr. Griffin. I remembered the way Dr. Griffin had zeroed in on my address during the office visit. That's how she had known Shadow could see ghosts. The puzzle pieces all fit.

The distant flush of a toilet sent a jolt of fear through me. My breath caught. I clicked off the site, closed the computer top, and rushed back to the counter.

I picked up a large spoon and stirred the fruit salad. I had to act normal, eat dinner, retrieve Dad's letter from the guest bedroom and find a plausible way to get the hell out of this house.

CHAPTER FOURTEEN

I managed to choke down another bite of pork chop even though I had no appetite. Dr. Griffin jabbed her fork at her own meat and pushed the fruit around her plate. Our dinner conversation felt more like a job interview. Where are you from? Why did you choose to come to Walnut Acres? Yada yada yada.

My dining partner hadn't reacted to my casual reference to the Canton family during the meal. My attempt to get her to admit that the ghost Shadow had seen at our house was Gregory Canton had failed. This secret, this "elephant in the room" stamped its feet and trumpeted, but Dr. Griffin only shrugged as if it didn't exist.

Her dog clock indicated another forty-five minutes must pass before the next scheduled picture. I still had no plan of where I might go once I left here. Returning home was out of the question even if the medicine stripped Shadow of her ghost-seeing power. David's former best friend, Gregory Canton, was an angry spirit who was fond of tossing chairs around. What about Margaret O'Shawnessy? I didn't want her disturbed by Shadow's barking and calling animal control.

It seemed like this night would never end. Three Polaroids, the baseline, the 6:45 p.m. and the 7:45 p.m., lay in a row on the table like a decorative centerpiece. The last image of my purple-eyed dog looked almost identical to the baseline photo except that one ear, tipped to the side, gave Shadow a comical appearance. Two hours since the last pill, and the medicine still hadn't worked. I wanted to leave, but I still needed to get Dad's letter. She actually followed me into the back hall during my one trip to the bathroom. Even though she entered her own room, I couldn't help feeling as if she knew I had an ulterior motive. She hovered near the bathroom door when I emerged.

A half-hour sped by while we watched a documentary about rhinos on the small television mounted on her kitchen wall. I learned three rhinos are killed each day for their horns. The problem seemed to stem from the belief by some Asian cultures that the rhino horn contains medicinal powder when it is the same material as fingernails. These people are even willing to pay thousands of dollars to get it. The high price triggered more and more rhino deaths. The poachers didn't even spare females with calves. The show host visited a rhino orphanage. The baby rhinos immediately stole my heart. I felt depressed when the show concluded that there was no end in sight. Humans could push rhinos into extinction if action wasn't taken soon.

"Wow," I said, feeling more tired than ever.

"It's hard to believe, isn't it?" Dr. Griffin's voice held a twinge of anger. "A species that's been around for 50 million years could disappear in our lifetime."

"Well, the show said the numbers of poached rhinos decreased last year," I said. "Maybe the species can still be saved."

"Maybe … I hope so," she said, but there was no conviction in her voice.

I looked around, desperate to change the subject. My emotions were too raw, and the plight of the rhino too sad. My gaze fell on the pile of journals. Every time I had headed over there, Dr. Griffin had found a way to distract me. This time she wouldn't sway me.

"I'd like to read the Dalmatian study article now," I said.

To my surprise, Dr. Griffin strode over to the stack.

"Yep, yep, yep," she said. "It's pretty dry stuff though."

One by one, she rifled through them. All had dull gray covers as if the publisher was afraid of using color or glossy paper lest the reader expect the contents might be interesting. Dr. Griffin scoured the stack. The way she snatched at each issue and tossed it aside communicated panic.

"It was here," she said. "I know I left it on top."

Her hand froze on a slender document then picked up the one underneath it. She rushed to where I still sat. If she found the article, why did she have two journals in her hand? Her glowing expression resembled the face of a kid in a candy shop about to purchase not one, but two, super-sized chocolate bars.

"You see, you see," she said, shaking the two publications so they flopped up and down. "Look. I have volumes four and six. Volume five is the one that contains the Dalmatian study."

I didn't see. Unease and doubt reared their ugly heads once more. Had Dr. Griffin made up the whole thing about the purple-eyed Dalmatians? After all, Shadow was her vehicle to David.

Dr. Griffin suddenly got all twitchy. She touched her hair, her nose, tucked her hair behind her ear.

"He ...I mean, I must have misplaced it," she said. "But it doesn't matter."

Yeah, right. If I had Dad's letter in my hand, I would have leashed up Shadow and left. I couldn't bolt into the next room plus take Shadow with me. She would know I was plotting my escape and barricade the front door. My voice within advised patience.

"Let's watch another show," she said.

She rushed into the kitchen and picked up the TV remote off the granite counter. I followed but remained in the archway, not quite entering the room. Images flashed as she flipped through the channels.

"Anything appeal to you?" she asked in a high voice.

Her discomfort smelled of desperation. She knew I wanted to leave.

"No," I said.

A gust of wind kicked up outside. A rash of windstorms

had plagued the town since I moved into my new home after Dad's death. Last week pulsing drafts of air shook the house sporadically throughout the night. I wasn't looking forward to driving home in this weather.

Shadow lay content on the floor by my feet. Dr. Griffin's house offered protection from the wind. If she had a say, I'm sure she would vote for sticking around.

Dr. Griffin settled on a sitcom I didn't recognize. My father had limited my television viewing. When I was younger, we would play board games on Friday and Saturday night. His favorite was Scrabble. Wait. The perfect plan. I could slip away, retrieve my envelope during her turn, take Shadow, and leave.

"Hey," I said, "do you have a Scrabble game?"

Dr. Griffin's head bobbed up. A twinkle shone in those turquoise eyes. Well, well, well. Who would have guessed we both loved this word game?

* * *

Dr. Griffin pulled an "a" from the bag of tiles as we drew for who would go first. I drew a "u."

"You're first, Dr. Griffin," I said, flipping my tile to show her my draw.

"Don't you think it's time you started calling me Claudia?" she said.

Claudia? What an old-fashioned name. Someone named Claudia should be stout and burly, not a frail, blonde woman.

"Really?" I blurted.

An image formed of my Dad lifting up a flash card showing the relevant part of Rule #8: Always demonstrate good manners. My face must have turned three shades of pink before it settled on crimson.

"I know, I know. Abysmal, isn't it?" she said with a laugh. "My great-aunt just had to be my mother's favorite relative."

Somehow calling her by her first name didn't feel right when I did not trust her. I glanced over my shoulder. As I was about to excuse myself and go look for Dad's letter, she played "worthy" for a score of 38. Ouch.

Dr. Griffin dipped her head to check on Shadow. The muscles in her face relaxed as she gazed at my dog. Could she be all that horrible if she cared so deeply for my dog?

Tiles clicked as she rearranged her letters, reminding me it was my turn. All of her letters were pushed together. Uh oh. Had she formed a seven-letter word? I drew a mix of vowels and consonants, but mostly "one pointers." I had an "h" and could capitalize on a triple letter if I spelled "horn" using the "r" in "worthy" for 15 points. Then another word assembled itself in my mind. A low-scoring word, but it might help us talk openly.

I glanced at the woman seated across from me and made up my mind. With four letters, including the precious "u" that I would prefer to save in case I drew the "q" on my next turn, I used the "t" in "worthy" to spell "trust."

Dr. Griffin pursed her lips. She stared hard at me for a moment then reached for her letters. Placing an "e" on the "w" in worthy to make "we" and working backwards on the horizontal, she spelled the word "able."

Able, as in able to trust? I had the sense that despite her lies, she was concerned about Shadow's well-being. If only she would tell me what was really going on with David the Ghost. I knew exactly what I wanted to do on my next move but didn't have the letters to spell "yes."

In the end, I added "reli" to the front of able, to make "reliable." My move set up Dr. Griffin for a triple word—a major faux pas for a serious Scrabble player.

To my surprise, she didn't use the triple. Instead, she used the "s" in trust to build "secret." My whole body stilled. I had been so focused on her secret that I forgot I had one too. Did she know? If she found Dad's letter, she could have Googled his name and figured out my true age.

Outside, the wind caused an eerie moan. Shadow stirred but did not awaken.

My draw left me with a great rack of letters that spelled hornets. I could use all seven letters and get 50 bonus points. Except winning had become less important now. I stacked "honest" on the "y" in worthy to make "honesty."

I put my elbows on the table, interlaced my fingers, and rested my chin on my interlocked hands. I gazed at Dr. Griffin with eyebrows raised. It was time for straight talk.

Dr. Griffin bit her lip. She studied her letters while her fingers fluttered over her tiles. She picked up the same letter twice, put it back, then snatched different letters from her tray. Using the "h" in honesty, her letters spelled "ashamed."

Ashamed. What a guilt-laden word. Ashamed of what? That she had read my private letter? That she had brought me here tonight under false pretenses? Lied about the Dalmatian study? Withheld information about the identity of the ghost in my house and the ghost in hers?

Maybe she meant that I should be ashamed. Maybe she was right. I had tried to enter a locked bedroom, and I snooped on her computer. I wasn't proud of either action. I even presumed the worst of her. Hadn't I been convinced she was intent on imprisoning me and wanted to steal my dog? There was shame enough for both of us.

Shadow stood and stretched then rested her head on my knee. I fingered her pointy ears while I examined my choices. I hadn't really planned to continue this dance of words, but my letters aligned with my goal. I had to know what she knew. I added "ivulge" to the "d "on "ashame*d*" to make "divulge" on the vertical.

Dr. Griffin picked up four letters. She didn't even try to add to the words forming on the board according to the game rules. She placed the word on an unused side of the board then lifted her head to face me. Her eyes held a question, but that wasn't what compelled me to answer. It was the completely vulnerable expression on her face—like a child who had done something wrong and was afraid to confess.

Her four-letter word spelled "safe." Did that mean my

secret was safe, or did she want to know if it was safe to tell me her secret? I decided that either way, a nod would work, so that's what I did.

Dr. Griffin pushed her chair back. Shadow came to her side as if she could sense her distress. For the first time I saw what an impossible situation she was in. Not many people would believe that she lived with a ghost. She bit her quivering lip, an evident sign of her inner turmoil. I no longer suspected that she had stumbled onto my secret. Whatever she was about to say related to her own undisclosed past. She was struggling with her own demons, or rather, her own ghosts.

I already knew about David, but she didn't know that. As we stared at each other, the elephant in the room roared and waved its ears before standing on its two hind legs, begging for acknowledgement.

"Claudia," I said. "Tell me about David."

CHAPTER FIFTEEN

I could almost see Dr. Griffin's mind turning. Twitching facial muscles and the nervous wringing of her hands gave away the extent of her anguish. Her spine lay ramrod straight against her chair back, like a young debutante learning proper posture. My admission that I knew about David the Ghost created a dilemma for her. She didn't know what or how much I knew, so she didn't know what to say.

"David and I met," I said. "Last night. In the hall."

Her mouth opened and closed and opened and closed like a fish that has leapt from its fishbowl onto the floor. Confusion simmered in her aquamarine eyes. She glanced at Shadow then back at me.

"Between Shadow's eyes," I said, placing my two fingers above the bridge of my nose between my eyebrows, confirming what I imagined she had already surmised. "When you thought I was still in the bathroom, I saw you do this to Shadow."

"How long..." she said, getting up from the table. "How long did you keep your fingers on her head?"

The way she towered above me, peering down through those horn-rimmed glasses, scared me. Even as I shrank away from her, she craned her neck, like a great blue heron about to strike.

"How did he tell you his name?" she pressed.

Was she kidding? She had introduced me to her lover boy ghost last night. Did she really not know? Before I could decide how to answer, she asked another question.

"Did he say anything else to you?"

Oh, yeah. He said you disabled my car. But I wasn't about to reveal that little tidbit. Besides, he hadn't *said* anything. He had only made hand gestures.

"It happened so fast," I said, avoiding a direct answer. "He was there . . . then he was gone."

"So, a few minutes?" she persisted.

It didn't matter how long I had chatted with a ghost. It was time she answered some of my questions.

"Why didn't you tell me about . . . this?" I asked, again holding up two fingers between my eyebrows.

This. What an inadequate word to describe Shadow's amazing ability to allow humans to see ghosts through her. None of Mrs. Lutz's vocab words fit. Not clairvoyance. Not psychic. Not mystic.

"How could I?" Dr. Griffin said. "Most people reject the concept of ghosts. The idea is too frightening. Fewer still can handle viewing a real supernatural being."

She was right. This wasn't something she could bring up while waiting in line at the grocery store. If she had explained what Shadow could do during her office visit yesterday, I probably wouldn't have called her back today.

"His name," she persisted. "How did you know?"

She really must not remember. I stared at the word honesty on the Scrabble board. Okay, okay. I could be truthful without telling all.

"You said his name last night," I said. "You didn't say he was a ghost. I figured that out."

"Really?" Her brow furrowed into a puzzled expression.

"Your turn," I said. "Tell me the truth. Is there a journal article or did you make it up so that I'd bring Shadow back here?"

Her hand fluttered to her mouth. She must not have expected this question.

"Oh, yes," she said, nodding vigorously. "The study is real."

I wanted to believe her. Yet, she was too … earnest. Mrs. Lutz' nasal voice completed my sentence with another of her vocab words.

"Then where is it?" I said.

"Volume five was here," she said. "I swear it was."

She stood and went to the bookshelf, just as she had done earlier in the evening. I followed and peered over her shoulder as one by one, she sifted through the publications. When she reached the bottom, she dropped the pile in disgust.

"I know this is where I left it," she said. She ogled the

journals as if she was staring at a zoo animal she had never seen before. "I left it on top." Her voice dropped. "He's clever, that David. He hides things. I think he does it to drive me crazy."

Crazy? Seemed like David was succeeding. The image of Dad's disapproving stare materialized in my mind. He would want me to be sympathetic.

"I'd feel the same way if things kept disappearing," I said.

She tipped her head back and laughed.

What a loony. I had to get out of here. I did a mental calculation on how much time had elapsed since the last photo. Only fifteen minutes till the next picture. After that, I would grab Dad's letter, take my dog, and leave. I'd had enough.

"Where is David anyway?" I said.

Back at the table, Dr. Griffin sank into her chair. She patted her leg. Shadow trotted over and leaned against her. I stayed standing, glancing at the hallway. Should I go find Dad's letter? Was this my big chance? Dr. Griffin turned to look at me, and the door to my escape route slammed shut.

"You know," she said, "I think David is up to something. He was here when you walked in the door yesterday. That's what upset Shadow. When Celeste was alive, ghosts didn't upset her. So David and I had a lot of time to develop a kind of sign language."

What would you talk about with a dead person? Hey, honey, how's death? Did you see the Pearly Gates? Is it hot where you live?

"David probably sees Shadow as an opportunity to communicate with us," Dr. Griffin added, "and he doesn't want you to take Shadow and leave, so he's keeping his distance so Shadow will stay calm. I toyed with the idea of not calling you after I reviewed the Dalmatian study results, but I decided it wouldn't be fair to Shadow. Celeste wasn't afraid of ghosts. She would bark, but in a friendly kind of way. Shadow is different. Your dog needs to be taught how to cope."

There was truth to that. But I no longer believed she was the one who could help my dog.

"I want you to know," she said with her blue eyes fixed on mine, "I only have Shadow's best interests in mind."

Sincerity shone through her words in the way honesty emerges when people think their world is ending, and they are going to die. On this point, I believed her. The rest of her story rang as false as a happily-ever-after fairy tale.

Shadow, sweet, sweet Shadow. I owed it to her to do everything I could to help her, even if it meant sticking around here until it was time to give her another pill. Except what if staying put my dog and me in some kind of danger? That wouldn't do either of us any good.

"I'll let her outside," Dr. Griffin said. "She can sniff around the backyard and take care of business. Then we can take her photo. It's almost time to see if the medicine has taken effect."

A breeze ruffled the cover of the scientific journal on

the top of the stack as Dr. Griffin opened the back door to let Shadow outside. Volume four. Volume six lay underneath. Where was volume five? Was David a poltergeist? Or was Dr. Griffin a liar?

CHAPTER SIXTEEN

The first and the latest Polaroid photos of Shadow lay side by side on Dr. Griffin's dining room table. Shadow's adorable face captured on two shiny squares. How could such a cute dog create so much havoc in my life?

"Look, her eyes are a redder shade of purple in this last picture," Dr. Griffin said.

A slight change in the intensity of the eye color might be present, but that could be because Dr. Griffin had taken the last photo in the living room where there was less light. Also, on the other pictures, she had said the word "Polaroid" aloud to make sure she extracted the overlying sheet on the picture at a moderate speed for optimum development. This time she remained quiet, and I could swear she pulled more slowly, which I presumed could alter the color.

"Let's take another photo in the kitchen to check," I said.

"Okee-dokee," Dr. Griffin said. "Shadow, come."

Shadow trotted to her side. She sat before her as though expecting a treat. Dr. Griffin raised the camera and pressed the button. The familiar click interrupted the silence, but no white pull-tab emerged.

"Oh dear." Dr. Griffin frowned. "The camera is out of film. How stupid of me. It'll take two hours before the extra pack in the refrigerator will warm to room temperature and be ready for use."

Was this a stall tactic to get me to stay? I had been playing cat and mouse with Dr. Griffin all night. Her ploy was about to backfire. While she retrieved the film, I would grab Dad's letter. But instead of going into the kitchen, she followed me into the living room, the way she had shadowed me all evening.

"Let's have a cup of coffee, shall we?" Dr. Griffin said.

"Actually, Shadow and I have got to get going."

"But you can't take Shadow with you. The motion of the car might affect her reaction to the medicine. It could skew the study."

Skew the study? What? Now Shadow was a lab animal? Besides, Shadow hadn't shown any side effects to the drug.

"Actually, it would be better if you didn't leave either." Her forceful words held an undercurrent of malice. "Let's give Shadow another treatment and wait till morning for the next picture. The Polaroid film will be ready by then."

I wasn't about to be bullied. I had already stayed longer than I wanted. Now she was concocting a reason to keep me here even longer. I felt foolish for coming here at all.

Outside, a gale storm blew. I was surrounded by turbulence inside and out. I marched into the kitchen, took

Shadow's canned food from the fridge, scooped out a table-spoon, and added a pill from the vial. I offered the morsel to Shadow under Dr. Griffin's watchful eye.

"By the way," with a nervous flick of her wrist, she pointed at the spare bedroom, "I brought your stuff in while you were doing the dishes."

She what? She had invaded my car, brought my gym bag in when I had purposely left it in the trunk of my Civic and combed through my purse contents without permission to get my keys? I bit my tongue to hide my outrage. I headed toward the coffee table where I had left my purse. I was out of here with or without Dad's letter.

"I kept your keys," Dr. Griffin said, "because I'm afraid I can't let you or Shadow leave."

I whirled around in time to see her hand emerge from her jeans pocket. A thumb-sized Eeyore surrounded by a set of silver keys confirmed my worst fear. She planned to hold us hostage. My jaw clenched. Shadow barked and pawed at my leg. My dog didn't like it when I was irritated.

"Stop it, Shadow," I said in a gruff voice.

Butterflies fluttered in my stomach. First, the missing journal and now she had confiscated my keys. This was her idea of trust? I was a pawn in a game where I didn't understand the rules.

I thought about the dead cell phone in my purse. She had probably seen that it was useless, or I'm sure she would have taken it too. I had violated Rule #3: Prepare for the worst.

"You look tired," she said. "Perhaps you should get some rest."

It seemed wise to agree, and I still needed to get Dad's letter out of the bedroom. I would sneak out after she fell asleep, even if it meant walking home. I resolved to push past David if he guarded the door. After all, he was just a patch of cold air. He couldn't really hurt me.

"You're right," I said. "I think Shadow and I will go to bed. We can take another picture in the morning just like you said."

My fingers itched to retrieve the leash from the coffee table, but I resisted the urge. Instead, I herded Shadow into the guestroom, shut the door, and engaged the lock. I never should have come back here. David the Ghost had warned me about her last night. If only I had listened.

CHAPTER SEVENTEEN

The bed had been made. I strode across the room and lifted the pillow with caution as if a spider might jump out from beneath it. No letter, no envelope. No. No, no, no. It had to be here.

I closed my eyes. How could I have been so careless with this last precious gift from my father? I stripped the linens, not caring about the jumbled mess of sheets that littered the floor. Shadow stood out of the way with ears tipped forward watching my every move. I lifted each mattress corner and checked underneath. Nothing.

I wanted to storm out into the hallway and demand its immediate return, except I knew that would be stupid. Who knew what she was capable of? If she had read the letter, and I bet that she had, she knew my secret. Now she had power over me.

There was nothing else to do. I picked up the sheets, remade the bed, and collapsed onto the covers. Shadow jumped up, licked my face, and curled up beside me. Outside, the air blew against the house.

David probably knew where my letter was. He might even know how I might go about getting it back. How much more bizarre could my life get? I was being held captive, actually hoping for Dr. Griffin's ex-boyfriend's spectral form to appear.

An hour passed, then two, then I lost track. I should have been a complete mess. I had gotten so little sleep that it was a miracle that I managed to keep my eyes open. Twice I could have sworn that I heard footsteps pause outside my door. Now, rustling noises down the hall suggested that Witchy Woman was still awake.

Something Dr. Griffin had said about David needled away at the edge of my thoughts. If only I wasn't so tired. Yet, try as I might, I couldn't quite grasp what bothered me about our conversation. Think, think, think. I pinched my arm and patted my cheeks to wake myself up. Feeling revived, I wracked my brain once again. She was upset that I knew David's name. David had answered my questions with gestures last night. Guessing his name would have been difficult.

Wait. Gestures. That was it. That's what didn't add up. I needed to see David with my eyes to talk to him. I needed to put my fingers between Shadow's eyes. But last night when Dr. Griffin was sleepwalking, she said, "I'll make sure he understands." How? Shadow was with me.

True, David could probably understand her spoken words, the same way he had understood mine. But how could she know if he agreed to her request if she couldn't see him? Dr. Griffin must have found another way to communicate with her ghost boyfriend since Celeste died. Why would she want to? Why would he want to talk to her? I shook my head. Relationships were complicated, even if they were between ghost and human.

I turned over on my side then flipped onto my stomach. Shadow grunted. Outside, wind-blown branches scraped the side of the house. The raspy noise was as nerve-wracking as the idea of a ghost hovering just outside my door.

Where was David? Perhaps his ghostly form hung out in the locked bedroom. Surely, she couldn't keep him prisoner though. I imagined David could walk through walls. The only reason to secure the door was to keep me out.

What was in that room? I envisioned crystal balls balanced on pedestals, photos of her with David in high school pasted on all four walls. I tried to squash the images, but thoughts exploded through my brain like the grand finale of a fireworks show. Maybe the room housed Celeste's bones reassembled into a skeleton. Or perhaps just her dog's skull so Dr. Griffin could put her fingers between the empty eye sockets in the hope the dog's essence lived on in her calcified remains.

I wanted my mind to shut up. I wanted to go home—not the house on Cherryglen—but the last home I had shared with my father. Most of all I wanted Dad to be alive again.

My hand reached over and flipped on the lamp, hoping the light would calm me. Shadow sighed and buried her nose and head under her back leg.

At 11:35, when I hadn't heard any more movement,

my voice within told me to make a run for it. I swung my legs over the edge of the bed. Shadow stood and stretched. She shook her whole body. The tags on her collar rattled—a loud, accusatory noise that broke the silence and threatened to bring Dr. Griffin knocking on the bedroom door, which would ruin my escape plans.

My fingers grappled with the switch and turned off the light. I tilted my head, listening. No sounds came from the hallway.

I tiptoed to the door and rotated the knob as carefully as if I were trying to crack a safe. The door inched open. I positioned my body to bar Shadow's view of the hall in case David stood watch. I peered through the slit. Dr. Griffin had placed a small nightlight in the bathroom across the way. The faint light illuminated the narrow passage. It was empty.

No blast of cold air, no warning growl from Shadow. Good signs that David wasn't lurking nearby. I planned to take Shadow's leash from the coffee table and come back for her. When I opened the door, she slipped out. Crap.

The sound of her dog tags made me cringe as she trotted toward the dining room. Moonlight seeped through the front window as I made my way in semi-darkness to the far end of the house. I followed her, noting that the coffee table was empty. Dr. Griffin had taken Shadow's leash and my purse. I had been a fool for not taking my belongings into the bedroom with me. I rounded the corner and found Shadow standing at the back entrance.

At least Dr. Griffin hadn't appeared. I should get the

hell out of here. But even if I were to walk home along darkened streets with Shadow heeling by my side, Dr. Griffin had my house key. She had my wallet, too. I didn't even have my credit card. Once again, I had violated Game Plan Rule #3: Prepare for the worst.

Shadow pawed at the door. I let her out so that she wouldn't wake Witchy Woman. A blast of wind hit my face as I opened the door. Normal cool air, not the paranormal, icy essence brought on by a ghost. I shut the door while Shadow did her business. It was too dark to see. What if Dr. Griffin had moved my purse and keys into this room? Dr. Griffin had lowered the light when we watched television, so I knew the chandelier over the dining table had a dimmer switch. I turned the knob to keep the light low before I turned it on. A yellow haze illuminated the room.

The Polaroid wasn't on the tabletop, although the extra film was there. The computer was gone too. What had she done? Taken the camera into her bedroom? Why? The Polaroid was useless without film. My fuzzy brain couldn't focus long enough to puzzle it out.

Shadow yipped, and I rushed to open the door before she roused Witchy Woman. My dog trotted inside the house, wiggling her body with enthusiasm. Apparently David was keeping his distance.

Now what? Should I risk sneaking into Claudia's bedroom for my purse and keys? No. Better to let a sleeping Dr. Griffin lie.

I cut the light and herded Shadow toward the guest

room. I needed to plan my next move. When I entered the hallway, I stopped short. The door to the locked room was open a crack. Had it been like that moments ago? I hadn't looked in that direction when I emerged from the bedroom.

Go back to bed and lock your bedroom door, my inner voice demanded. But what if Dad's letter, the leash, and my purse lay inside the room at the end of the hall?

Shadow entered the guest bedroom. My voice within said I should follow her. Instead, my hand shut the door, closing Shadow in our assigned room.

My feet strode down the hall, while my brain chanted a repeating mantra of "bad idea, bad idea, bad idea." When I reached the door to the mystery room, I noticed the difference between this door and the others on the hall. The nightlight from the bathroom illuminated a double panel design rather than the single panel that decorated my bedroom door. That was odd.

With a bass drum hammering in my ears, I extended one finger and pushed. The opening widened, but not by much because the door was so heavy. At least no cold drafts seeped through the crack. I put the flat of my palm against the door and shoved harder until there was enough space for me to peer inside.

Darkness cloaked the contents of the room. My shoulder pressed against the door until it swung fully open. Shapes unfolded, but I was too impatient to let my eyes fully adjust. I entered the foreboding room with my arms outstretched as though I were blind.

CHAPTER EIGHTEEN

A large desk stood dead center in the mysterious room. Perhaps Dr. Griffin kept confidential patient files here. If so, it would make sense to keep the door locked. Dad always claimed I created drama unnecessarily.

LEAVE, my inner voice commanded. Yet, I had to be sure my possessions weren't here. I squinted at the dark shape to the left of the room. A bureau. Everything else was in silhouette.

I tiptoed into the room. I had entered only a few feet, when outside, a gust of wind whistled through the trees, and I lost my nerve. I took a step backward then another.

The bluish haze of moonlight infiltrated the room. A glint of light brought my attention to the desk. The wooden top was bare except for four objects: a frayed envelope, the silver eagle hood ornament, a Polaroid camera, and a thin document, no doubt the missing volume five. I had found Dad's letter. No car keys or purse though. Dr. Griffin must have squirreled those away in her bedroom.

Something about the way the items lay perfectly spaced

from each other frightened me. My inner voice warned me to leave now and forget the letter. My rattled brain started a new mantra: get out, get out, GET OUT.

My feet refused to cooperate though as if my body demanded that I retrieve Dad's letter, over-riding my flight instinct. Yet, I couldn't find the courage to grab it.

The door behind me closed with a decisive thud and released me from the spell. Holy mother. Was I locked in? I scrambled backward while my hand reached behind to locate the doorknob. My fingers encircled the cold, round metal.

I tried to swallow, but my throat had constricted. My head was going to explode if I didn't take a breath soon. I opened my mouth as if to scream. No sound came out. I gulped air, yet I couldn't breathe. Then, when I thought things couldn't get any worse, I heard the unmistakable creak of a door opening somewhere in the house. Dr. Griffin must have emerged from her bedroom.

What would she do if she caught me in here? There wasn't time to get back to my bedroom or even the bathroom. My shoulder leaned into the heavy door so if she tried to enter she wouldn't be able to gain access. Moments ago I had wanted out, now I wished I could seal myself inside this forbidden room. If she had left the door ajar as a trap, she would know I violated her privacy.

Those arranged objects... she was unstable. I envisioned a long silver knife concealed in her hand as she marched down the narrow corridor. Would I be joining

David in the afterworld?

The soft swish, swish of slippered feet grew louder. I held my breath. Barricading the door now seemed like a bad idea. Maybe she didn't know I was inside.

A cloud must have covered the moon because the blue haze disappeared. The room went black. I sidled over to the side near the door hinge so the door could open, but I would be hidden behind it.

A gentle knock sent a tremor of fear through me. Why was she knocking? It was her house. The door opened inward a crack.

"David?" Dr. Griffin whispered. "Are you there?"

The hall light illuminated the room. My breath caught once again. Posters covered the right wall: motocross, a surfer catching a wave, the Grateful Dead. Typical decorations for a teen boy. Holy crap. This was no office. This was David's room.

Dr. Griffin stepped inside and headed straight for the desk. I sucked in my stomach, trying to make myself smaller. She picked up the hood ornament. My brain began a new mantra, "don't scream, don't scream, don't …" With her free hand, her fingertips touched first the journal then the Polaroid camera. I couldn't tell by her actions if she had just discovered them or if she knew they were there because she had put them there herself.

She fingered the envelope. Her head turned to the right, away from where I cowered. She stiffened.

"David," Dr. Griffin said. She had the tone of a teacher

reprimanding a student. "Remember what we talked about? You need to stop. Enough already."

She dropped the hood ornament back on the desk. It tipped over with a thud. The fallen eagle looked out of place on the immaculate desk. Her hand reached out and grasped the camera, an angry move that left me trembling.

Moonlight highlighted the curve of her spine and the set of her clenched jaw. Her body was wound so tight she could probably launch herself into orbit. Now I understood David's nervous glances. What would she do to me if she spotted me in her ghost boyfriend's room?

She swiveled around like a U.S. Marine practicing a drill and strode from the room. Through a stroke of good luck, she didn't see me. The door closed with a quiet click. I heard the jangle of keys and the twist of metal.

I had escaped one situation, only to find myself in another precarious circumstance. Locked in the shrine of Dr. Griffin's dead boyfriend.

I moved to the door to examine the doorknob. The metal ridge in the center lay horizontal. I almost laughed my relief was so great. Even though she had locked me in this ghost room with David, I could get out. Duh. The door could be unlocked from the inside and relocked without a key. Nothing prevented me from turning the knob and making my escape.

Not yet though. Dr. Griffin must return to her bedroom and I should linger long enough for her to doze off. Then I would take back what belonged to me. Keys or no car keys, purse or no purse, I was taking Dad's letter and leaving this wacky house.

I counted to one hundred then impatience got the better of me. I strode to the desk and grabbed the envelope. The familiar crinkle of paper inside gave me courage, but when a cold breeze passed by me, heading for the door. I faltered.

David. Where was he going? The guest bedroom? If so, Shadow would bark, and I'd be caught.

"Wait," I whispered.

The draft settled into a motionless cold, like heavy air in a Tule marsh. Wet, thick, and still. He was listening.

"Please. Let me go to Shadow," I said. "Then I can see you, and we can talk."

The cold retreated. I took that as permission to leave to prepare Shadow for a spectral visitor. My quaking knees skirted the frigid spot. I somehow managed to grasp the knob and ease open the door without a sound. I hesitated at the threshold. What I wouldn't give to take that journal off the desk, too. But I had the impression that such an action would anger David.

I turned away from the temptation even though it would show me once and for all if the Dalmatian study were real or if Dr. Griffin was playing games. I stepped into the hall, reached around, and twisted the inside button on the knob. With the locking mechanism engaged, I closed the door.

Back in my room, Shadow lay curled up in a tight ball on the bed. Her tail thumped a greeting as I entered.

I didn't know how much time David would grant me, so I went straight to my gym bag, extracted the headband and tucked the precious envelope underneath my spare clothes. Crooning "good dog" to Shadow, I slipped the restraint over her head then secured her muzzle in a figure eight pattern. Soon enough I would know if Shadow were cured. If I could see David, then the medicine hadn't worked.

Exhausted, I crawled onto the bed next to my beloved pooch to wait. Moments later Shadow tensed then rose to her feet. A low growl erupted from her throat. Her tail twitched at a pace that even the fiercest rattlesnake would respect. Well, no need for a picture. Shadow's capability had not diminished. Her head tracked from the doorway in the direction of the closet. I inhaled and placed my fingers between her eyes.

Just as last time, white lines flickered. The image waxed and waned like I was looking through a microscope and fiddling with the focus knob. Slowly, a shape materialized in the chair across the room. I felt myself relax a little. I expected him to be standing over me, stiff and annoyed. But David leaned back in his seat with one ankle hooked on top of his knee. He intertwined his hands and placed them behind his head—the posture of a boss who has called an employee in to chat. A man who wants the other person to feel at ease, but also communicates that he is in control. David's tuxedo still appeared pressed, a crease visible down the front of his slacks.

"Hello again," I said.

CHAPTER NINETEEN

David's spectral form lifted his index finger to his lips. A universal signal. He wanted me to be quiet. He smiled and shrugged as if to assure me that he wasn't angry. Yet, there was a jaggedness to his manner that left me uneasy but at the same time intrigued. Was I a moth being drawn to the flame?

David extended his arm, a single finger pointing up toward the ceiling. What was he trying to say? Communicating with a ghost was a lot like playing charades. Wait, maybe that was exactly what he was trying to do.

"First word?" I said.

He shook his head side to side. What else could he mean?

"One?" I said.

He nodded. Shadow took a deep breath as if to say, "not this again." Her whole body quivered. At least David hadn't moved from the chair. Shadow probably wouldn't tolerate him coming closer.

David splayed his fingers and showed me his palm.

He pumped the air once with his hand outstretched like a crossing guard telling a car to stop then he went back to one visible finger. He repeated the actions in rapid succession. Shadow tried to stand, but I leaned into her.

"One, five," I said. He continued his movements.

"Fifteen?" I said.

He nodded and smiled, revealing straight even teeth. That boyish grin had probably melted many a girl's heart. David pointed at his wrist where a watch would be.

Time? Seconds would be too short. Hours would be too long.

"Fifteen minutes?" I said

He grinned, clearly pleased, added his middle finger to his index, and placed them between his eyebrows.

"I need to keep my fingers between Shadow's eyes for fifteen minutes?"

His head nodded with enthusiasm. Shadow squirmed at the sound of her name. David went through the motions of one and five, two fingers between his eyes, then pointed at his ear. This time I hadn't a clue. Ear? Sound. Hearing? His meaning dawned on me.

"I'll be able to hear you speak after fifteen minutes?"

His head tilted left then right. I presumed that meant I was close enough.

An idea formed. Maybe I could get David to help me. Gregory Canton and David had been best friends. If David knew that I could take him to see his former buddy, would he help me get my keys back?

"You were Gregory Canton's best friend," I said.

He sat up straight and leaned forward. Boyish nonchalance evaporated. I had his undivided attention. Shadow moaned. Every muscle tensed.

"I know where his ghost lives," I said.

David's eyes widened. Or at least I thought they did. His ethereal form faded slightly. His features blurred for a moment before coming back into perspective, this time in color. His cheeks held a peach tone, his lips were a pale pink, and, as I had suspected, his eyes were brown, his hair a sandy shade of umber. It occurred to me that maybe he had to work at being visible.

The ghost pointed at me then put his hands in the ten-and-two position as he had done last night. A moment later he pointed back at himself. Perfect. Just as I had hoped, he wanted me to drive him to where Greg was.

"You want me to drive you there?" I repeated aloud.

He nodded. Shadow twitched and groaned. I hadn't thought this through. Even if I got my car keys back, I wasn't about to traumatize my dog by forcing her to sit in the back seat with a spiritual being that frightened her.

"I have a better idea," I said. "You get my keys from Dr. Griffin. I'll get Greg and bring him back here."

David's form turned rigid as if he suddenly remembered what rigor mortis was like. The white highlights of his whole body turned a dark shade of pink. I would never have guessed that the body and face of an angry ghost would turn a rose color. When David shook his head, the pink tones around his cheeks flushed magenta.

This wasn't good. I had underestimated him and the ease with which his temper flared. How had he guessed that I had no intention of returning and had just hoped to use him to get my car keys? Was my face as transparent as his translucent spirit?

If spirits could move objects, and had the ability to throw chairs, David could harm me. He didn't even have to worry about getting caught. I doubted that a ghost could leave DNA at the crime scene. Even if he did, no investigator would name a guy who had been dead for eight or nine years as a suspect. They would have to create new nomenclature: spirit of interest.

"Okay, okay," I said. "Bad idea."

David sat up straight. The magenta hues turned a softer shade of pink as he settled down. I couldn't believe I had entered into negotiations with a ghost. I still had another problem if I somehow managed to get to my house. Maybe David could fix that too.

"If I agree to take you over there," I continued, "will you ask Greg to leave my house?"

Crap. I hadn't meant to tell David that Greg was at my house. What if he could just float over there? He wouldn't need my help. Unless he didn't know where I lived.

The rosy aura that surrounded David's ghostly form faded into white highlights. That was promising. David's pale lips pursed as he pondered my proposal.

What was taking him so long to respond? Did asking

another ghost to vacate a property violate some kind of spiritual etiquette? David lifted his shoulders into a shrug. Did that mean that he didn't know? Or maybe death had taught David not to make impulsive decisions just like Game Plan Rule #1. Then again, he had all eternity, so why not stretch this out?

Shadow stiffened and growled. I wasn't sure how much longer my dog would allow me to indulge in this conversation. I gave her a reassuring squeeze.

I still needed to solve the logistical problem of transporting David and Shadow in the same vehicle. I didn't relish the idea of suggesting David ride in the trunk. Did ghosts get claustrophobic? Maybe he could ride on the roof. Did wind move through ghosts or would it unravel his essence like a skein of yarn?

"I don't think Shadow can handle being too close to you. Can you—"

I felt it then. It was like cold fingers crawling across the surface of my brain. David still sat on the chair across the room, but he was also inside my head. I heard a chuckle. It felt like someone was whispering in my ear.

"Ghosts don't need to breathe," the male voice announced in a whisper.

Was this what David meant by hearing him? Except he had entered my skull. I glanced at the bedside clock. Fifteen minutes had passed. How could so much time have elapsed? I didn't like this sensation. A new fear surfaced. Maybe David could hear my thoughts.

David's eyes widened but at the same moment as the unmistakable click of Dr. Griffin's doorknob turning. I didn't know if my thoughts or Dr. Griffin's approach caused David's surprised reaction. He brought his index finger to his lips again, though he didn't need to, because I heard the "shush" in a husky, male voice as clear as if he had spoken aloud.

Neither his actions, nor his verbal warning were necessary. No way did I want Dr. Griffin to know I was conversing with her boyfriend in a bedroom. I tried to pull my hand away from Shadow.

"Don't give Shadow any more medicine," the voice hissed. "Then you'll get your keys." The muted sound seemed to stem from within a distant cavern, as if we were at opposite ends of a long tunnel.

Pain throbbed in my head as if I had eaten ice cream too fast then everything went white. Milky white—as if I had been submerged in a vat of milk with my eyes open. A screech filled my head. This was followed by intense pressure, as though David clutched my brain in his fist and squeezed tight. A flash of pain roared through my entire body. Something or someone pulled me toward a dark abyss.

"This way." Somehow David's voice remained inside my head.

No way. I shut my eyes tight, gasped, and using my other hand, jerked my fingers away from Shadow's head. I heard a sucking noise followed by a gurgle like the last swirl of water disappearing down a drain.

The room appeared blurry when I first opened my eyes, then gradually came into focus. Shadow rumbled with displeasure. I kissed her head to reassure her.

A gentle knock at the door startled me. I put my fingers back between Shadow's eyes and glanced at the chair. David had vanished.

"Are you awake?" Dr. Griffin asked. "I heard voices."

"Yes," I said. "I was ... talking to Shadow. She seemed scared, but she's fine now."

I pulled the headband off Shadow's head. My sweet, cooperative dog gave me an appreciative lick. Then she jumped from the bed and went to the door.

"Oh," Dr. Griffin said. "Since you're awake, can we take a quick photo?"

No need. I already knew the outcome. Still, I wouldn't mind her taking another picture. In fact, I was curious to see if the purple had faded. Shadow's ability was intact, but maybe the white light, that vat of milk thing, hadn't been David's doing. Maybe that's what happened when Shadow's ghost-seeing power faded. Well, no harm in a photo. David hadn't forbidden a Polaroid. He had only mentioned the pill.

"Sarah?" Dr. Griffin said.

"A photo is a good idea," I said. "I'll be right out."

I scrambled off the bed and unlocked the door. Dr. Griffin stood in the hall with the Polaroid in one hand and the medicine bottle in the other.

CHAPTER TWENTY

I followed Dr. Griffin into the dining room. Shadow sneezed, shook her head, and sneezed again. Dr. Griffin paused mid-step and stared at Shadow. Her brow knitted together with concern, but she said nothing. The film pack still lay atop the kitchen counter. She frowned then flipped over the package.

"Shoot," she said. "The film's expired." She shrugged. "Well, that's okay, the other film we've been using was probably outdated too, and those exposures came out fine."

I sank into the wooden dining room chair. My lids grew heavy, and I felt myself fighting the tiredness. It's amazing what a body can endure. I had probably had two hours of sleep in the last two days and averaged six hours of solid rest at most since my father died. I had reached the edge, and now exhaustion threatened to push me into the abyss. My eyes fluttered closed, and my chin dropped to my chest. Shadow rested her head on my thigh. I massaged her neck. I wanted to curl up in a bed under the roof of a house that wasn't a haunted shell inhabited by a whacko vet.

"Let's take the picture then," I said, too weary to care about the useless photo.

My dog stiffened and expelled air through her nose, leaving moist droplets on my hand. Eww! She shook her head then nudged me several times until I resumed petting her.

I pondered my next move. Bad film was a great excuse to give in to David's demand that I not medicate Shadow further. Why give my pet a drug if we couldn't be sure she needed it? Better yet, I could argue that all this sneezing could be a side effect of the medicine and Shadow needed to go home to rest.

David and Dr. Griffin would be out of my life. They could exist in their own weird world, and I would inhabit mine. In this fantasy, I even envisioned Greg-the-Ghost leaving my house to move in here with David once he knew where his friend now lived.

"Ready?" Dr. Griffin said.

"Yes," I said. "Shadow, stay."

Dr. Griffin leaned in to take the photo. A flash then a whir. Dr. Griffin peeled back the white coversheet. This time she enunciated each syllable of Polaroid as she stripped the plastic off to expose the print.

We leaned over the square picture. The surface was black. Not a trace of gray or white highlights. I knew right away that this meant the film was defective, but Dr. Griffin stared at the photo with such intensity I expected her to will the desired image into appearing. She picked up a black pen to label the useless documentation.

She glanced at her kitchen clock. The second hand passed the beagle, the pug, and a boxer. When the arrow rotated back to the beagle, and a full minute passed, the picture remained unchanged. Her arched eyebrows drooped. She ran her hand through her blonde hair.

"This is horrible," she said. "Just horrible. My study is ruined."

I picked up the glossy photo by the edges and tilted it away from the harsh light. Multiple shades of gray appeared on the square film. The outline of Shadow's body was apparent, but her central form was as black as coal.

The eyes were dark, too. Wait. Oh-my-gosh. If I could convince her this meant something, she would have no reason to give Shadow another dose. This was my way out.

I stood up so fast the chair toppled onto the hardwood floor. Shadow startled and scrambled to the corner of the room.

"What is it?" Dr. Griffin asked.

My finger jabbed at the photo. I turned the film so she could see. Her hand snatched at the white square. She collapsed into a chair like a balloon deflating.

"It doesn't matter," she said, tossing the photo onto the table. "Expired film."

"But, but, but," I said, shaking with forced excitement. "Look. Eyes. All black." I inhaled a lungful of air as if to steady myself. Dr. Griffin's medicine had worked after all. "If her brown eyes were caught on this film, they would be black. Purple eyes would show gray. I'm sure of it."

She shook her head. I had another idea. I crossed my fingers hoping she wouldn't call my bluff.

"If you don't believe it," I said, "call David out here. If Shadow doesn't react to his presence, we'll have proof."

Dr. Griffin squinted at me from behind her turquoise glasses, as though I had just asked her to hurt a kitten. She opened her mouth to say something, her shoulders slumped, and she sighed. Shadow rushed to her side to reassure her damsel in distress.

"It doesn't work that way," she said, patting Shadow's head. "David comes when he feels like it. I don't know what prompts his appearances."

Dr. Griffin spoke that last sentence without conviction. She was lying. Maybe I should suggest that we all go into David's room. But she would discover that I had snooped.

Witchy Woman went to the counter and grabbed the pill bottle. Shadow meandered over to me. I rubbed her head, which prompted her to crawl atop my lap. I hugged her close. I could not allow this woman to administer another dose.

"Shadow," Dr. Griffin called.

I clutched my dog tight so she couldn't go.

"Uh," I said. "I don't want her to have any more."

Dr. Griffin's whole body stiffened. Her lower lip trembled as she glared at me through cloudy lenses.

"What?" Dr. Griffin slammed the vial down. "I thought you wanted my help."

I sucked in a breath to control my rising anger.

"You said so yourself," I said. "The medicine didn't work. You don't want to call David out here. I don't see the point in continuing. Besides, the film isn't reliable, so we don't know if she needs it." I rose from the chair, keeping a firm grip on Shadow's collar. "We're going home. Even if we have to walk."

Dr. Griffin lurched around the counter. I thought she might try to wrench Shadow out of my grasp. Instead she grabbed my arm. For a frail woman, she had a strong grip.

"Please," she said, and her voice cracked. "Sit down. Just for a moment. So I can explain." Those aquamarine eyes didn't hold anger now. Those pinpoint irises communicated desperation. "For Shadow's sake," she pleaded. "It could save her life."

"If I listen, will you promise to return my purse and car keys?"

She let go of my arm. "If you hear me out till the end."

My fingers uncurled from Shadow's collar. The next thing I knew I was sitting again. Dr. Griffin sat in the chair across the table from me. The amber vial stood between us, next to the dark, half-developed photo.

"You don't understand. Celeste ... my sweet, loyal dog," Dr. Griffin pulled her body rigid. "She was only six when she died. Brain hemorrhage. The same thing could happen to Shadow."

Brain damage? Her ghost-seeing abilities could hurt her? I patted my leg, and when Shadow jumped up, I gathered her close. Was all this head shaking and sneezing because of her encounter with David? Maybe she was trying to clear her muddled thoughts.

"When," I said, forcing the words through clenched teeth. "When were you planning on telling me her ghost-viewing talent could be hazardous to her health?"

Dr. Griffin set her jaw. She stared at me, pulling in her bottom lip and biting down as though forcing herself not to reveal more bad news.

"What would you have done differently?" she said.

"I wouldn't have talked to David—"

Crap. I hadn't meant to tell her that. Her ghostly complexion turned a healthy shade of pink, but rather than anger, anxiety laced her eyes.

"What?" she said. "You talked to David again. Tonight?"

"Yes, tonight."

"Oh, Sarah," she said. "For how long? Over fifteen minutes?"

I nodded. Dr. Griffin stared at Shadow.

"That's really dangerous. The longer you communicate with the ghost through Shadow, the more likely she'll suffer brain damage."

I chewed on my lower lip as I thought about that. If what Dr. Griffin said was true, something didn't quite fit. If giving Shadow pills wouldn't affect David's ability to communicate through my dog, why had David insisted I avoid giving Shadow another one? He wouldn't want Shadow harmed if he could use my dog to communicate with Dr. Griffin. She must be lying again.

"The pills won't stop Shadow's ability to see ghosts," Griffin said. "I'm sorry, I'm really, really sorry I lied about that. But the medicine might protect her brain."

"That doesn't make any sense," I said. "Why wouldn't David want Shadow to have more?"

"He said that?" Dr. Griffin furrowed her brow and then shook her head. "You have to stay away from him. You don't know what he's like. He's cruel. He's bitter. And angry. And he doesn't care about your dog."

"Well," I said. Shadow squirmed, and I released my grip. "Thanks for introducing Shadow and me to him."

"He was supposed to stay away," she said. "We had an agreement." Dr. Griffin waved the pill container. "Please, let me give Shadow another dose. There really is a footnote on the Dalmatian study about metronidazole being administered to one dog during the clinical trial due to diarrhea. This lucky dog was the only animal in the study that didn't suffer brain damage. I don't know if it will help Shadow but let me try. I couldn't save Celeste…" Dr. Griffin's hand shook. She put her head on the table. "Maybe I can help Shadow."

"Why didn't you tell me?" I said, snatching the vial of pills from her hand.

"Would you have believed me?" she said.

She was probably right. I wouldn't have believed her, but that didn't change anything. She wasn't getting near

Shadow until I had proof she wasn't lying.

"Let me see the journal article," I said.

"I don't know where it is."

I couldn't believe it. All this talk about being sorry, and here she was lying again.

"You know damn well where it is." A freight train pounded in my head. I couldn't believe the ... the ... audacity, Mrs. Lutz filled in the blank. My breath came in ragged spurts. "Go. Try. His. Room."

Dr. Griffin's eyebrows arched. Crap. Why the hell couldn't I keep my mouth shut? I wasn't supposed to know about her dead boyfriend's little sanctuary.

"How do you know about David's room?" Dr. Griffin's tone was heavy and menacing all at once. "And ... I haven't been in there all weekend. It's another part of our agreement."

Yeah, right.

"We're done here," I said. "You were in David's room tonight. I saw you with my own eyes. You even touched the journal."

Dr. Griffin's blue eyes widened. The corner of her mouth twitched.

"Oh. Oh, no," she said at last. "The old and weak. I knew he could ... but I'm strong. I thought I was safe from his influence."

She thought David exerted some kind of power over her without her knowledge. Was that possible? It would explain a few things such as her glazed expression last night. And what about the white I saw, the pain in my head, the way David's thoughts had been inside me? If I hadn't broken the connection, would David have controlled my actions? Would he have brainwashed me as well?

I backed away, keeping a firm grip on Shadow's collar with one hand and the pill container in the other. The fur around my dog's hackles rose and she planted her feet. The growl came next. I knew this pattern. David must have come into the dining area.

My feet edged toward the doorway separating the living and dining rooms. Shadow contorted her body and lurched sideways. I lost my hold as she launched into a barking fit, aiming her displeasure at the archway into the living room. David, no doubt, blocked the exit.

Shadow lifted her nose up and howled. A quiet settled in the room as Shadow backed under the table. I thought David had gone and my shoulders relaxed. Then Shadow gathered her feet underneath her and ran through the doorway.

"Shadow, no," I screeched.

It was too late. My dog jogged to the left as if going around something, before diving into the living room. I heard the muffled sound of paws traverse the carpet then a thud. What the hell was that?

I hesitated, envisioning David standing in the doorway, each hand clutching the doorframe. The idea of propelling my body through his ghostly essence held me immobile.

"Shadow?" I called.

Dr. Griffin's eyebrows knitted together in genuine concern. Her white knuckles gripped the edge of the table. She listened with a cocked head.

"Shadow. Come," I said, using my happy voice to let her know she wasn't in trouble.

No patter of dog feet answered my command. Shadow usually came when I called. The kitchen clock ticked away the seconds. Something was wrong and I had to brave crossing that threshold to find out if my dog was okay.

With the theme of *Jaws* hammering through my head, I steeled myself. Duh-da, duh-da, duh-da. I ducked through the doorway. A blast of cold air grazed my cheek as if David had stolen a kiss as I passed. Dr. Griffin scrambled to her feet and followed on my heels.

My body moved in slow motion as though I walked through a swimming pool. I blinked twice not believing my eyes. On the far side of the coffee table, Shadow lay on her side. Her pink tongue lolled out of her mouth as she panted—too spent to even lift her head.

"No, no, no," I screamed.

I rushed to her limp form. I should have let Dr. Griffin give her the pill sooner. I should have listened.

"Shadow?" Dr. Griffin's voice came out as a squeak.

She didn't move. Was she dead? Dying? No, she couldn't die. I couldn't bear it. She was all I had now. The hurricane of grief I so carefully suppressed since my father passed threatened to descend. Not now. Not now. I will not cry. I will pull myself together. I am a Brazil nut. I will NOT CRY.

"I'll get my medical bag," Dr. Griffin said.

Thump, thump went the tail, but my dog didn't rise. What was I thinking coming back to this place? I didn't need Dad's letter. I had memorized the words. I could have written them down verbatim. Why had I been so sentimental? The content of the letter wasn't any more valuable in his handwriting. If ripping up that piece of paper would spare Shadow, I would do it right now.

I lay down beside my dog, patting her with my fingertips as if the weight of my hand might hurt her. I curled my body around hers. She loved me. She wouldn't leave me. Shadow moaned, tilted her head back and licked my face. I didn't deserve a kiss. I had failed her.

"She's going to be okay," Dr. Griffin said as she re-entered the room. A stethoscope dangled from her neck. "Celeste did this once. She was up and about in less than ten minutes without any lasting problems. She'll be fine. But we should give her another pill."

I squeezed the pill vial in my hand. I had already lost Dad. I would not, could not, lose Shadow, too.

"Sarah." Dr. Griffin's voice was firm. The urgency in her voice jarred me.

I fumbled with the child-proof cap on the bottle. My shaking hands couldn't open it, so I passed the container to Dr. Griffin. In moments she had extracted a small white pill.

Dr. Griffin opened Shadow's jaws and forced the medicine down her throat. My sweet, gentle dog growled. Her lip curled back to reveal sharp white teeth. Dr. Griffin re-coiled. I couldn't believe it.

"You'll have to hold her head," Dr. Griffin said.

I didn't hesitate. I clasped her neck in a firm grip. The instant I touched her it was as if I had thrust my hand in a bucket of ice. David. Yet I held tight as Dr. Griffin managed to get the pill into Shadow's mouth and held her muzzle until she swallowed.

A draft of icy air traveled up my arm like a spider. When I released Shadow, the cold sensation disappeared, but Shadow remained lethargic. It was too late.

CHAPTER TWENTY~ONE

Ten minutes passed. Shadow still lay unmoving on the carpeted living room floor. I stroked my dog's head, but she didn't seem to notice my touch. Dr. Griffin paced the room, periodically assuring me that my pooch would recover quickly. I was unconvinced. My dog's nose remained ice cold. I covered her with a leopard-patterned fleece throw.

"I'm taking her to the emergency vet clinic," I announced.

Dr. Griffin froze. Then her hand fluttered to her throat. Those discerning blue eyes darted around the room..

"I don't think David will let you leave," she said, shaking her head no. "You don't know what he's capable of."

Greg had flung my dining room chairs to the ground during his ghostly fit of temper back at my house. But even if David pitched kitchen knives at me, I would get Shadow the help she needed.

"Let's wait another ten minutes," she said.

"No. I'm not going to stand here and let my dog die,"

I said.

Squatting next to her, I gathered Shadow in my arms and lifted her, blanket and all. Her body remained limp like wilted lettuce. Her ribcage expanded and contracted against my stomach. The medicine had not stopped my dog's heavy panting.

Dr. Griffin moved to my side and put her hand on Shadow's chest.

"You're right," she whispered in my ear. "Shadow needs a brain scan. If you let me come along, I'll pay the bill."

I hadn't even thought about the cost. What if the clinic demanded payment up front? Game Plan Rule #6: Don't spend money you don't have flashed through my mind before I squashed the thought.

Then there was the transportation problem. Dr. Griffin still had my car keys. Like it or not, I needed the woman's help. I nodded my assent.

The front door was only steps away. I mouthed the words, "let's go." Dr. Griffin disappeared then returned with my leather bag slung over her shoulder. With her hands stretched out before her like a zombie in a bad horror flick, she dove for the doorknob.

Dr. Griffin pulled the door open and crossed the threshold without any problems. Wind whipped hair into her face as she beckoned me. I lunged outside with Shadow clutched in my arms. Behind me, the door slammed shut of its own accord. Perhaps David was glad to be rid of us.

"We need my keys," I said, sprinting toward my Civic. "I'm blocking you. We'll have to take my car."

She rummaged around in the bowels of my leather bag and I realized that she must have returned my keys. At last Dr. Griffin's hand emerged from the depths of my purse with the Eeyore key chain.

"You drive," I said.

A nervous glance over her shoulder was her only hesitation. In moments, the passenger door had been unlocked, and I had settled Shadow on my lap. Her eyes remained half-closed. At least her breathing slowed. A warm nose and a heart thumping with a regular rhythm were also good signs, though none of these physical improvements would tell me whether she had suffered brain damage.

Dr. Griffin slipped into the driver's seat, depressed the brake pedal, and turned the ignition. Click, click, click. The engine wouldn't catch.

"Well, that explains why David let us leave the house," Dr. Griffin said.

I remembered how David claimed that Dr. Griffin had tampered with my car. Had she done it again tonight? Or had he?

What were we going to do now? The odd angle of my car blocked Dr. Griffin's VW bug. Waiting for a cab or Lyft might mean the difference between life and death for Shadow.

"Don't worry. He's pulled this stunt before." Dr. Griffin said as she located the hood release and pulled. "Last time,

I had to have the car towed, but the auto mechanic showed me what to do if this happened again. David doesn't know I learned how to deal with his latest prank."

She hopped out of the car. The car tilted as Dr. Griffin leaned against the fender. Moments later, the hood fell into place with a thud. The vet plopped back in the driver's seat.

"Okay," she said.

The engine roared to life with the twist of the key. Shadow startled out of her sleepy state, growled, then placed her head on my chest. It seemed a little too convenient that Dr. Griffin knew how to fix the problem. Not that it mattered. I was too relieved that we were on our way to dwell on it.

We navigated residential streets without incident. Only after we were barreling along the highway did I allow myself to relax.

"What are you going to say to the vet?" she asked.

Good question. I would have to omit the part about ghost-induced trauma.

"I'll just say she collapsed ... and she hit her head really hard so they'll be sure to order a brain scan. How does that sound?"

"Perfect."

We exited onto Claremont Drive. Two blocks later, the car pulled into a poorly lit parking lot. A sign on the side of a one-story brick building indicated that we had arrived at the emergency vet hospital.

I hefted all sixty-five pounds of my dog and myself out

of the front seat and rushed Shadow inside with Dr. Griffin on my heels. As I stepped through the clinic's glass door, the smell of bleach accosted my nostrils. Harsh fluorescent lighting made me squint.

The place was deserted. The front counter was bare except for a metal bell. A note instructed customers to ring for service. Dr. Griffin rushed by me and hit the ringer twice. Swinging doors burst open. A young woman with frizzy red hair wearing a kelly-green smock and scrub pants appeared. White letters on her black nametag spelled Leah.

"Oh, dear," Leah said, when her eyes fell on Shadow's limp body.

"She collapsed," I said.

Leah shoved a clipboard with the requisite forms at Dr. Griffin and navigated around the check-in counter to stand next to me. I clutched Shadow closer.

"I'll take her back to Dr. Pullman," she said, petting Shadow's head. "You two get the paperwork done then I'll bring you into the exam room. Is there anything else I should tell the vet?"

"Shadow was running," Dr. Griffin said. "The kitchen floor was wet, and she slid into the wall and hit her head."

"Oh, poor Shadow," she said.

My dog rewarded her with a half-hearted wag of the tail. She wasn't growling anymore. A good sign.

"Can't I go with you?" I said.

"Not yet. But don't worry," she said. "Dr. Pullman is a top-notch vet."

She carried Shadow into the back room. I turned my attention to the paperwork. Dr. Griffin leaned over, watching my progress. When I got to the alternate phone, I remembered my cell phone had died. When I hesitated, Dr. Griffin rattled off her mobile number. She must have noticed the status of my cell phone when she invaded my purse. I should have been upset at this revelation, but I didn't care. All I wanted was my dog to be okay.

"I've heard of Dr. Pullman," Dr. Griffin whispered. "He's supposed to be good."

Headlights flashed outside, casting a yellow haze in the lobby. A squeal of tires followed. Then a heavy-set man stumbled from the cab of a white pickup. This whale of a guy must have weighed 350 pounds. He staggered to the passenger side.

Moments later he crashed through the front door carrying a large dog. The hindquarters of the yellow lab were coated in blood.

"Help," he shouted. "Help, God dammit. My dog's been shot."

Leah's red hair and flushed face appeared through the double doors. Her eyes darted from the dog to the man's face.

"Mr. Crogan?" she gasped. "Is that Brutus?"

"Yes," he said. "I brought him in with a foxtail up his nose just last week."

"What happened?" she said, already herding man and dog toward the back. "This way, this way."

"Shot. Back leg." Whatever else Mr. Crogan said was lost behind closed doors.

I scanned the clipboard once more. Dr. Griffin had just filled in her VISA number in the payment box when Leah re-emerged from the back. The Labrador's owner followed behind.

"Have a seat, Mr. Crogan," Leah said.

Perspiration flowed down his temples and dribbled down his double chin. He collapsed on a plastic chair, but immediately rose to his feet. He picked up a magazine and thumbed through the pages.

"Shadow's stable," Leah removed my forms from the clipboard and reviewed the contents. "Good. I see you have a cell phone. Candice, the other technician, will be monitoring her vitals. Dr. Pullman thinks Shadow will be fine, but he's concerned about the head injury. He wants to run a few tests. Right now, he needs to do surgery on the Labrador though. I'm sorry. Normally, we have two vets on duty, but Dr. Eliza went into labor tonight. Two weeks early. Jeez, what a night, this is turning into."

What a night, indeed. She had no idea. Leah disappeared then stuck her head back through the doorway.

"It'll be a while before Dr. Pullman will be available. Why don't you go to the coffee shop a few blocks down? We'll call your cell if there's any change in Shadow's condition."

Mr. Crogan tossed the magazine aside. He staggered back and forth in the small waiting area, mumbling curse words that would have had any preacher reaching for his Bible. I wondered if he had shot his dog in a drunken rage. A giant brick-red stain covered one leg of his jeans. I didn't want to be around if his dog didn't survive.

Dr. Griffin raised her eyebrows. She motioned at the door with her head. That was all the encouragement I needed.

CHAPTER TWENTY~TWO

I insisted on driving. To my surprise, Dr. Griffin handed the keys over without a fuss. I guided my Civic out of the parking lot onto the main road. Dr. Griffin pointed to a red, neon sign in the distance that advertised Joe's Coffee Shop. I squinted through tired eyes. Now that Shadow was safe and being cared for, the weight of fatigue came crashing down. A double espresso would help, but this diner probably wouldn't offer anything that fancy.

The windstorm increased its fervor. I kept both hands on the steering wheel to adjust for the crosswind. Even so, my car's wheels spewed gravel as the Honda veered toward the curb. I slowed and guided the vehicle toward the center divider once again.

"Uh...are you okay to drive?" Dr. Griffin said.

I nodded even though I had never driven in wind like this before. Leaves skittered across the road, while trees tilted away from the gale force.

Various businesses lined either side of the street. A lighted plastic sign announcing Chuck's Tires and Gas flickered, the internal bulb peering out through cracks. Claremont Drive must have been a hopping business district at some point.

My car clock said 12:27 when we pulled into the restaurant lot. It seemed like a lifetime ago that Shadow had collapsed. Only two other cars occupied parking spaces. Getting a table wouldn't be a problem.

Wind lashed at my hair as I made my way to the entrance. How could it be calm one moment and blustery the next? The gusts threatened to pull the coffee shop door off its hinges. Dr. Griffin grabbed the doorknob with both hands to shut the heavy glass door. I smoothed my tangled hair. Dr. Griffin plucked a leaf off her shoulder.

A faded sign suggested we seat ourselves. We had a choice of booth sectionals with Formica tables or swivel chairs at the counter. Either option came with olive-green vinyl seating. Joe's Coffee Shop was overdue for an update. My hope for an espresso vanished.

I headed for a booth near the window. The red carpet had been worn to a white-ribbed fiber in some spots. We were the only customers.

A sixty-something woman appeared through a set of wooden double doors. She offered me a menu. I shook my head. Upside-down yellow coffee mugs with matching saucers were already on the table.

"Just coffee for me," I said, turning my cup up.

Dr. Griffin held out her hand for a menu. The server gave Dr. Griffin an odd look, before tossing the plastic menu on the table. She strode away with her nose in the air.

"Do you know her?" I whispered.

"That's Gloria. She's married to a Canton," she said. "All the Cantons know me."

Another Canton. The old lady who had almost crashed my car was a Canton. Plus Gregory Canton, the ghost in my house. How many were there?

"If I were you," I said, "I'd only order prepackaged items here. She looks annoyed enough to spit in your food. Better yet, I'll order for you. What do you want?"

She studied the menu. "I'm not hungry anymore."

"I have to tell you something," I said. "I was late for dinner because I was almost in a head-on collision accident with an old woman. A Canton."

"What?" Claudia said.

The Canton waitress appeared with a pot of coffee, interrupting our conversation. I scooted my mug to the edge of the table. Dr. Griffin did the same. She smiled up at our server without a trace of reservation.

"Just coffee for me, too."

Gloria grunted and filled my cup.

"I'm going on my break," she said. "I'll leave the pot." She glared at Dr. Griffin. "You can pour your own. It's prom night, you know."

"Wow," I said after she had disappeared. "What's the deal about prom night?"

Dr. Griffin's shoulders drooped.

"The Cantons have a right to hate me." She shrugged

then shook her head.

I took a long sip of the strong, black coffee, feeling the welcome surge of energy enter my veins.

Her lower lip quivered. I had originally thought tragic was a fitting description of her. Now, I knew why. All of a sudden the newspaper article I read on her computer made sense. I felt sorry for her.

"Because of the car accident?" I said without thinking. "Greg and David were playing chicken. They were trying to impress you, right?"

"How do you know that?" The plate underneath Dr. Griffin's coffee mug clattered against the saucer as she attempted to lift her cup. Her hand trembled, and brown liquid sloshed onto the table.

Crap. I should have kept quiet. I didn't want to admit that I had looked at the contents of her computer. Lying might be the better path. Except my deception had cost Shadow too much already. I pictured my dog huddled in a metal cage at the vet. If I had been up front with Dr. Griffin from the beginning about my contact with David, my beloved pet might not have needed a trip to an emergency clinic.

"I'm sorry." The truth poured out before I could change my mind. "I snooped on your computer when you went to the bathroom tonight."

Dr. Griffin's jaw slackened. Her expression held a mixture of anger and maybe disappointment. She sighed.

"I suppose I deserved that," she said. "I did take your

keys. I was so worried about Shadow. But I see now that I should have told you the truth."

She did seem sorry. Could I have misjudged her? Well, the least I could do was to let her know that I hadn't invaded too much of her privacy.

"You had Googled my address," I said, "and I was curious. I saw the newspaper article. But I didn't look at anything else on your computer. I swear."

Dr. Griffin looked away. Dishes clanked together in the back of the restaurant. I studied a chip in the Formica table while the silence stretched on as if we were in a room full of nervous students taking the SAT test.

A cluster of Shadow's short red hair clung to my sleeve. Shadow. She had growled at David and welcomed Dr. Griffin. Should I trust my dog's instincts?

"I ... I haven't known who to believe," I said. "You or David. David told me you had sabotaged my car, so I couldn't leave."

"You trusted a ghost over me." Dr. Griffin let her breath out slowly.

Hurt materialized in liquid pools at the corners of her eyes. Even those thick horned-rimmed glasses couldn't hide her raw emotion. Great. I'd made her cry.

I, a naïve teenager without any connection to her sordid history, even I had betrayed her trust after she had opened her home up to me. I wished she would yell at me. I deserved it.

"Holler at your boy," I blurted. This had been one of

Tess' favorite sayings. The thought of my friend sent a pang of longing through me. Perhaps using her slang was my subconscious clinging to my old life when hanging out after school with my best friend was so important to me.

"What?" Dr. Griffin said.

I imagined Dad rolling over in his grave at my blatant violation of the part of Game Plan Rule #8 that said to always use proper English.

"It means," I said, "go ahead and yell at me, if you want."

"I'm not angry," she said with a sigh.

"I'm not here to judge you, Dr. Griffin," I said, repeating what my grief counselor had said to me. "Do you want to tell me about that night?"

She gazed into her coffee mug then raised her eyes to meet mine.

"It's about time I told someone what really happened on prom night," she said. "I've never spoken of it to anyone. But I always thought my confidant would be either my husband ..." Her face grew wistful. She took in a deep breath. "Or a police officer. Never in my wildest dreams did I imagine I would confide in a young woman I had only known a few days."

"Well," I said, "I never dreamed I'd own a dog that saw ghosts. For whatever reason, Shadow has brought us together."

My mouth went dry at the thought of Shadow. Would she pull through? What if I had caused her permanent harm? My lower lip trembled.

Dr. Griffin picked up her coffee mug.

"Don't worry, she's going to be fine," Dr. Griffin said.

She saluted the steaming cup in my direction. I wanted to believe her so I lifted mine, and we clinked the ceramic sides together.

"To Shadow's health," we said together.

"How about we start fresh?" Dr. Griffin said. "It's nice to meet you, Sarah."

I should give her a second chance. Dad used to tell me that we could never really know a person until we walked a mile in their shoes. Sitting here across from this woman, I could see how this could be true. She had been living with a ghost. That could make anyone act odd. Despite everything, her concern for Shadow had always been genuine and, besides, Shadow liked her. Dr. Griffin had asked me to use her given name. I really should honor her request.

"Okay, Claudia," I said. I set down my mug and stared into her vibrant blue eyes. "Tell me about prom night."

CHAPTER TWENTY~THREE

Our corner booth had windows on two sides. A street lamp outside the coffee shop illuminated the sidewalk that fronted the main drag. The yellow haze of light shimmered in the night wind. Leaves flew by, trapped in a flurry of moving air.

Claudia's gaze fell behind me toward the cracked vinyl backrest. I was beginning to suspect that she wasn't going to tell me what happened on her prom night. Then her shoulders tensed, and she sat up straight. I had been humbled watching my dad endure the pain and humility that death demanded. I suspected it might be just as painful for Dr. Griffin to speak of the night that changed her life forever. Courage was admirable whether from a dying man, or a woman steeling herself to reveal her deepest secret.

I leaned back against the cold seat and folded both my hands around the warm coffee mug, while outside the dance of leaf litter continued.

"I live with regret every day," Claudia said at last. "I am reminded everywhere. In the strangest places. Cantons seem to populate this entire town. I swear there are two degrees of separation, not six, where the Cantons are concerned."

Claudia gripped the Formica table and turned sideways in her seat. She ground her index finger into the sixties-era vinyl. An indentation formed in the supple material.

"This booth. My fault." She pointed at the red carpet. "Worn rugs. My fault. Ancient fixtures?" She pointed at the rickety ceiling fan. "You guessed it—my fault. All the buildings along Claremont Drive were owned by Greg's father."

Her eyebrows pinched together. She resembled an egret about to spear a fish. If birds wore tortoiseshell glasses, that is.

"The Canton fortune dwindled in the 70s and 80s. The family moved into a smaller home. Cooks and drivers were let go. Then Greg's father made a killing during the dot com boom. In a newspaper interview a week before the accident, Mr. Canton announced how he had planned to sell some assets and invest in a major renovation of the town businesses. After his son died, or more accurately after I caused Greg's death, Mr. Canton lost all interest in the redevelopment plan and his investments. The dot com stock tanked, so none of the town improvements ever happened. The Canton wealth had kept this community alive. Without it, well, look around. I didn't just ruin the lives of David's and Greg's families; I destroyed the whole town."

Wow. If that's what she thought, why in the world had

she returned here? Veterinarians could find jobs just about anywhere.

"What made you come back after college?" I said.

"David." She shrugged. "And guilt, of course. When they started developing the land near where the accident happened, bad things started occurring. I knew he—his spirit—was involved."

Just like that she had drawn a connection to a ghost? Then I remembered her university research involved a study of the paranormal. She would have drawn that conclusion.

"After I figured out how to talk to David through Celeste, after even more deaths, I made a deal with him. I would stay here if he would quit harassing people. I fixed up a room for him and promised I would keep him company for the rest of my life. David was a location-bound ghost—unable to move beyond the accident scene. At least, he had been. But something has changed."

"Location-bound?" I said. "Like he can't leave your house?"

Her gaze shifted to meet mine, and she nodded. She looked as sad as a basset hound puppy. I'd be depressed, too. She had given herself a life sentence.

"Now that he has figured out how to wander, he's become a danger again. Worse, he's learned to get inside people without using a dog."

It must be true. I had seen him take over Dr. Griffin. Maybe that's why he didn't care if Shadow died. He had learned how to inhabit people. Could David have been controlling the old Canton woman's actions when she tried to run me down in her Mercedes? The incident had happened a block from Dr. Griffin's house. Apparently, as long as he could control Dr. Griffin, I was disposable too. Or maybe he sensed I was stronger than his old high school sweetheart. He tried to get inside me using Shadow and I barely escaped.

Shadow. I felt the pressure of tears behind my eyelids. I bit my lower lip to keep them from spilling over. I had hurt my dog because I had used her to talk to David.

"Oh, Sarah. I'm sorry. I shouldn't have mentioned dogs. Shadow's going to fully recover," she said. "Celeste came through her first few episodes without any long-term health issues, even without the medicine. Shadow will too."

I believed her. Not because she was a vet, not because of Celeste. I believed her because even though I was young, I knew what she needed was someone to believe her.

"Go on," I said. "Tell me what happened that night."

Claudia's blue eyes cleared as if my encouragement had given her the fortitude to continue her story. There was no masking her strong, inner core. She may not be big, but I wouldn't want to arm wrestle her willpower.

"Every high school girl dreams of prom night. The shopping. The dress. Finding the perfect shoes, the matching purse, having her hair and makeup done."

She was right, of course. Junior prom was supposed to be one of the highlights of high school. Because of my dad's death, I didn't attend mine. My big mouth had ruined Margaret's special night tonight and that had triggered Paul to break up with her.

"She imagines the boy she wants to go with," Dr. Griffin continued. "She fantasizes about the circumstances under which he will ask her. I wanted to go with Greg Canton. Problem was, David had already told everyone we were going to the dance together, even though I hadn't said yes."

Claudia stared at the table. A few booths away, our server appeared through the kitchen doorway. Gloria. Nothing glorious about her. She scowled in our direction, surveyed the room, shrugged her shoulders as if she had determined there weren't any real customers—at least not any worth bothering with—and slunk back through the double doors.

"David was a cliché," Claudia continued. "Really good looking. The quarterback of the football team. The guy you would vote most likely to succeed. Every girl's dream date." Claudia picked up her napkin and twisted it around her finger. "My girlfriends thought I was crazy, mooning over Greg Canton when I could have David."

Dr. Griffin's friends had a point. Even in his spectral form, David was a hottie.

"Greg was the thin, intellectual type," Dr. Griffin continued. "He held the confidence of one whose place was set in the world by money, but he lacked arrogance. He was solicitous and polite. At seventeen, I thought he was everything I wanted. Unfortunately, he and David were best friends. I didn't want to destroy their friendship, so I agreed to go with David. If only I had skipped prom, if only I had told David I wasn't going to the dance with him and stayed home that night, they would both still be alive, and my life would be different."

Outside, a flash of headlights illuminated the dim restaurant. I looked out the window. A line of three stretch limos passed by like a funeral procession. Margaret's high school prom night must have just ended.

"I never even made it to the dance. David and I went out to dinner. Greg showed up at the restaurant. He was dressed in a retro diamond-patterned shirt and bell bottoms."

I knew it. I totally knew it was Greg haunting my house. He was dressed in his prom-night clothes, just like David.

"Formal dress was optional for prom, because there were a number of low-income families at the school. The organizers decided on a 1970s theme. Greg chose the informal dress option. That was who he was. Greg never flaunted his family's wealth. He was going stag, but he showed up at the restaurant to drop off his cousin who was working that night. He spotted me across the room and smiled. My face must have betrayed my feelings for Greg. David was furious. He practically dragged me out to the car."

Claudia's lower lip trembled. Her fingertips massaged her temples, making her glasses bob up and down. I leaned forward, willing her to finish her story.

"David floored the accelerator," she said in a low voice. "We sped out of the parking lot. Greg must have feared for my safety, because he followed us. David spotted him in the rearview mirror. The next thing I knew David pulled over. Greg stopped too. I jumped out of the car and told David I wasn't getting back inside until he calmed down. I stood on the side of the road while these testosterone-crazed boys revved their engines. When David squealed away, I thought the ordeal was over and took a few steps toward Greg's car. Then in the distance, David's car made a U-turn. The old Chevy rumbled down the road in our direction. I'll never forget the way the moonlight flashed on that silver eagle hood ornament."

Silver eagle? Like the one on her coffee table? I shuddered. Did she keep a replica like a shrine?

"Greg yelled at me to stay put and peeled out," Claudia continued, "heading straight for David's car. I watched from the roadside, powerless to do anything as these boys played their lethal game of chicken. The cars hit. I'll never forget the screech of metal colliding with metal, the explosion of shattered glass, the blood—"

The sound of dogs barking "Jingle Bells" rang out from Claudia's purse making us both jump. She scrambled for her cell phone and glanced at caller ID.

"It's the vet," she said as she pushed the button then handed the phone to me.

Had Shadow collapsed? Died? Claudia leaned forward. Her blue eyes zeroed in on mine.

"Hello," I said. My heart pounded like a jackhammer in overdrive. "This is Sarah. Is Shadow okay?"

"Shadow is doing great," Leah said.

Tension flowed out of my shoulders. I gave a thumbs-up sign to Claudia. She smiled and leaned back from the table.

"But the operation on the Labrador may take hours. Dr. Pullman suggested I call and tell you to come get Shadow. We've done a brain scan and have been monitoring her closely. Her test results were normal. Dr. Pullman sees no reason to keep her overnight. I've got some paperwork to wrap up, but you can pick her up in about twenty minutes or so."

"Thank you so much," I said and pushed the off button.

"Shadow's being released," I said to Claudia. "Dr. Pullman's still in surgery, but we can take Shadow home."

Home. What a joke. My house was haunted and so was Claudia's. Neither of us had anywhere to go.

"Great," Claudia said. "I'm ready to get out of here."

"There's no hurry. They still have to fill out some paperwork on Shadow," I said. "Tell me the rest."

"You already know how it ends," Dr. Griffin said. "Both boys died."

Wind rattled the window. I had the sense that Claudia's words had set something in motion. She must have felt it, too. Her sad, blue eyes held wariness, like a deer before it bends down to drink.

"Since we have a moment," Claudia said, standing.

"I'm going to use the restroom."

I nodded and reached into my purse for my car keys. My fingers glanced across the laminated card that outlined the Game Plan rules. Dr. Griffin had shared her darkest secret. Did she know mine?

"Wait. I have to ask you something," I said. "That envelope that I left under my pillow, did you read the letter inside?"

Claudia sunk back into the seat. "I'm so sorry. I shouldn't have, but I did. I found the article online, too. I know you're only sixteen."

She knew my age. It was easy enough to figure out with an internet search. Dad had insisted that I not post an obituary. Neither one of us had anticipated that in an article about a rise in cancer deaths in fifty-something men that the local newspaper would note that Gerald Whitman was survived by his sixteen-year-old daughter, Sarah. That must be how she figured it out.

A quiet settled between us. We were like two dogs licking our wounds.

"You won't tell anyone, will you?" I said.

"No, but your father should have never left you to fend for yourself," Claudia said.

What? Who was she to judge? What choice had there been? He only wanted to protect me.

"I've been living on my own because my dad didn't want me to be placed in foster care after he died. My aunt couldn't take me. There was no one else."

"What about your sister?" Claudia said.

Warmth flushed my cheeks, remembering how I had told her I was going to Sacramento. "I lied. I don't have a sister."

"Oh, Sarah," Claudia said. "How awful to lose your father and have to deal with everything when there are other options."

Like what? The government? Dad had good reason to distrust social services.

"My aunt and father were raised by separate foster parents," I said. "They both had awful experiences."

I didn't add that my aunt had been physically abused, and as Dad had put it, had never been "right in the head" after that. Or how my dad was fed table scraps like a dog.

"He wanted to protect me," I continued, trying to suppress the defensive edge to my voice, "so he bought me a house, helped me find a job, and pulled me out of high school. He said I could get my GED instead. When I turned eighteen, I would go to college like any other high school graduate. No one had to know."

Claudia frowned, unconvinced.

"We moved around a lot because of Dad's job," I added. "He jump-started restaurant chains in new cities. In a major urban area, we would stick around for six months to a year. In a small town, we might be stuck in a hotel room for a couple of months before moving on. He didn't have any close adult friends—"

"Oh, Sarah. What an unstable childhood you have

lived. Well, your secret is safe with me. I just hope I'm making the right decision."

"You are," I said. "Without a mother, well, I had to grow up fast. I can cook, I know how to clean, and I can balance a checkbook. Dad thought I could handle it. I probably would have been fine ... if I hadn't kept Shadow."

Claudia shook her head and muttered something that reeked of disapproval. Here I had opened up to her, and all she had done was criticize my father. I wished I had kept my mouth shut. She stood and tossed a twenty-dollar bill onto the Formica tabletop then disappeared around a corner. Gloria emerged from the kitchen and strode straight over to me.

"I overheard a little of Claudia's version of what happened," the woman whispered, "but I'm sure that woman hasn't given you the whole picture. Make no mistake about it. She's a liar and a murderer and crazier than that schizophrenic mother of hers. She must have goaded Greg into playing chicken with David to defend her honor or some such nonsense. There was no question that sweet boy died in that horrible accident. But David. I swear that ... that witch killed him after the crash. How else had his eye been dislodged by a sharp object?"

"Killed him?" I scoffed. This Canton lady obviously didn't like Claudia, but this was ridiculous. "He died in the car wreck."

"Hah! I read the coroner's report myself. It said that David died from a blow to his head from a pointed object.

You ask me, he survived the crash, and she was probably mad that Greg had been killed, so she decided David deserved to die, too. She's not right in the head, just like her mom. Bad things happen to the people around her. You better watch your back, little miss."

I didn't know what to say so I nodded.

Claudia appeared a moment later. Gloria swiped the money off the table. I wanted to believe that this server was a bitter old woman with a grudge against Claudia, but I couldn't shake the feeling that Gloria's words held truth.

CHAPTER TWENTY-FOUR

The wind had taken its fury to a new level. We both tumbled into the Civic and slammed the doors shut. Gusts pounded the car, as though I were revving the engine. Our server stood inside the restaurant, watching us from the window. Her presence set me on edge. Was she worried for my safety? I wasn't sure who or what to believe.

What if it were true that Claudia had been so angry over Greg's death that she had gone nuts and killed an injured, but still alive, David? I had heard that mental illness runs in families. If her mother was crazy, Claudia could be, too. During dinner the night before, Claudia had whispered to Shadow that she wasn't used to being around people. I assumed that meant that she didn't have many friends. What if she had been institutionalized and kept away from other people because she was a danger to herself and others?

Then again, the hood ornament could have flown off the car and hit her sweetheart in the head during the collision. Then David's ghost could have taken the hood ornament from the scene, which would explain how it ended up in Claudia's house. I squeezed my eyes shut. This all sounded so crazy and I was too tired to puzzle it out.

We still had a few minutes until it was time to pick up Shadow so I didn't start the car. Stalling seemed like a good idea. As long as we remained under Gloria's watchful eyes, I felt safe. Besides, since Dad told me not to believe rumors, I wanted to hear more from Claudia. Dad said that if you wanted to catch someone in a lie, just keep them talking. Sooner or later they will slip up.

"It must be horrible being surrounded by these Canton people," I said, looking at Claudia. "And hard on your parents too. Did the Cantons give them a hard time?"

Claudia adjusted her horn-rimmed glasses. Her eyes tracked the migration of a tree branch skittering across the asphalt. She would not meet my gaze—the behavior of a liar.

"My parents? No, the Cantons didn't blame them. But, well, it sounds crazy," she said, "so you'll have to hear me out."

Crazy? Had she overheard Gloria speaking to me? I glanced over my shoulder. The woman hadn't budged from her spot by the window. Hopefully, she would stay there.

Claudia took a deep breath. "On the first anniversary of David's car accident, my parents' van slammed into a telephone pole less than fifty feet from where David had died. Mom died instantly. Father survived, though the collision left him paralyzed from the waist down. The cops ruled it a freak accident."

"I'm so sorry," I gasped.

Here I'd been thinking this woman was a monster, but I could tell from the expression on her face that it pained her to speak of her loss. I knew what it was like to lose a parent. The accident would explain why Gloria said that bad things happened around Claudia. But how could this tragedy have been Claudia's fault?

"It was bad," Claudia said, shaking her head. "Real bad. I'd been following them in my car and saw the whole thing. And guess what I found clutched in my dead mother's hand?"

I held my breath. The wind jostled the car's body as I waited for the dreaded answer. Don't let it be the silver eagle.

"The hood ornament," Claudia said.

Something seemed off. It didn't add up. Why had she been following them? Why would her mother have been holding the hood ornament from a car accident they didn't even witness? Unless ... maybe her parents found the eagle stashed in their daughter's bedroom and had been on their way to turn it in to the police. The coroner's finding ... if the shape of the ornament matched the ragged wounds around David's eye socket, and Claudia had the silver eagle in her possession she could be in real trouble.

I envisioned a desperate Claudia passing the van, pulling in front, and forcing her father to swerve into the telephone pole to avoid a collision. Would this woman have been so desperate she would have risked hurting herself and her parents? Had the death of her mother sent her over the edge?

"I knew David had planted the eagle," she said, pushing her glasses up her nose, "to let me know that he had been responsible. My father was in a coma for a few days after the accident. When he finally did wake up, he couldn't remember a thing about the night of the crash. Father had lost the use of his legs. He was wheelchair-bound. I didn't have any extended family I could turn to for help. So, after I finished high school, I lived at home and commuted to college. That way I could visit my father at the managed care facility every day."

More likely she wanted to keep tabs on what daddy might suddenly remember or might say to his nurses. Claudia closed her eyes and leaned back against the car seat. Moonlight blanched her skin to a grayish hue. She could have been a ghost herself.

The parallel between my life and Claudia's unnerved me. Her mother was deceased and Claudia had been helping an ailing father. Was that a coincidence or was she making it up?

"Without my knowledge" Claudia continued with an edge to her voice, "my father bought us a new house—the one I live in now. He said he kept dreaming of that very house and decided it was fate when he saw it for sale online. It was supposed to be a college graduation present, and because it had wheelchair access, he was convinced that now that I had my degree, he and I would live there happily ever after. My father closed the deal before he'd even told me what he had done."

We had this in common, too: Her father had purchased a haunted house. Was this a lie to show me how similar our lives were? Claudia's blank stare unnerved me. Was she lost in the past or in her own twisted version of the truth? It took all my willpower, not to lean into the car door to put as much distance between us as possible.

"I didn't realize it then, but now I know that David," Claudia spat the name, "had somehow wheedled his way into my father's subconscious."

Yeah, sure he did. Another gust of wind slammed into the car. I glanced at the restaurant, Gloria stood next to the window booth, arms crossed. Claudia was too absorbed in her tale to notice the weather or the waiter.

"The moment I stepped through the door of that house," Claudia said. "I knew David's ghost occupied the premises. I'd feel a draft or find something moved out of place. We had been in the home less than a week when Father died of a heart attack. I never told anyone that I found the silver eagle in his shirt pocket. I removed David's calling card and hid it before the mortuary picked up the body."

A chill traversed the length of my spinal cord. David's calling card or hers? The hood ornament had been on her coffee table when I first arrived at her house. Was she marking me as her next victim?

"I wanted to leave town," Claudia said, "but I had college debt, and the housing market crashed, so I couldn't afford to sell. Meanwhile, I met Barry. We dated for about six months. I fell hard for him. We went out to dinner one night, and when he drove me home, he asked to use the bathroom. How could I say no? Barry kissed me in the living room. I never guessed David would be jealous, but Barry died in a car accident later that night. He, too, had the hood ornament in his possession. I'll never know if Barry took it out of the medicine cabinet in the hall bathroom where I had hidden it or if David planted it on him."

The hairs on my arm rose to spikes. This time I did lean against the car door. No one could be surrounded by all this death by chance. Was there a different scenario? One where she had been so smitten that she had shown Barry the eagle and confessed what she had done, thinking that he loved her so much that he would forgive her? Maybe when he didn't, she took matters into her own hands again, the same way she had with her parents. The hood ornament connected all of them.

I positioned my arm so that my fingers were just inches from the door latch. If Claudia noticed, she didn't show it. She still had that glazed look to her.

"After Celeste had grown through her puppy stage," she added, "and I discovered how to talk to David through her, David told me that if I sold my house, he would kill the new homeowners. So I made my deal with the devil. No more killing if I kept him company for the rest of my life."

Yep, uh huh. David was now a blackmailer as well as a murderer. This woman was definitely not well in the head. Regardless of whether David or Claudia was behind the deaths, I feared my life was in danger. David's or Claudia's weapon of choice was an automobile, and here we were together in one.

A loud snap crackled through the air, making me jump. A wire on an electric pole across the street came down, and the loose end writhed on the ground like an agitated snake. The whole world seemed dangerous.

A passing car swerved around the wire and then pulled over. The interior car light came on and I could see the man punching in numbers on his cell phone, no doubt reporting the hazard to the authorities.

Claudia shook her head beside me. "So you see, I'm being blackmailed by a ghost."

"How awful," I said, hoping that I sounded sympathetic.

I had to get the hell away from this woman, and I knew just how I was going to make my escape. I inserted the key in the ignition and started the car. As I pulled out of the restaurant parking lot, I vowed that I would take Shadow and run. She could take a taxi home for all I cared.

"There's one more thing I should tell you." Claudia said. "I can see David without Shadow now. Something happened after I touched Shadow that first time. But I've been pretending nothing's changed. We can't let David know I can see him."

Movement caught my eye. Gloria still watched us from the restaurant window. Dr. Griffin followed my gaze then lifted her hand and waved. The woman stepped backward. Her rear hit the side of the booth and she stumbled. Gloria and I both had good cause to be afraid.

CHAPTER TWENTY-FIVE

My Civic accelerated toward the emergency vet clinic as wind tossed leaves and twigs into our path. I should have slowed down, yet fear drove me onward. I pulled into the parking lot, noting the white truck was still out front.

Leah smiled at us when we walked in. Mr. Crogan paced the reception area. At least I would not have to wait alone with Claudia. Leah disappeared and moments later appeared with an energetic Shadow. My dog strained against the leash, dragging Leah over to me. Shadow leaned her body against mine as soon as she got close. Leah handed me a brown paper bag.

"There's a sedative in there for Shadow if she needs it," she said. "Since your friend is a vet, she can give it to Shadow when you get home. It would be best to keep her calm."

At the word "home," Shadow's claws scrambled for purchase as she tried to force me toward the door that led outside. She was as anxious to get out of here as I was.

Claudia patted Shadow's head.

"It looks like Shadow is feeling better," Claudia said.

"At least someone's dog's okay," Mr. Crogan grumbled.

"I hope Brutus pulls through," I said to the distraught man.

"We need to settle the bill," Leah said to us.

"Of course," Claudia said.

This was my moment. As Claudia went to the counter to sign off on the billing charges, I fled the building and rushed to my Civic. Shadow jumped into the front seat. Normally, I insisted she stay in the back, but there was nothing normal about tonight. Putting distance between Claudia and us was more important.

I gunned the engine and squealed out of the parking lot as Claudia rushed through the glass doors. A few quick turns and my Civic merged onto the freeway on-ramp. Instinct took me toward home, and maybe that was my best option. If I kept the house lights off and gave Shadow the sedative, maybe my dog's silence and a dark house would make Claudia think I wasn't there. Not much of a plan, but I didn't have money for a hotel.

My car exited the freeway without incident. After a few stop signs and a right turn, I arrived on Cherryglen. No porch lights illuminated the street. Although I noted an unfamiliar car was parked out front of Mr. O'Shawnessy's house, the interior house lights were off. Wind whipped the trees around, but otherwise, the street felt oddly still, as though time had stopped.

I shifted into park, cut the engine, then realized I would need to hide the car in the garage. The garage door opener was broken, so I would have to lift the heavy door myself. The last time I had tried, I couldn't do it, so I had been parking in the driveway, but that wouldn't work tonight. Claudia would know we were here.

Outside, the wind whistled. I thrust open the car door, told Shadow to stay, and closed the car door. As I whirled around to rush into the house, I recoiled and my hand flew to my mouth, somehow managing to suppress my scream. Kyle stood in front of me. His red curls whipping around his ears and forehead.

"Kyle," I gasped.

Everything was going so terribly wrong. Dr. Griffin could arrive any minute. Would she hurt Kyle if she found him lingering on my driveway?

"I'm so sorry," he shouted over the wind. "I didn't mean to frighten you."

He shrugged and smiled, dimples creasing his cheeks.

"Margaret and Paul didn't show up to prom," Kyle said, "and neither answered my texts. I was crazy with worry. So I left the dance and found Margaret here. She's ... err ... can we talk inside for a minute? I can't hear myself think in this wind."

I closed my eyes. There was no way I could invite Kyle into a haunted house. A home that was also missing the father I claimed to have.

I shook my head no.

"Please? Just five minutes."

How much time did I have until Dr. Griffin showed up? Uber, Lyft, and even taxis were probably backlogged due to prom. The best thing would be to let him say what he wanted then to ask him to leave. I glanced at Shadow. Her glazed eyes stared back. No need to worry about her being overly-protective of me.

"Get in," I gestured at the car and stepped back into the driver's seat.

Kyle slid into the front passenger seat. Shadow sniffed the back of Kyle's offered hand, groaned and lay down.

"Good dog," Kyle said then gave her an affectionate pat before sitting down.

"Thanks," Kyle said. "I won't keep you. It's just that Margaret told me about how it was all your fault that she and Paul fought and broke up. I wanted to let you know that I can see through her finger pointing. I think it was nice of you to offer to stay with Margaret's grandfather."

As he spoke, his eyes drank me in. The attraction between us was as thick as syrup. My tongue seemed to have swollen making it impossible to speak. His timing was horrible. I had to get inside and hide before Dr. Griffin figured out where we had gone. I swallowed hard, unable to pull my eyes away from his gaze.

"Thanks," I squeaked. "I'm so sorry I ruined your prom night."

"Honestly," he said, "I was hoping you'd be home. Um … I wanted to ask you something." Kyle fidgeted, glanced at Shadow, then took a deep breath. "Can we get together tomorrow morning around eleven? We can meet at the open space and go on a hike with Shadow."

His eyes glittered with hope. I wasn't supposed to get involved. Not with anyone. Not for another year and a half.

"Yes," the word popped out before I could stop it.

"Great," Kyle fidgeted. He glanced at the house. "Is your dad asleep?"

This was my opportunity.

"Dad always waits up for me. He's probably watching TV in the living room wondering where I am."

"He's not being a helicopter parent then." Kyle leaned close, tucked a strand of hair behind my ear, and delivered a peck on my cheek. "I can't wait till tomorrow."

Oh, how I wanted to pull his face close and give him a proper kiss, but for his sake as well as mine, he needed to leave.

"Me either," I said, "but you better go before my dad starts to worry and peeks out the kitchen window."

"Right," he said, grinning. He stepped out of the car then poked his head back in. "I don't think I'm going to be able to sleep tonight."

Such a sweet thing to say. I wasn't getting any shut-eye either but for a very different reason. Under different circumstances, thinking about him would keep me awake too.

"Me neither," I said.

Then he shut the door. Moments later, his car's headlights flashed and the car pulled away. I plunged out of the Civic and sprinted into the house. I raced through the dining room, past the broken glass and spilled wine in the kitchen and headed to the interior garage door. No thud of chairs. No cool air. If Greg was annoyed by my return, he wasn't announcing his displeasure.

How much time did I have? Even if she figured out that I had come here, I was pretty sure Dr. Griffin would go home first to get her car since she couldn't know for sure whether or not I had returned to my house.

I pulled the manual lock inside the garage, then squatting to use the strength in my legs, I tried to lift the heavy door. It didn't budge. If only I could have asked Kyle for help.

I tried again and gained about an inch clearance. I picked up a few wooden blocks. If I could get the door a foot or two off the ground, I was sure I could get the leverage I needed to pull it all the way up. I managed to wedge in two pieces of scrap wood, but it was no use. I hadn't eaten much today, and the lack of sleep didn't help. It was hopeless. I undid my hard work, allowing the door to crash to the ground.

Now what? Leaving my car outside wasn't an option. My tired brain tried to think as I walked, defeated, through the house. By the time I reached the front door, the obvious solution came to me. I would leave Shadow in the house for the few minutes it took to drive the Civic up the street and park around the corner. Her barking would be masked by this crazy wind, and I would only be gone a short time. I wished that I had thought of that in the first place. I raced through my house and out the front door.

As I approached the car, I saw that my new plan wasn't going to work. Shadow was in a panic, barking and jumping between the front and back seats. When I opened the car door, she cowered. Nothing had changed. She had no intention of voluntarily entering the house. How foolish of me to think now would be any different. I closed my eyes as a wave of exhaustion coursed through me. If only I could think straight.

Pull it together, Sarah, my inner voice demanded. *Get your dog inside the house. Do what it takes.*

Suddenly I knew what I had to do. I would knock Shadow out with the sedative then carry her inside. I grabbed the brown bag and extracted the syringe loaded with sedative. I pulled off the protective plastic tip, inserted the needle under the loose skin near Shadow's back and depressed the plunger. OMG. OMG. What if there was an air bubble? In my exhausted state I hadn't thought about the consequences. My hand jerked the needle out and dropped the syringe on the seat. A heavy fist of dread knotted my stomach. I stared at Shadow looking for signs that she might die. But she only slurped my face.

I retrieved the syringe. No bubbles. But that didn't mean there hadn't been air in it. I had only given her about two-thirds of the dose, but already she was swaying. Tears welled in my eyes. I could never forgive myself if I killed her. Please, please, please, let her be okay. I hugged her to me, putting my hand on her chest. Her heartbeat drummed under my fingertips but already I felt a calmness coming over her. She rested her muzzle on my shoulder as her muscles relaxed, and her breath slowed gradually—a good sign that the medicine was working as it should, and she was merely falling asleep.

A flash of headlights turned onto the street. Crap. Crap. Crap. That couldn't be Dr. Griffin, could it? How much time had passed? Thirty minutes? I hunkered down in the seat, my hand on the ignition, but if she blocked the drive-way, I would be trapped. To my relief, the car sped by my house without slowing down.

Get the dog in the house, my inner voice commanded. *NOW.*

I shoved open the car door then picked Shadow up. My dog's spiky fur pancaked into her skin from the gale storm wind as we made our way to the front door. As I stepped inside, she fell limp in my arms. I could still feel the steady beat of her heart though, so I knew she was asleep. I set her down in the entry, shut the door, and jogged to the car.

In moments, my Civic traveled down the street. I pulled around the corner at the end of the block. When I got out, a glint of light caught my eye. A silver wing tip jutted out from under the back seat. The hood ornament. Claudia must have shoved it under the seat. Without thinking, I grabbed the object, locked the car, and raced back toward my home.

The wind lashed hair into my eyes. As I rounded the

corner, a yellow VW bug turned into my driveway. Claudia's car. No, no, no. I had left the front door unlocked. I tucked my head against the wind and ran as I never had before. Why hadn't I told Kyle I couldn't talk? Why had I bothered trying to open the garage door? I had wasted precious time, and now Shadow would pay the price. Stupid, stupid, stupid.

By the time I reached my porch, Claudia had already let herself inside. I held the hood ornament behind my back, wondering if I should toss it into the bushes or keep it as a weapon to protect myself. Claudia squatted next to Shadow, and when she looked up at me, her eyes only held sorrow.

"Why did you run off?"

I had no answer. At least none that she would want to hear.

"I think you should leave, Claudia," I said.

Her blue eyes widened behind her turquoise spectacles. She stood so that we were facing each other.

"Oh …Oh …" she said, staring over my shoulder. "How did he …No …No …Noooooo."

Her gaze then focused on the arm I held behind my back.

"Is that it?" Claudia said. "How could you be such an idiot?"

Her hand lashed out and clutched my forearm. Her grip was as strong as if she dangled over the edge of a cliff and my arm was the only thing saving her from a fatal fall.

She tugged so hard that I lost my grasp on the hood ornament, and the silver object tumbled to the ground.

I could have sworn a wave of cold passed by at that moment. David? Greg? I didn't know what to believe.

"Oh, Sarah, you brought him here. David travels with it." Her index finger pointed at the eagle.

Did he? Or was she insane?

A cold breeze rushed by my face then Claudia's hands flailed at the air as if she were trying to ward off a swarm of mosquitoes. Her glasses wiggled on the bridge of her nose.

I was too petrified to move. Had I really brought David with me? She reached out and clasped both her hands over mine. As those blue eyes latched onto mine, a cold crept across my skull, like water oozing under a SCUBA diver's wetsuit. Holy mother. Either David was here or Claudia had some kind of psychic power. Her eyes flicked toward Shadow. The cold that resided inside my brain withdrew at that exact moment. I pulled my hands away and stepped backward.

"He's so strong," she whispered. "It's as if he's found a portal into me."

Claudia reached down and grabbed the hood ornament from where I had dropped it. What she had said earlier this evening came flooding back: You don't know what he's capable of. Oh, crap. What if she had multiple personality disorder? Could she be calling David her second personality, and somehow in her confusion, attributing her own actions to a ghost? If so, I could be her next murder victim.

CHAPTER TWENTY-SIX

I took a step backward, but instead of bringing the hood ornament crashing down on my skull, Claudia turned abruptly and ran toward my living room. I took a step inside. Arctic air streamed in through my open front doorway. Was that David coming inside too?

I looked behind me. A cluster of leaves swirled in a tornado-like pattern on my porch. Shadow lay at my feet. She woofed in her sleep as though she sensed danger.

I inched toward the living room. Claudia stood in the center of the room. I eyed the fire poker I kept next to the fireplace, but there was no way to get to it without passing Claudia. The woman's eyes had glazed over wearing that same odd expression I had seen the first night I met David. She put her arms up above her head, lifting the hood ornament like a priest raising a crucifix. I couldn't quite believe my eyes when she balanced on her tiptoes and turned in a circle in the manner of a ballerina. Was the woman possessed or insane?

Claudia's arms fell to her side then lifted in slow motion. She took a tentative step closer to me. I stumbled backward. Her arms levitated to shoulder height, then splayed outward as though she welcomed a hug. The ornament remained clutched in her left hand.

Taking baby steps as though her ankles were bound, Claudia lurched then turned in the direction of the dining room. I considered returning to the entryway, picking up my dog, and bolting for my car, but if I took Shadow, she might rouse out of her trance. I couldn't outrun her. I doubted I could get as far as Mr. O'Shawnessy's porch, and even then, if Margaret answered, she probably wouldn't open the door to the person who had ruined her prom night.

Claudia turned toward the kitchen, now holding the hood ornament in cupped hands in front of her. She pursed her lips as she studied the broken glass and spilled wine then turned around and retraced her steps through the dining room in the direction of the living room.

"Greg? Are you here?" she called with a twinge of hope in her voice.

I headed for the kitchen intending to grab a knife. I navigated through the jumble of glass fragments and was about to open a drawer when Claudia screamed.

"Sarah," Claudia yelled. "He's headed for Shadow."

Shadow? My fear morphed into full blown panic. No, no, no. Not my dog. A quick hop over the broken wine bottle. I rounded the corner and saw that Shadow remained in the entry unharmed. But straight ahead in the dining room,

Claudia's body had buckled backwards while her hands curled around her own neck, thumbs pressed into her larynx. Her elbows jutted toward the ceiling like chicken wings. The hood ornament lay at her feet.

I thought about calling 911. Except how would I explain that a woman was choking herself to death in my house? A strange gurgling noise erupted from Claudia's throat. Her face had turned the color of pewter. The whites of her eyes showed like the eyes of a temperamental horse. I sprung to action, clawing at Claudia's hands, but only succeeded in knocking off her glasses. Cold air encased my hands. That lingering doubt surfaced again. Was David the Ghost trying to kill her? Claudia's eyes bulged.

The bark from the entryway made me jump. My muddled brain thought a stranger's dog must have walked into the house because Shadow was sedated. But the muscled, red body that streaked past me was unmistakable. Shadow jumped on Claudia knocking her to the ground and dislodging her hands from her throat.

A wave of chilly air passed by. Claudia wheezed in a lungful of air then launched into a coughing fit.

Behind me, the thwack, thwack, thwack announced my dining chairs were once again crashing to the ground. Greg had returned. He liked to hurl furniture. Or was it David this time? I knew one way to find out.

I pulled Shadow to me, placed two fingers in the space between her eyes, and scanned the area. The sedative I had given my dog apparently hadn't interfered with her ghost-seeing ability. The ethereal forms of two teenage boys with hands wrapped around each other's throats formed. Greg, in his John Travolta garb, crushed the starched collar of David's tuxedo shirt. Behind them a glow of white light illuminated their translucent forms. David appeared to be pushing Greg toward the hazy light. They spun in increasingly tight circles. Watching the two of them made me dizzy.

I had to get out of here. I let go of Shadow. I had only managed to take a few steps when a wave of cold hit me as though I had been slapped. Shadow lunged at the wall of cool air. I pulled her to me and placed my fingers between my dog's eyes once more.

David's milky white face loomed inches from mine. He smiled and puckered his lips. I leaned backward.

"Go pick on someone your own ... in your own world," I said and blew coffee breath at him.

David recoiled, so he was no longer in kissing distance. Greg was nowhere in sight. Had David sent Greg on to the next level of death? Was it possible to re-kill someone?

Icy air numbed my fingers. Shadow yelped and jerked free. Hands encircled my throat. Everything swirled around me as if I had been swept up in a tornado. Shadow's barking reverberated in my ears.

My vision blurred. I couldn't swallow, I couldn't breathe. It was as if I was being pulled underwater.

Shadow's barking faded. I was going to die. I was so tired I didn't even care anymore. Life without my dad was a miserable existence anyway. I would finally get to rest. A wet nose jarred me awake. *"WHAT ABOUT SHADOW?"* my voice within screamed. Fight back. Do it for your dog.

I dug deep knowing that the voice was right. I had to protect Shadow. I twisted my head to the right and lifted my shoulders. The pressure eased, and I sucked in air.

Cold crept along my skull as though an icy rain trickled through my hair. My index fingers and thumbs started flicking each other like a shrewd homemaker thumping watermelon to find a ripe one. I couldn't stop. What was happening?

"Go away," I screeched.

I regained control of my hands. But I felt untethered to this world and couldn't bring my surroundings into focus. I reached out to grab Shadow, but she dodged away and rushed back toward the living room.

"Shadow," I tried to yell, but all I managed was a hoarse whisper.

A fire poker registered in my side vision. I scrambled backward as it dawned on me that who or what held that black rod with a sharp point meant to hit me. The metal shaft rose higher, ready to come down and crack my skull open. Shadow appeared, barking at the raised weapon. The object shifted so that it hovered over Shadow's head. I pulled her to my chest, planting my hand over her skull so that the metal would slam into my hand, not my dog's head.

"No," I cried. "Please, no."

The air crackled, and an ethereal form appeared. Knobby knees, a thin hospital gown. My eyes traveled upward, my heart swelling with hope. Those familiar, brown eyes connected with mine. The face that I never thought I would see again.

"Daddy," I cried out trying to warn him.

It was too late. The fire poker swung in the arc of a baseball bat. It sliced through my father like a saw blade. His ghostly form swirled and evaporated.

"Daddy," I screamed. "Daddy, come back."

The weapon descended toward me in slow motion. I shifted my body to protect Shadow then tucked my chin to duck. The sharp hook suddenly shifted direction. A clicking sound filled my brain, like someone opening and closing wooden shutters at a rapid rate. The black object connected with my temple. Jarring pain flooded my senses until a strange blanket of light absorbed all feeling. I lurched forward but remained on my feet.

Across the room, a flickering light expanded into a vacuum-like cavern. I wondered if I might be hallucinating as I saw David move toward this white hole. I shouldn't be able to see this without my dog. Wait. Hadn't Claudia said Shadow had transferred her ghost-seeing ability to Claudia? Maybe the same thing had happened to me.

David turned an ugly shade of brown as his body neared the light. He took a step back as though he had changed his mind, but at that moment, the ethereal image of Dad reappeared. My father shoved David into the light. A sucking noise like the last bit of water disappearing down the drain filled the room. The light became the size of a flashlight beam as the hole swallowed him. Like a searchlight coming back around, the glow widened as Greg approached. My father nodded to the young man as his spirit spun in a circle, legs disappearing first. They became translucent, as though he was dissolving. The reverse of a genie coming out of a lamp. Oh, the look of rapture on Greg's face. He waved to me and saluted my father. Then, the light disappeared. Both David and Greg were gone.

My dad turned and blew me a kiss then reached his arms out as if to hug me. I reached a toward him. As he leaned in my direction, my father's body moved backwards as if someone had grabbed him by his hips pulling him further away from me. He paddled the air as though fighting against a strong headwind, but the more he fought, the more his image retreated. His ghostly form faded to a wisp of fog before disappearing altogether.

The wind quieted and left an eerie silence in its wake. For a moment, I hung in space and time. Not floating, for gravity still anchored me. Yet, I felt weightless. Pain shot through my head as though it just remembered that it had been whacked with a metal poker. My body tilted. The ground reached up to meet me. My head thudded against the floor.

The image of my dog's pointy muzzle and her distinctive ridgeline materialized under my closed lids. Her dejected brown eyes peered out through cage bars, reminding me just how much I had failed her. My red dog's form shimmered, melted into orange, faded to yellow, until all that remained was white.

CHAPTER TWENTY-SEVEN

Frenetic throbbing pulsed against my temple. Except for the pounding in my brain, I heard nothing. What had happened? Was I dead? Did dead people feel pain? That would suck.

"Please, Sarah. Open your eyes." A woman's voice came from a great distance. "It's okay. David is gone."

I opened one eye. I lay on a cold floor. A porch light illuminated the entry in a yellow haze. My eyes zeroed in on a fire poker lying by my head. The nightmare came flooding back in an avalanche of memories.

Movement caught my attention. Oh, no. Claudia's face came into focus. Not her. I tried to scramble backward.

"Help," I croaked. My throat felt as if it had been subjected to a cheese grater.

"Thank God," Claudia whispered. "You're okay."

I looked around for Shadow and realized her warm, muscular body lay nestled beside me. I touched her sleek coat and was rewarded with the thump of a tail and a flick of her tongue across my cheek. Moisture pooled in the corners of my eyes. Shadow had survived, too.

I tried to sit up. Ow. Ow. Ow. Bad idea. Shadow whined and tried to crawl atop me as if she knew I shouldn't move.

"It's okay," Claudia said. "Lay still. The paramedics are on their way."

"Help," I wheezed.

Even this whisper caused unbearable twangs of protest, surging through my brain. Oh, holy mother. I lifted my head again, but a searing jab of pain convinced me to ease my shoulders back to the ground.

"What happened?" I whispered.

"David's gone," Claudia said with a tinge of wonder. "Greg, too."

The world was alternately blurry then double.

"I assume David hit you," Claudia said. "But I can't say for sure. I remember David was making me choke myself, and I passed out. When I awoke, I didn't know where I was at first. I heard you groan, and I crawled to the entry. That's when I saw the poker near you. You were out cold. I thought David had killed you."

Not David. He had already been gone, hadn't he? Claudia had to have hit me with the poker.

I didn't know what to believe anymore. My head ached. I couldn't think straight. My thoughts seemed to sink deep into my brain before I could grasp their meaning. I closed my eyes.

"I've called 911," she said. "They're coming any minute now. Just stay awake. You shouldn't sleep."

The muscles in my back relaxed. Help was on the way. Claudia wouldn't dare harm me now.

"I told them you were unconscious," Claudia said. "I said an intruder hit you on your head and ran off. I gave them your address. I answered all their questions. They asked if you were breathing. I felt your warm breath on the back of my hand. Yes, you were breathing. Yes, you had a pulse. No, I didn't see any blood. I told them that I didn't know of any medication allergies. You aren't taking anything, are you? I didn't see any pills in your purse.

"No," I croaked.

I nodded then turned my head to the side. The poker still lay within arm's reach. I couldn't see any red on the weapon. I would probably have a nasty bruise though.

"Everything's going to be fine now," Claudia said. "Greg went through the white tunnel. He said the opening would only appear tonight, and if he didn't go, he would be stuck between two worlds for another year."

More of Claudia's delusions. I wished my head would stop hurting so I could think straight.

"Greg said it took him years to figure out that his portal opened on prom night," Claudia continued. "One night each year to step into the next realm. Before he could leave, though, he had to settle his unfinished business. His duty was to get David to cross over. And he did."

Another lie. My father pushed David through. Claudia placed her hand on my forehead as though checking for a fever. I forced myself not to flinch at her touch. The wail of a siren announced that an emergency vehicle approached.

"Greg said he was sorry for hitting you with the poker," Claudia continued. "Sorry for scaring you and Shadow. I wish you could have seen him leave. He faded until all that was left was a ribbon of light."

Wait. Didn't she say she was passed out until after I had been whacked in the head. Except I had seen the ghosts, hadn't I? When I had been sitting in the restaurant with the wind rattling the windows, I had felt as if something was about to happen. It seems I was right.

Shadow whimpered and scratched at her ear with a front paw.

"Don't worry, sweet girl," Claudia leaned forward and whispered in my ear. "They're gone for good. Greg said that once you cross over, there is no coming back. He took the hood ornament with him."

Greg hadn't taken the ornament. I didn't see anything in his hands when he disappeared. Another lie.

The siren chirped off, and bright lights illuminated my driveway. My breath steadied. Help had arrived. As much as I was relieved not to be alone with Claudia, I felt doomed. I had failed my father. My age would be revealed when the authorities arrived. So much for Game Plan Rule #5: Keep a low profile. The thought of my secret being discovered made my head hurt worse. I tried again to right myself.

"Stay still," Claudia said.

My hand touched my forehead. A large lump had formed. I eased back down. Oh, crap. I was going to puke.

Don't let me puke. I bit my lip until the urge passed.

"Don't worry," Claudia said in a low, raspy voice. "Everything will work out. You'll see."

I didn't know what she meant by that, but I felt too awful to care. Red and yellow lights churned through the darkness. Claudia moved to the front door to let in the emergency staff.

* * *

A pinch roused me. A needle had been thrust under the sensitive skin on the back of my hand. Cool liquid chilled my fingers—an odd sensation as though ice crystals had melted in my blood. I opened one eye and squinted. Night still coated everything in darkness. How much time had passed?

"Sarah." The voice was deep and masculine. "Sarah, can you hear me?"

My limbs had been straightened, and I had been rolled flat on my back. The male voice came from my left. I tried to twist my head to see who was speaking. The hard plastic of a neck brace poked into my chin.

Panic swelled up. Not my spine. I wasn't paralyzed, was I? I wiggled my toes. They moved.

"Sarah," Deep Voice said. "We are going to lift you onto a gurney on the count of three."

Before I could respond, the man counted "One, two, three." My body landed on a thin mattress. Someone pulled a sheet up to my chin. It reminded me of how my dad used to tuck me in. Just like that the grief descended. Tears rolled down my cheeks.

"Are you in pain?" Deep Voice asked.

How could I explain? I ached for my father more than anything. His death had ripped me apart, and though I had reassembled myself, somehow I had put myself together all wrong. Without Dad's big, bear-paw hand to cover mine, I felt I would never be whole again. I needed Dad to tell me I was going to be okay and that he forgave me for breaking my promise by not following the Game Plan. I wanted him to reappear. I wanted the impossible.

"Miss? Where does it hurt?"

I did know how to answer. My heart hurt. Everything hurt. All the time. This man could put me out with drugs but each time I awoke, I would still be in pain. Even Shadow only offered temporary relief. Shadow. Panic spread like ice through my veins.

"Where's my dog?" I said, trying to sit up. "Where's Shadow?"

"Take it easy," Deep Voice said, guiding my shoulders back onto the stretcher. "Your dog is safe," he said. "It was growling at your vet friend. It didn't have a problem with Officer Stone though. Shadow is in the back of his patrol car."

Officer Stone from the Mercedes incident? The police were here? What kind of story had Claudia concocted? Would they see through her story and arrest her?

Wait. Had he said that Shadow growled at Claudia? That didn't make any sense. Unless, Claudia really had tried to hurt me. I had to keep my dog away from that woman.

"Please, promise me you'll take my dog back to the emergency vet," I said, gripping his arm.

A wave of nausea hit. I closed my eyes. Colors started to spin around in my head creating spirographs under my eyelids. The world tilted.

From somewhere far away, a voice said, "Sure, calm down. Don't you worry about a thing."

The gurney moved then stopped. Some kind of commotion occurred at my side.

"I think you should wait," Deep Voice said.

"Ms. Whitman." Warm breath that smelled of a cigar whisked by my ear. The voice was low and kind. "It's Officer Stone. I need to ask you a few questions."

I opened an eye. No questions. Not yet. I grimaced. I wanted to ask about Shadow, but just opening my mouth sent missiles of protest to my brain.

"Not now," Deep Voice said, emphasizing the word "now." He sounded annoyed. "She's going to the hospital."

The gurney moved forward. No. They shouldn't let Claudia get away. What if she skipped town before they discovered how sick she was?

"Claudia," I whispered.

"Claudia," Deep Voice called. "She wants you to ride with us."

What? Oh, no. No, no, no. But my tongue got tangled

in my mouth, and the words wouldn't form. The gurney's wheels clattered as we proceeded down the porch steps. I found my voice, but all I could manage was to cry out. My mobile bed stopped. I opened one eye to see that a needle had been inserted into the IV attached to my hand. My body was too exhausted to worry about what that meant. My eyes closed and I slipped away.

* * *

The smell of disinfectant and ammonia accosted my nose. Hospital odors. A cold metal bar pressed against my shoulder.

My dry throat thirsted for water. I lifted my hand. A white bandage covered the injection site where the IV needle poked into my skin. I fingered the bulge. They must have left it there in case I needed IV fluids later. Muted voices wafted in from the hallway.

I tucked my chin. No hard plastic restricted my movement. The neck brace had been removed. Good. I hadn't suffered a spinal injury.

Folds in the light brown, privacy curtain swirled in and out of focus. I relaxed my head back onto the pillow, noticing the other bed in the room was empty. My head didn't feel as bad as it had before. Maybe I had been given pain medicine.

What had happened? I had been on the entryway floor with Shadow. Oh, no. Where was she?

"Shadow," I mumbled aloud.

"What?" Claudia appeared at my side. She leaned across the bed, so that she towered over me. Her eyes were sunken. Bruises had formed on her neck where she had choked herself. A pale hand brushed a strand of her hair off her brow. "How are you feeling?"

I tried to swallow to ask about Shadow but my throat was too dry.

"Water?" I squeaked.

Claudia offered a paper straw. The cool liquid eased my throat and helped clear my head.

"Shadow?" I blurted when I found my voice. "Where is she?"

"She's fine. The police took her back to the emergency clinic."

Thank goodness she hadn't run off with her.

"We'll get her soon." Claudia smoothed the sheet, petting it like a dog.

I took another sip of water. At least she had said "we'll" and not "I'll." Claudia had pulled her hair back into a ponytail. A few errant strands fell in wisps about her face. Two half-moons of gray skin lay below her blue eyes. She looked beyond tired.

"What time is it?" I asked.

"About six a.m."

That meant I had been here at least five hours. I wondered if the hospital would consider releasing me later this morning.

I turned my head away from Claudia and stared at my dingy hospital gown. Dad's ghost had been clad in similar garb, and David and Greg's ghosts had worn the clothes they wore when killed in the car accident. If I had died, would I have been stuck wearing this through all eternity?

"I'm trying to get you released," she said. "There's a problem though. Sarah, they know you're underage."

My heart sank. All Dad's planning. The Game Plan was supposed to help me cover up my age. I only needed to keep my secret for another year and a half. I had barely made it through a month. I had failed.

"How did they find out?"

"Oh, I told them."

The witch. I had trusted her with my secret, and she had betrayed me. Whatever doubt I had harbored that she was a victim of David the Ghost vanished. She did what she wanted or what served her needs, and she didn't care who she hurt. She probably thought she could keep Shadow now.

"Thanks a lot," I spat.

Claudia's blue eyes hardened. Her lips formed a thin line. She reached down and pulled a tattered envelope out of her purse. Dad's letter to me. She waved it as a child might tease a dog with a bone then tucked it away in her bag.

"If you want your letter back," she said, "you'll go along with my version of events. I kept our story simple." She leaned in close and whispered. "Shadow was my patient, and you called me when she collapsed. I met you at the clinic then came home with you so that I could give Shadow her sedative. We had just gotten back from taking her to the emergency vet clinic. We entered the dining room when some guy in a ski mask wrapped his hands around my neck and started to choke me. You ran into the living room and picked up the fireplace poker, but when you reached the entryway, a second intruder appeared, grabbed the weapon out of your hand, and hit you instead. I escaped from the first guy. They fled, and I called 911. The police will probably ask you whether you got a good look at them."

She was a skilled liar. Her fabrication seemed plausible. Had she been plotting this scenario when she was choking herself? The cops would think we had surprised a couple of burglars. They would do a cursory investigation, find no fingerprints, and assume the men wore gloves. Nobody died. No evidence, no leads, no distinguishing description of the perps. Nothing stolen. No similar home invasions would occur. In a few months, they would call it a cold case and shove the paperwork into a dusty file cabinet.

Now that my head felt less fuzzy and I had finally slept, the events of the last few days seemed surreal. Had there ever been ghosts? Could everything that I had experienced been the result of this woman's power of suggestion and my exhausted state of mind? If she swung the fire poker like I believed she had, she would have been smart enough to wipe off fingerprints. If ever someone was a threat to herself or others, it was Claudia. How would I ever feel safe if she wasn't locked up?

"All right," I said, knowing it would be better if she thought I was cooperative. "That's easy enough to remember. I'll say my attacker was short and stocky."

"Excellent," she grinned. "I've already told them my guy was average height and weight."

Claudia's dark silhouette settled into a chair next to my bed.

"If the cop comes in," she whispered, "you will pretend that you're still asleep as though we haven't had a chance to talk."

Resentment reared its head at the way she ordered me around. I should have controlled my temper, but I was tired, I felt awful, and I was sick of her lies.

"Okay, okay," I snarled.

Claudia took a deep breath. She leaned into the vinyl chair. I settled back onto my pillow.

"Don't even think about telling a different story," she said in a low voice. "Or you'll never see the letter or Shadow again."

My breath caught. The letter I could live without, but I would never let her take Shadow from me. I imagined it would be easy enough for her to deliver on her threat. She had paid the first vet bill. She could pick her up and disappear before the hospital released me. I heard a deep, male voice outside the door.

"That's Officer Roderick," Claudia whispered. "Remember what I said."

It didn't really matter whether I was supposed to recall the details of her fake story or her threat to take Shadow from me. I had to do exactly what Claudia demanded until I was sure that Shadow was safe. I closed my eyes and feigned sleep.

"Hey," Officer Roderick said. "What are you doing in here?"

"I was worried," Claudia said. "She just had head trauma. She shouldn't be left alone."

"What?" I mumbled.

"Out," the cop said.

"I'll just—"

"Now."

I opened my eyes. Claudia's gaze darted to her purse under the visitor chair. But the officer ushered her out empty-handed.

CHAPTER TWENTY-EIGHT

The cop asked questions about what had happened at my house. Fewer than I had expected. I avoided looking at Claudia's purse throughout the interview.

"One more thing," he said.

"The doc told me that you're suffering from acute exhaustion." He checked his notes. "Possibly mono."

"Why does that matter?" I asked.

"One of the side effects of extreme exhaustion is hallucinations. It will affect your credibility as a witness."

Hallucinations? Like seeing ghosts. Feeling cold air. Once again, doubts surfaced about what had really happened to me these last few days.

"Look, Sarah," Officer Roderick said. "It's not that big of a deal. Your version of tonight's events match Claudia's story.

"That's good," I said. "Because I remember what happened clearly."

He made a notation in his book then snapped it shut.

"Okay. No need to worry. Social services will be by

later this morning to discuss your living situation."

Not worry? Easy for him to say. He wasn't going to be forced into foster care.

Now that everything was falling apart, more than ever I wanted Dad's letter. I was going to get it as soon as I was alone.

"Could you close the door and tell the nurse that I need some sleep? I'm really tired."

"Of course," he said. "Get some rest."

He shut the door behind him as he left, enfolding the room in darkness. Only a sliver of light slipped under the doorway. Other than a dull ache, my head felt normal. I sat up and wasn't dizzy.

I scooted to the end of the bed to avoid lowering the rail and possibly alerting the nurse to my movements. My feet hit cold floor. After a bit of groping, I found Claudia's soft leather purse under the chair. It was huge with only a snap to keep the contents from spilling. I located the frayed paper envelope and was about to shove the bag back under the chair when my fingers hit cold, grooved metal that tapered to a point. I knew what it was. An eagle's wing. Claudia had taken the hood ornament.

Claudia must have said Greg had taken the object with him to the other side because she didn't want me to know the object was still around. I suspected she feared the ornament could implicate her in David's death. I stashed both letter and silver eagle inside the pillow under my head.

I remembered something Dad had told me about the

procedures of the foster care program. They did back-ground checks, though those weren't foolproof in his opin-ion. An idea formed—one that could solve all my problems. It would be risky, but it could work.

* * *

I crawled back into the bed. Claudia's voice filtered in from outside. I could make out hushed protests of the nurse here and there: "No visitors." "Rest."

Claudia responded. "Just long enough to get my purse." "I'll be quiet." "Just take a moment."

The door opened a crack, flooding the room with light. I turned my head to face the purse and groaned. I watched through slitted eyelids as Claudia snatched up her purse. The nurse grabbed her arm and escorted Witchy-Woman out. The door closed once again, encasing me in darkness. In moments, Claudia would know what I had done.

I waited a minute longer then pressed the call button. The nurse poked her head through the door.

"I'm so sorry about that," she whispered. "Do you need something?"

"Yes," I said. "Can you come over here?"

"Sure," she said. "Close your eyes. I'm going to turn up the lights."

The nurse flicked on the light, shutting the door behind her. By the time she moved to my bedside, my eyes had ad-justed. I glanced at her photo nametag that she wore like a necklace. The picture showed a 30-something, smiling woman with big hair. The woman before me had aged a few years since the photo had been taken and had straight hair, but the kindness in her eyes remained the same. The name on the badge said Marie Hatcher.

"Marie," I said. "My cell phone is dead, and I need you to make a very important phone call for me. Can you call the emergency vet clinic and ask them not to release my dog to anyone but me? Make sure they put it in writing on her chart. She is not to go home with anyone else, especially Dr. Griffin."

"Of course," Marie said, glancing over her shoulder. "She is a bit odd, isn't she? I wouldn't want her caring for my dog either. Anyway, don't worry about a thing. I'll take care of it right now. Just focus on getting some rest, okay?"

"Thank you," I said. "Thank you so much."

Marie dimmed the light as she left. I closed my eyes and snuggled under the covers. For better or worse, the first step of my plan had been implemented. I reviewed Dad's Game Plan Rules. My idea complied with Dad's guidelines. For a change, I hadn't made a rash decision. Dad would be proud.

My chest tightened, and I felt that familiar ache press against my heart. Dad had returned last night to help me. But what if that was the last time I would ever see him? Had he crossed over like Greg and David? What if he were really gone and he would never be able to come back to save me if I was in trouble?

Fissures splintered the hard shell of my Brazil-nut exterior. I closed my eyes, trying not to cry. If I wasn't Dad's nut, if I wasn't his pumpkin, who was I? I thrust my face into my pillow giving into the pain and frustration and bawled, pummeling the filling with my fists.

When at last I regained control, I felt as though I had shed the hard outer layer and all that remained was the soft core that I had worked so hard to protect. Through hitching breaths, I marveled that nothing had changed. I still had my inner strength. I remembered a part of one of my favorite Winnie the Pooh stories where Christopher Robin tells Pooh he was stronger than he knew. If Dad were alive, he might have said the same thing to me.

* * *

I awoke with a start. My whole bed shuddered. I thought at first of an earthquake. Light from the bathroom filtered in. The clock on the wall said it was 9:00 a.m. I had gotten three glorious hours of sleep.

I rolled onto my side still dazed and not fully awake. Claudia's arms were shoved deep under my mattress. Blue eyes flaming with anger bore through me, just inches from my face. Raw fear cleared my head. I sat up, stealthily groping for my call button.

"Where is it?" she hissed.

"Somewhere safe," I said.

At least for the moment. The hood ornament was still

stuffed in the pillowcase under my head along with Dad's letter. The silver object was necessary for the success of my plan so I couldn't let her find it. Now it was time to take the second step. I took a deep breath.

"This is what's going to happen," I said. "You'll do as I say if you don't want the cops involved. You're going to go to social services and request to become my legal guardian."

"What?" Claudia snorted. "That fire poker must have damaged your brain."

"I think you should—" I said.

"No, you listen to me," Claudia said, jerking her arms out from under the mattress. "You're going to hand over the hood ornament right now, or you'll never see Shadow again."

The hell I was. I had anticipated this threat. But I had followed Rule #3. I was prepared for the worst. I finally located the nurse call button under the sheet though I would only use it if she tried to take my pillow.

"I'm going to lose her anyway," I said. "Even if by some miracle social services finds a foster home that will take a teen girl, I won't be able to keep Shadow. You won't get to keep her either. She doesn't even like you anymore. Besides, once I turn over the hood ornament to the police, you'll be in jail. So, I suggest you do as I say."

Claudia's face flushed scarlet with rage. Her blonde hair was a wind-whipped mess. Blue eyes jabbed daggers into mine, but I didn't look away.

"Foolish girl," Claudia said. "You're in way over your head."

I hadn't expected this reaction. I thought as long as I had the hood ornament that I had the power. Claudia had been so paranoid about the eagle that I had been sure she would go along with my demand. I steeled myself with Winnie-the-Pooh courage.

"Think about it, Claudia," I continued. "As long as you cooperate and don't hurt anyone else, I won't tell anyone what I know. You'll be my guardian in name only. The hood ornament will stay hidden. In a year and a half, I'll be an adult and you'll be free of me. I don't like the arrangement any more than you do, but it's your fault I'm in this mess. You're the one who told them I'm underage."

"That doesn't give you the right to take what is mine," Claudia said as she stormed to the light switch and turned the dimmer all the way up.

I squinted at the brightness, but Claudia's eyes darted around the room. I took this as a good sign. She could pretend all she wanted, but she was afraid of what might happen if the ornament fell into the hands of the police. The empty bed next to mine was disheveled. She must have searched it while I slept. End table drawers gaped open. As far as I could tell, she had exhausted all the obvious hiding places, except the one that mattered. How long till she zeroed in on the real hiding place?

Doubts about my scheme surfaced. Big ones. I had underestimated the woman. She might be unstable, but she was clever. I had anticipated that Claudia would agree to sign the papers. I had also assumed the background check would eventually disqualify her from being my guardian. The plan had been that during the procedural delays about my guardianship, my inheritance would come through, and I could take Shadow and leave town. I hadn't considered that Claudia might not be afraid of my threat.

Fear gripped my center then coursed through me in waves. Without Claudia's cooperation, I would lose Shadow. Claudia was right. I was a foolish girl.

The door burst open and a tall, heavy-set woman entered. Behind her, sunshine streamed in from an outside window across the hall. The woman had a kind smile and a confident gait. She strode to my bed and thrust her hand out.

"Good morning. I'm Mrs. Wright of social services," she said. "You must be Sarah."

She seemed nice enough. I wanted to make a good first impression. I wanted her to see that I could solve my own problems.

"Yes, I'm Sarah, and this," I said pointing to Claudia, "is Dr. Claudia Griffin."

I had hoped Claudia would chime in about wanting guardianship. Instead, her eyes darted about the room before her lips drew back to expose her teeth in a fake smile. She offered her hand to Mrs. Wright.

"Ah," Mrs. Wright said, shaking Claudia's fingertips, as if she was already wary of the woman. "I understand you saved Sarah. It was good you scared off the burglars. Who knows what would have happened if you hadn't been there?"

The last sentence dashed all hope that I would be allowed to return home without adult supervision.

"I was glad I was able to help," Claudia said. "Sarah is such a sweet girl."

The words flowed off her tongue with such ease. I could almost believe she was sincere. Moments ticked by. The vet didn't add anything about becoming my guardian. My plan wasn't going to work.

Mrs. Wright nodded. "Well, I have some things to discuss with Sarah. Claudia, would you mind stepping out of the room?"

I could have sworn Claudia's blue eyes turned a shade darker. She gave me a warning look, smiled at Mrs. Wright, and exited without a word, leaving the door open.

Mrs. Wright shut the door then sat in the visitor's seat. I chewed on my fingernail. Without the possibility of Claudia becoming my guardian, I no longer wanted to talk to this social worker. Dad had warned me to avoid these people. She had probably changed many lives, maybe some for the better. If she took away Shadow and forced me into foster care, she would change mine for the worse.

"I can only imagine," Mrs. Wright said, "how difficult it has been for you since your father died. I'm really sorry for your loss."

I didn't know what to say. She seemed sincere, but

would Dad want me to be nice to a woman from social services? When I didn't respond, the woman reclined in her chair. Her black pants held errant strands of white animal fur. She tried to brush them off to no avail then she met my eyes. I leaned back into my pillows, averted my gaze, and used my peripheral vision to see what she was doing.

"My Sasha sheds all the time. I understand you have a dog," Mrs. Wright said. "What's its name?"

I liked the way her whole face softened when she talked about her pet. She watched me with an expectant expression, still waiting for an answer. Dad's rule about being polite reared its head. I couldn't see any harm in answering.

"Shadow," I said, turning my head to look at her.

"What a nice name. What breed?" she said.

"Doberman," I said.

"Sasha's a blue merle Australian shepherd. She means the world to me, so I know how scared you must feel about being separated from Shadow. I promise I'll do everything I can to find a way to help both you and Shadow."

I believed that she really would try to find a way to help me keep Shadow. Maybe if she knew how well-behaved she was now, it would make a difference.

"Shadow is housetrained. She doesn't chew or dig holes in the yard. She wouldn't cause any trouble. Please, let me keep her. I'll pay for all her food and any other expenses. I have a job, and I have an inheritance coming, too."

"Well, that's all good news," she said with a smile. "But before we talk about your and Shadow's options, can you tell me how you came to be living on your own?"

My fingers plucked at a loose thread on the blanket. I noticed red spiky fur dotting my hospital gown. Shadow's hairs were always sticking to me. Was this a sign that I should trust this woman? I took a giant leap and decided to confide in her. If she understood how well I had handled ordinary day-to-day problems and how much I loved Shadow, there might be a chance that she'd let me go back to my house.

So I told her the truth, describing my father's illness, my deceased mother, and my unwell aunt. As I spoke, she leaned forward. Her eyes misted. I liked the way she just listened. She wasn't taking notes. I had her undivided attention. I told her about my dad's work travel and how his job had kept him from establishing close friendships. I even shared about Dad's bad foster experiences that had poisoned him against placing me in the care of strangers.

She nodded but didn't say anything, so I added how I was used to taking care of the house. I knew how to manage a checkbook and cook and clean. My money problems were temporary and would be resolved soon.

"So, you would prefer to continue holding on to all these adult responsibilities all by yourself?"

"Yes," I said without hesitation.

Though I had struggled to learn my job, I had managed to do all the things that Dad used to take care of before he got ill, like cooking and laundry. And there were lots of good things about living at my new house: Mr. O'Shawnessy, the open space at the end of the street—Oh god. Kyle. I was supposed to meet him.

"What time is it?" I said.

"A little after ten," she said after consulting her watch.

So Kyle wasn't waiting for her and Shadow yet. But I didn't have any way to contact him to cancel. I didn't even know his last name to find him on social media. He was going to think I stood him up. I couldn't exactly confide in Mrs. Wright that I had made a date to meet a boy that I just met.

"Something wrong?" Mrs. Wright asked.

"No, sorry. I—I've always been independent," I said remembering what I had been about to say about not minding the adult responsibilities. "Dad taught me how to take care of myself."

Mrs. Wright rested her chin on tented fingers. She nodded.

"What about school?" she said.

I laughed.

"I never thought I'd say this. I kind of miss it. A normal school routine sounds pretty good. Leaving high school was the one aspect of Dad's Game Plan that I never thought would be a problem for me.."

"Dad's Game Plan?"

How much more should I tell this woman? Then again Dad's rules didn't matter now that my secret was out, so I described how Dad had devised his plan to help me keep my age hidden. I added that I was going to have to get a

GED to finish high school, but I always planned to go to college.

Mrs. Wright pursed her lips and nodded.

"You seem very mature," Mrs. Wright said.

"I really want to go back to school and be a regular student," I said. "I don't need to work. Dad left me plenty of money. As an orphan I'll get some support from Social Security, but he thought it would be too suspicious if I didn't have an obvious income. He had also decided that being in school was too risky. School officials were bound to learn that I was living alone when it was report card time or back to school night."

"So, your dad didn't know?" she said in a quiet voice.

"Didn't know what?" I asked.

"That if you can demonstrate financial independence and both your parents are deceased or deemed unfit to raise you, and if you are sixteen or older, the system sometimes allows you to live alone."

"What?" I sat up straight in bed.

I was sure I had heard wrong. Why hadn't Dad researched this? He must have been too ill. Or maybe he had been afraid to contact social services to even ask questions that might alert them to my situation.

She smiled. "You're probably more prepared to live on your own than a lot of eighteen-year-olds. It's rare to allow a minor to live alone, but if you are willing to enroll in the local high school, I'd be willing to support your emancipation."

"Really?"

"Don't get too excited yet," Mrs. Wright added. "You will still need to be deemed competent by an adult who will vouch for you. This requires a formal proceeding and scheduling it can take weeks, maybe even months. So, I'm afraid social services will still need to assign you to a temporary custodial family. I've reviewed our files of available families, but none of them would allow a dog."

The room shrank in on me. Mrs. Wright's lips continued to move, but I didn't understand a word. This couldn't be happening. I never really believed I would have to give up Shadow. I had just begun to accept that my father was gone. I couldn't handle losing my dog, too. I clutched my bedsheet in frustration.

"Sarah," she said. "I wish there was another solution. Don't worry, though. I promise that Shadow's not going to the shelter. I'll find her a temporary home."

"No," I said.

My throat felt so tight, I thought I might not be able to catch my breath. My hands came up to hide the tears trickling down my face. I didn't want her to see me cry.

"No, please," I croaked. "Don't take my dog. She's all I have."

Mrs. Wright frowned. "What about your veterinarian friend? Maybe she would take her."

"No." I had spoken with such force that the woman recoiled. I wiped my nose with the back of my hand. I took a deep breath then choose my words carefully. "She's not my friend."

I didn't want to say anything more about Claudia. If social services knew this woman was crazy, they might fear for my safety and not let me go home.

"Okay, scratch that idea," Mrs. Wright said. "I'm sure we can figure something out. I'm really sorry about this. With a little luck, I should be able to find a living situation for Shadow until the new foster family deems you capable of supporting yourself."

"Capable?" I blurted. "Where was social services when I had been keeping house, paying bills, while caring for my sick father and going to school?"

I stopped myself, though I wanted to say more. Outbursts wouldn't help my case.

Think, Sarah. Think. I didn't really know any adults in this town, except Mr. O'Shawnessy. He had seen me every day since I had moved here, and he didn't suspect my true age. Wait. What if he would vouch for me? Could things stay the same then?

I described my friendship with my neighbor. I explained that living next door would almost be the same as sharing the same house with him. I didn't add that the man was old, and his health was failing and that his granddaughter despised me.

"I can't let you stay by yourself." Mrs. Wright stood to leave. "But if you give me your neighbor's phone number, I'll contact this Mr. O'Shawnessy and ask on your behalf if he would agree to consider letting you stay with him until we get this sorted out. Shadow could stay next door in your house or maybe your neighbor will let the dog come, too."

Mr. O'Shawnessy had an easy phone number to remember, and I knew it by heart. I rattled it off while Mrs. Wright scribbled down the information. She took a few steps toward the door then turned back to face me.

"Social services usually places minors in the direct care of another relative, but since you don't have any suitable options, this might be a good solution. I'm convinced that it is not in your best interest to take away your dog." Mrs. Wright gave me a parting smile then added, "Let's hope for the best."

She was on my side. I had been right to trust her. At least I had made one good decision today. I eased back onto my pillow and its hidden contents, relieved that Dr. Griffin hadn't offered to become my legal guardian. I still had to figure out what I was going to do about her though. If I alerted social services or the police to this woman's obsession with me and my dog, they would probably never agree to let me live alone. As long as I had the hood ornament, I might be able to control her. But I still had to get the silver eagle out of the hospital without Claudia's interference.

Nurse Marie bopped into the room. "I have a surprise for you," she said.

She approached with an arm hidden behind her back. I expected an extra serving of pudding. Instead she presented me with a plant blooming with yellow flowers.

"What do you think? Would you like to take them

home? Room 118 left them behind."

I stared at the golden mums in their clay pot and smiled as an idea formed. The wingspan of the eagle was about the width of my thumb to pinky when my fingers were spread. When placed on the diagonal in the pot, the hood ornament would just fit inside.

"Oh, yes," I gushed. "They're lovely."

The moment Marie left I unzipped the inner pillowcase and extracted Dad's letter and the hood ornament. I left the envelope under my pillow but picked up the potted plant and the silver eagle, taking them with me to the bathroom. After I buried the ornament inside the pot, I rinsed the sink well, flushed the extra soil down the toilet, and returned the flowers to my tray table.

I had only just climbed back into bed when Nurse Marie came in with a food tray.

"You must be starving," she said. "You slept through breakfast, but I made special arrangement to get you an early lunch plate."

"What time is it?" I asked.

"A little after eleven."

I imagined Kyle perched on the slatted fence near the open space entrance waiting for me. He didn't have my cell either. Would he walk to my house and knock on the door or would he be afraid that my supposed father would open the door? Or worse would he think I was a flake or a cruel person who enjoyed leading boys on only to dump them?

"Eat up," the nurse chirped as she headed to the door.

"I've seen release papers floating around. You should be able to go home soon. I'll be back in a bit with an update."

I lifted my fork. The plate contained mashed potatoes, apple wedges, and a fleshy, brown tube thing that I supposed was a sausage. At least the apple slices looked edible. I nibbled the fruit then pushed my plate to the side. I didn't need food. I needed to know that I could keep Shadow.

I picked up the two unused napkins grateful that I had accidentally been given an extra one. I shoved them under my pillow. I had an idea and I would need these.

The door opened. A smiling Mrs. Wright appeared. I sat up and allowed myself to hope.

"I wanted to tell you right away," she said, "that Mr. O'Shawnessy has agreed to take temporary custody of you."

My heart swelled with gratitude. Mrs. Wright went on to say that she had pulled in some favors and expected to get a background check done on Mr. O'Shawnessy by this afternoon. Since he lived near here, she had also arranged to drive to his house and check out his guest room to see if it met acceptable standards.

"Unfortunately," Mrs. Wright added, "Shadow will need to stay next door in your house because of his granddaughter's allergies."

I forced myself not to roll my eyes, but I was too happy to let Margaret dampen my mood. Shadow would be right next door and it would only be a short time before I could move back into my house.

Mrs. Wright explained that if all went according to

plan, Mr. O'Shawnessy and his granddaughter would meet her in the social services office on the fourth floor of the hospital to sign some papers late this afternoon. After that they would drive me to the vet clinic to get Shadow.

"Assuming Mr. O'Shawnessy finds you competent to handle adult responsibilities, he will have to appear at a legal hearing and report that you have demonstrated that you are capable of independent living. You'll need to be patient. Scheduling a court date can take a month or more."

After she left, I prodded a cold sausage with my butter knife. I wondered if Mr. O'Shawnessy realized how much Margaret was going to resent this arrangement. I wondered if Claudia would figure out where I had stashed the hood ornament before the hospital released me. Would Shadow think I abandoned her when I left her alone next door every night? Would Kyle speak to me again if I ever ran into him in the open space? Would I ever feel normal again?

CHAPTER TWENTY~NINE

I touched my face. Not too bad, just a little twitch of pain under the thick layer of coverup makeup I had borrowed from Nurse Marie to hide the purple bruise on my temple. My head felt clear. I was ready to leave.

It felt good to be back in my own clothes. Somehow having Dad's letter stashed under my shirt with my bra strap securing it against my chest, gave me a boost of confidence. I hadn't felt any dizziness, but Nurse Marie said hospital procedures required that I be escorted out of the hospital in a wheelchair. She assured me Mr. O'Shawnessy and his granddaughter had arrived to take me home and that they would be done with paperwork and would arrive soon. I sat on the edge of the bed. I had one more thing to do.

I removed the unused napkins from under my pillow. I twisted them into the shape of the eagle ornament and stuffed it into my pants pocket so that Claudia would think that was where I had stashed the object. Even if she forced her hand into my jeans and tried to take what she presumed was the ornament, the real silver eagle would be safe. I knew it was a gamble keeping Claudia's trophy or whatever it meant to her twisted mind. It had seemed like my best chance to keep the woman under control and out of my life. I wanted her to know without a doubt that I had the ornament.

Now, more than ever, I couldn't hand it over to the police. Even if they arrested her, if she made bail, she might retaliate and set fire to Mr. O'Shawnessy's house. I couldn't risk putting us all in danger.

I inspected my face one more time, satisfied that the bruising wasn't noticeable. I snapped the compact mirror shut as Marie walked in the door.

Marie smiled. "Now you are ready for your second surprise of the day." She poked her head out into the hall and said, "You can come in now."

Kyle's mop of red hair and the dimpled smile appeared as he poked his head through the doorway.

"Hey," he said as he entered the room. "You didn't think I'd let you off the hook that easily, did you?"

"How did you find me? I wanted to call but I didn't have your number. I don't even know your last name."

"I went to your house and, when there was no answer, I walked next door. Mr. O'Shawnessy explained what was going on and when you might be able to see visitors. I'm so glad you're going to be okay."

"Me too," I said. "I want a raincheck on that hike. How about tomorrow?"

"Deal," he grinned, slipping his hand into mine.

The warmth of his touch spread up my arm and into my heart. Curly red hair fell over one of his eyes. The effect was ever so sexy. He tilted his head the way Shadow did when she was curious. I was falling hard, but I felt confident Kyle would be there to catch me.

Marie knocked and my red-headed dreamboat quickly pulled his hand away.

"Dr. Griffin is insisting on see you," she said. "Are you up for another visit—"

"Of course, she is," Claudia said, pushing past the nurse.

Marie opened her mouth to protest, but I shook my head.

"I need to talk to her," I said and turned to Kyle. "See you tomorrow?"

He nodded, and as he reached the door added, "Wouldn't miss it."

My eyes lingered at his back as he skirted around Dr. Griffin and out the door. She frowned at Kyle no doubt trying to figure out who he was. The vet moved to my bedside as Marie followed on her heels.

"It's fine," I said to Marie. "Can you give us a moment?"

Marie hesitated, but I waved her away. I had something to say to Claudia.

"All right," Marie said. "Use the call button if you need anything."

"I heard you were about to be discharged," Claudia

said loud enough for Marie to hear. "I'll just pull my car around, and then we can go pick up Shadow."

"No, thanks," I said. "My legal guardian is taking care of that."

"What legal guardian?" Claudia asked, with a hint of panic in her voice. "Never mind. You'll still need my help with the vet bill."

"That won't be necessary," I said. "I spoke with Leah and they've agreed to take the charges off your credit card and bill me later."

Claudia shook her head. Her whole body tensed. I hadn't really made any arrangements, but I was confident I could work out a payment schedule.

"I have everything I need." I patted my pants pocket.

Claudia frowned at the bulge.

I lowered my voice. "You are to stay away from me and Shadow. I don't even want to see you on my block. If you don't listen, if you try to break into my house, if you come anywhere near Shadow, I will turn the hood ornament over to the police and my memory of last night's events will suddenly change. I'll remember that you hit me with the fire poker. That's assault with a deadly weapon. And who knows what they'll decide about what really happened to David."

Uncertainty flickered in Claudia's eyes. She glanced around the room, resting for one horrible moment on the yellow mums. When her gaze met mine, she straightened her shoulders and her back stiffened.

"You have no proof," she said through gritted teeth.

"Well, there is a hole in your story about what happened last night. You told the police that I called you to my house when Shadow collapsed, but the police officer who witnessed Mrs. Canton trying to mow me down yesterday evening, saw me turn onto your street. The same officer showed up to investigate the break-in. You see, I told Officer Stone I was going to stay with you for the evening. He and Roderick are probably checking their notes. I bet the two officers are wondering why you said I called you when I told Stone that I was staying at your place. I doubt that I would need too much more evidence than that to convince the police that you're a liar. You and I both know they won't find any sign of intruders. You admitted that a lot of people in this town don't like you. I'd bet they would believe you are capable of harming a helpless teen girl."

"I'll say you never showed up," Claudia said. "You've got nothing on me."

She fidgeted; her eyes once again riveted on my pocket. I could see her weighing whether or not to grab what she thought was the hood ornament.

"If you leave me and Shadow alone, the hood ornament stays hidden, and I keep my mouth shut. Unlike you, I can keep a secret. You're the one that blabbed about my age. Now I have to live with a guardian. I could have gone home if you had kept your mouth shut."

I let that soak in.

"I understand Shadow growled at you," I added. "My

dog knows the truth and doesn't want anything to do with you either. Don't even think about showing up at my house. You know what she's capable of. You saw her attack David."

I saw the recognition in her eyes. She had lost. She didn't have time to respond—not that it mattered. I could see we had an understanding. An orderly entered the room pushing a wheelchair.

"Your chariot has arrived, Madam," the burly man said to me. "Excuse me," he added, stepping next to the bed and forcing Claudia to retreat. "I need to assist this little lady into her fancy transport."

I shrugged and smiled at Claudia. "You heard the man."

"Well, I guess that's the way it has to be," Claudia mumbled.

"You're sure you don't feel dizzy?" the orderly asked.

"Nope," I said. "I feel great."

Nurse Marie sashayed into the room followed by Mr. O'Shawnessy and Margaret linked at the elbows. My new guardian and his granddaughter.

"Sarah," Mr. O'Shawnessy exclaimed. "A glorious day, indeed. Welcome to the family."

I could see the color had returned to my elderly neighbor's cheeks. I hoped that staying with him would not cause him too much stress.

"Hello, Margaret," I said then reached over and squeezed Mr. O'Shawnessy's hand. Margaret gave me her classic eye roll.

"I can't thank you enough for taking me in," I said to Mr. O'Shawnessy.

Behind her, Claudia, now backed into a corner in the crowded room, slunk around the perimeter walls to the door. As she slipped from view, I felt confident that I wouldn't be seeing her again.

"'Tis nothing. And I brought something for Shaddie." Mr. O'Shawnessy reached into his pocket, no doubt fishing for a biscuit. He glanced around confused then his eyes cleared as if he remembered where he was. "Ah, yes. We'll fetch her next. Right, Maggie?"

"That's right," she said, patting his arm with affection while scowling at me.

"Thanks for driving to pick up Shadow and me, Margaret," I said.

I couldn't blame her for not being happy about the arrangement. Shadow and I had ruined her high school prom night, and now we were invading her home. The skin under her eyes had darkened. Being the sole caregiver for her grandfather must be tough.

"Come on, Grandpa," Margaret said. "We have to bring the car around."

"Ready?" the attendant asked.

I nodded. The orderly guided me into the wheelchair. Nurse Marie smiled and placed the potted flowers on my lap.

"It was a pleasure having you as a patient," Marie said.

"Chad here will escort you to the car."

Chad grunted and navigated the wheelchair out into the hall, down the elevator and through glass sliding doors into fresh air. No ammonia, no lemon. No stifling hush of ill people. And best of all, no sign of Claudia. The potted mums in my lap glowed yellow with promise.

* * *

Margaret held her car below the speed limit as she drove to the emergency vet clinic. It seemed to take forever to get there. At last, the car slid into an empty space in front of the building. The parking lot held a silver Lexus, a white Buick, and a battered VW bus. The white pickup from last night was gone. I hoped Mr. Crogan's yellow Labrador had survived the night.

"I'll just be a few minutes," I said to Mr. O'Shawnessy and Margaret. "Do you want to come inside?"

"We'll wait here," Margaret said, her voice laced with impatience.

I pushed open the glass door to the vet clinic. The avocado green flooring didn't look half as bad in daylight. In fact, the whole place seemed pleasant and welcoming. But why wouldn't it? Last night, I had feared for Shadow's health and my life. Today, I knew my dog was fine. If there had ever been any ghosts, they were now gone, and Claudia had been booted out of my life.

I didn't even have to ring the bell. Leah brandished a

cheery smile from behind the counter. I couldn't believe she was still here.

"Good afternoon," she said.

"Are you back on duty already?" I said.

"Yep," she said. "No rest for the wicked. I came in early to check on Brutus. He's doing fine. Dr. Pullman wants a brief consult before Shadow goes home."

"Err, I need to discuss the bill," I said.

After I explained my situation, Leah promised that she would discuss the matter with the practice's accounting manager. She felt confident that a suitable financial arrangement could be made.

"Now, if you would follow me," Leah said.

The perky red-head opened a door that led into a small examination room. She disappeared, and moments later she returned with Shadow.

My dog, my sweet, sweet pooch looked fully recovered from last night's ordeal. She was on her feet, ears pricked forward, brown eyes keen and bright. Leah handed me the looped end of her lead and left the room. I sank down to the floor and Shadow sat on my lap. I held her close, letting her lick the tears of relief from my face.

"Oh, Shadow." I said then sniffled, wiping my dog-slobbery face with the back of my hand. "Shadow, Shadow, Shadow ..."

Dr. Pullman entered the room, placing a manila folder on the metal exam table.

"You must be Miss ..." He checked the chart. "Whitman."

"Call me Sarah," I said, brushing away my tears and standing to face the vet.

"Shadow has charmed us all," he said, shaking my hand. "What a nice dog."

Dr. Pullman turned his attention to my pup. "This girl seems just fine. Here. Let me show you the brain scan."

He pulled a glossy sheet from an envelope and clipped the image to a white box on the wall. A flip of a switch and the image revealed nooks and crannies of my dog's brain.

"Everything's as it should be," he said. "Shadow's scan appears normal. No need for any restrictions. Normal food and exercise today. I don't think you even need a follow-up appointment, unless she starts to behave strangely."

* * *

Out in the parking lot, I headed for Mr. O'Shawnessy and Margaret standing in the shade by their car. Shadow strained at the leash to reach my new guardian. The sweet old man fumbled in his pocket for a treat. Shadow sat in front of him and raised a paw off the ground offering to shake hands in exchange for the morsel.

"There's a good dog," Mr. O'Shawnessy said. "Here, Shaddie." He tossed a biscuit to her and she caught the morsel in mid-air.

"I think the session with the animal behaviorist has fixed her barking problem," I said to Margaret.

Margaret's features relaxed a little though I sensed a healthy bit of skepticism remained. Although I doubted she would ever find it in her heart to like Shadow, perhaps she might come to tolerate my dog. And even though my sweet pet would be forced to stay next door, she still had a home. Before long, I would be back sharing my house with my dog.

I inhaled the fresh air. For the first time since Dad died, I felt like myself. Game Plan Rule #10 was to listen to my voice within. My inner voice was telling me that living with Mr. O'Shawnessy for a while was the right decision. Being around his cheery self would help ease me into this new life. Claudia would keep her distance as long as I had the hood ornament. Witchy-Woman wouldn't dare come snooping around now that I was living in a house surrounded by other people.

A car full of rowdy teens honked at Margaret as they passed the clinic. She lifted her hand and waved. It was the first time I had seen her look happy. Her smile faded as her eyes tracked the car's progress. Game Plan Rule #4 came to mind. If you have a chance to fix a wrong, do it. I had ruined her prom date, the least I could do was give her the opportunity to spend time with her friends.

"I'll keep your grandpa company tonight," I said. "You could go hang out with them later."

"Aye," Mr. O'Shawnessy said. "That's a bonny idea."

Margaret shrugged. Her eyes met mine. I could have sworn her green eyes softened just a tad.

"This lassie will be all settled in before its time for afternoon tea," Mr. O'Shawnessy said to me.

Settled. I liked the sound of that. I opened the rear car door for Shadow and joined her in the backseat. She crawled onto my lap and gave me a sloppy kiss.

When Mr. O'Shawnessy pulled into his driveway, I told him I was going next door to give Shadow a special treat and pack a few belongings, promising that I wouldn't take long, and that I would call if I started to feel dizzy.

As I anticipated, Shadow trotted inside without protest. The police had apparently gathered up all the evidence they needed and taken pictures. Someone had even cleaned up the wine and glass in the kitchen. I placed the flowers from the hospital on the window sill where the silver eagle would remain hidden in plain sight.

Shadow asked to go out. I let her do her business while I packed a few belongings. As she came in, I gave her a giant chew bone though I was confident that she wouldn't be making a nuisance of herself by barking anymore.

I sat at the dining room table, watching my dog gnaw on her prize. I didn't like that I would be sleeping next door, but I would buy a baby monitor later today so I could hear if Shadow was distressed. I would only be a few steps away. This arrangement wasn't a perfect solution, but it would be temporary. I would return to live in my house soon enough. Even though this wasn't the path Dad envisioned, I avoided being placed in a foster home with potentially unkind parents. It all worked out in the end.

I could return to school and the challenges of math problems and studying vocabulary lists. On weekends I would have time to sketch pencil drawings of Shadow and eat junk food with girlfriends that I would make at my new high school. Maybe Tess could come for a sleepover after she wasn't grounded anymore. I looked forward to hiking with Kyle. I could tell him stories about my dad and apologize for lying to him about a phantom father. A relationship built on falsehood would never have worked. A smile formed as I felt a glimmer of happiness seep through my sadness for the first time since Dad told me about his cancer diagnosis. Because my age had been revealed to social services, I had been given a second chance to become an ordinary teenager.

I reached into my blouse and removed the frayed envelope. When I pulled out Dad's letter, the laminated card with the Game Plan Rules and a Polaroid fell to the table. I sucked in air as I examined the picture of Shadow. Instead of purple, her eyes displayed a typical red-eye effect. It had been the batch that I printed and had planned to put in a collage frame and the Polaroids of expired film that showed her eyes as lavender. Had everything I went through these last few days been orchestrated by Dr. Griffin and experienced through a lens of fear and grief?

Setting the photo down, my attention turned to the Game Plan Rules. It was as though I read them for the first time. How could I have been so blind? They had never been intended to only be a blueprint to keep my secret, his guidelines were meant to last a lifetime. My father's parting words were the greatest gift he could have possibly given me. It was time to let go. I ran my fingers along the edge of my new table. How foolish I had been thinking that removing the old one would lessen my pain. The memories I shared with Dad would always be there. Knowing that, I could accept that he would never say "Morning, Pumpkin" over breakfast anymore. Knowing that, I could let the grief I felt for my father go.

"Hey, Dad," I said aloud. "Your Pumpkin is ready to say goodnight now."

Shadow's tail thumped the ground as if she agreed. I stood up straight, shoulders back and tucked the card into my purse secure in the knowledge that Dad's Game Plan Rules would guide me throughout life's challenges.

Afterword

In October 2017, a red zipper-nosed Doberman became the icon for my newly launched, dog-rescue column in the San Francisco East Bay local arts and entertainment magazine, *The Diablo Gazette*. The column titled "Ruby_dooby_Do to the Rescue" features a hard-to-place rescue dog each month. In September 2018, I ran a special tribute to Ruby, her owner, Charles Lindsey, and the Doberman breed. During my research, I learned a lot about this often-maligned breed.

Initially bred to be guard dogs, Doberman pinschers can also be rescue or therapy dogs as well as assistants to police or military personnel. Hollywood has been particularly negligent in portraying the positive side of Dobermans. As noted by John Walter in his Doberman Planet blog (www.DobermanPlanet.com), "Famous Dobermans in Movies and Television: The Complete List," the breed is often portrayed as vicious animals despite the modern day Doberman possessing a very friendly disposition. In the 2009 Disney movie, *Up,* Alpha spends a great deal of time baring his teeth. Worse, the 1978 American horror flick, *Dracula's Dog*, depicts a Doberman on a killing spree in a national forest. The breed also appears in these well-known movies: *Father of the Bride, The Other, First Blood,* and *Flags of our Fathers* to name a few. A comprehensive list of movies that include everything from cameos to major roles including foreign films can be found at (http://www.reeldogs.com/doberman-pinscher/). The best example of the breed's softer nature is the 1946 movie, *It Shouldn't Happen to a Dog*, where Rodney the Doberman is portrayed as an intelligent, loyal, and lovable dog.

Ruby is a tribute to the gentle side of her breed. She is a smart, mellow Doberman pinscher with a knack for attracting attention, largely due to a combination of her regal appearance and her owner's photographic skills. I was thrilled when Charles, an incredibly generous and talented photographer, agreed to allow me to use Ruby's image on my book cover. Ruby's regal characteristics of a long head, cropped, erect ears, and a sleek, muscular body are indicative of her breed. Her reddish-copper coat with golden eyebrows makes her a perfect photography model. Her ability to shine under the lens has made her a social media celebrity with over 84,000 followers and growing on Instagram at the time of this publication.

In earlier drafts of my novel, I had portrayed Shadow as a male border collie mix, a replica of one of my fostered rescue dogs also named Shadow. All the adopters of my foster dogs were offered an open-door return policy. I would always take them back. Shadow-the-border-collie came back to me about six months later. A sensitive dog with a heart the size of Mount Rushmore, I couldn't send him away again so I kept him, ended my fostering career.

Shadow has since crossed the rainbow bridge, but I currently have the privilege of sharing my life with three rescued dogs, which puts me at the legal limit of number of dogs I'm allowed to own. According to the American Society for the Prevention of Cruelty to Animals, approximately 3.3 million dogs enter U.S. animal shelters nationwide every year. Of those, 670,000 dogs are euthanized annually. The number would be much higher without the dedication of many dog rescue organizations and the volunteers who run them.

If you are now smitten with the Doberman breed and are considering adopting or purchasing a dog, as with any pet, take a look at your lifestyle, along with your living situation such as space restrictions and amount of time you spend away from home. If purchasing a puppy is your preference, please go through a reputable breeder who will take a dog back if you find yourself in dire straits due to a health, financial or other crisis. Likewise, many rescue organizations will require that a pet be returned to them should irreconcilable problems arise. Though I hope, like Sarah in *Between Shadow's Eyes*, once you take on the responsibility, you will move heaven and earth to keep your dog.

Dear readers, if you enjoyed *Between Shadow's Eyes*, please go to my website www.jillhedgecock.com to sign up to receive news on the release date of the sequel, *From Shadow's Perspective*, and other novels. Please also consider posting a review on www.goodreads.com and Amazon.

Many thanks!

Book Club Questions and Discussion Guide

1. Choose one character: What do you like about Sarah or Mr. O'Shawnessey? What do you not like about either of them?

2. If you had no close friends and were a single and widowed parent, would you trust the foster care system to raise your child in the event of your death?

3. Do you think Sarah made a good choice by keeping the hood ornament rather than turning it in to the police?

4. Name several key similarities in Sarah's and Claudia's lives. In what ways did their fathers' health challenges affect them?

5. Shadow's behavior toward Dr. Griffin changes at the end of the book. Do you think dogs can sense when they need a person's help? Do you think dogs can tell whether humans are fundamentally good or evil?

6. Do you believe Sarah really saw ghosts or were these spirits the product of exhaustion, grief, and/or fear of Dr. Griffin?

7. Sarah grapples with feelings about using dogs for scientific research. How do you feel about this issue?

8. Did you find Dad's Game Plan Rules insightful? Do you see ways that you can apply them to your own life?

9. Do you have preconceived notions about dogs that end up in the shelter? Did you know that purebred dogs sometimes land in the shelter? Would you consider adopting a pet rather than purchasing a dog from a breeder?

10. Did reading the book change your opinion about the Doberman breed?

* * *

I LOVE book clubs. I am happy to Skype into your meeting (or visit in person if possible).
Contact me through my website to coordinate:
www.jillhedgecock.com

Acknowledgements

It takes a village to raise a family and it takes a village to write a book. First and foremost, I must thank Karen Grencik of Red Fox Literary for believing in an early version of the manuscript nearly a decade ago and providing valuable input. This novel would not have been possible without the help of the support of the talented members of my critique group: Elisabeth Tuck for her editorial eye, Cheryl Spanos for her spot-on plotting suggestions, Fran Cain who champions my work, David George for his knack for setting, Susan Berman for her wit and eye for comedic relief, Melanie Denman for her ability to capture the big picture and hone it into a succinct description, and Nannette Carroll and Jack Russ for catching everything in-between in the early drafts, and to Dana Barry for spotting typos in the proof. Many thanks to Karen Stanton, John Randolph, Lee Paulson, Laurel Anne Hill, Charlotte Cook and other members of Charlotte's writing classes, and to Elizabeth Koehler-Pentacoff for suggestions in character development and advice on early versions of the book.

Much gratitude goes to Charles Lindsey for allowing his dog Ruby to grace the cover of the book. I must also express my gratitude to the members of Avid Readers Book

Club. Through book discussions, you all have taught me so much about writing and what constitutes a good read. So thank you Mary Anderson, Miriam Belsa, Carla Bergez, Susan Bruno, Ann Gray, Cheryl Monroe, Amy Pennington, Joy Pinsky, Terry Pixton, Catherine Stafford, Laura Walsh, and Tamara Wickland. And Tammy Jacobson who is no longer with us. I am also indebted to my young manuscript readers, Charlie Greenlee, Bronwyn Austin, and Nathan Ures. Many thanks to my patient and supportive family, my husband Eric and daughters Kelly and Lindsay. Lastly, I hope that my prose has done justice to the many, many dogs that have enriched my life.

About the Author

Jill Hedgecock is an award-winning and internationally-published author. Her love of dogs led her to start a dog rescue column for *The Diablo Gazette*, a local newspaper, in 2017. *Rhino in the Room*, Jill's debut novel, was a Solo Medalist Winner in Travel/Adventures Abroad for New Apple's Book Awards for Excellence. She lives in California with her husband and three rescue dogs. Visit www.jill-hedgecock.com to learn more.

If you enjoyed the book, please consider
posting a review on www.goodreads.com and
other platforms such as Amazon.

Many thanks!

Also by Jill Hedgecock

RHINO IN THE ROOM

The last place seventeen-year-old fashionista, Claire, wants to go is on a South African safari with her father who she is angry with after discovering his extramarital affair. Claire's safari experience improves after meeting Junior, a handsome young guide. But when Junior takes them on a special excursion and Claire breaks a critical game drive rule, she and her father are pulled into the crosshairs of rhino poachers. Can Claire and her dad overcome their broken relationship in order to save themselves and the last two black rhinos from extinction?